DARK ANGELS

THE SONS OF THE LION

CONTENTS

THE FIRST LEGION 4
Dark Heritage...6
The Hunt for the Fallen.......................8
Chapter Organisation.........................10
The Battle Companies........................12
The Ravenwing....................................14
The Deathwing....................................16
Strike Forces.......................................18
The Unforgiven...................................20
Dark Angels Successor Chapters.........22
In the Name of Absolution 26
Company Masters...............................30
Chaplains...31
Company Veterans Squad 32
Command Squads...............................34
Tactical Squads 35
Assault Squads....................................36
Devastator Squads..............................37
Transports 38
Battle Tanks..39
Land Raiders 40
Dreadnoughts.....................................41
Techmarines..42
Scout Squads 43
Ravenwing Bike Squads......................44
Ravenwing Land Speeders 45
Ravenwing Vengeance Land Speeders...46
Ravenwing Black Knights 47
Nephilim Jetfighters 48
Ravenwing Dark Talons......................49
Deathwing Terminators......................50
Deathwing Knights.............................51
Venerable Dreadnoughts 52
Deathwing Land Raiders....................53
Librarians 54
Interrogator-Chaplains.......................55
Battle & Reserve Companies..............56
Deathwing..60
Ravenwing 64
Successor Chapters 70

SONS OF THE LION 74

FORCES OF THE DARK ANGELS 94
Lion's Blade Strike Force 95
Datasheets..96
Dark Angels Wargear List...................97
Belial 99
Sammael 100
Sableclaw 101
Interrogator-Chaplain 102
Asmodai 103
Librarian..104
Ezekiel..105
Company Master 106
Chaplain 107
Techmarine 108
Tactical Squad....................................110
Scout Squad.......................................111
Company Veterans Squad 112
Command Squad 113
Dreadnoughts.....................................114
Venerable Dreadnoughts 115
Deathwing Terminator Squad 116
Deathwing Command Squad 117
Deathwing Knights............................118
Ravenwing Command Squad...........119
Rhino 120
Razorback 121
Drop Pod 122
Assault Squad 123
Ravenwing Bike Squad 124
Ravenwing Attack Bike Squad..........125
Ravenwing Land Speeders 126
Ravenwing Darkshroud 127
Nephilim Jetfighter............................128
Ravenwing Dark Talon 129
Ravenwing Black Knights 130
Ravenwing Land Speeder Vengeance..131
Devastator Squad 132
Predators 133
Whirlwinds...134
Vindicators 135
Land Raider..136
Land Raider Crusader 137
Land Raider Redeemer 138
Azrael 139
Battle Demi-company 140
Deathwing Redemption Force..........141
Ravenwing Attack Squadron 142
Ravenwing Support Squadron 143
Ravenwing Silence Squadron...........144
The Hammer of Caliban 145

APPENDIX.........................148
Army Special Rules 148
Warlord Traits....................................148
Armoury of the Rock.........................149
Ranged Weapons 149
Melee Weapons.................................150
Special Issue Wargear.......................151
Armour 154
Dark Angels Vehicle Equipment 154
Relics of Caliban 155
Interromancy Discipline...................156
Tactical Objectives............................157
Deathwing Strike Force 158
Ravenwing Strike Force....................159
Profiles...160

PRODUCED BY GAMES WORKSHOP IN NOTTINGHAM

British Cataloguing-in-Publication Data. A catalogue record for this book is available from the British Library. Pictures used for illustrative purposes only.

Games Workshop Ltd, Willow Rd, Lenton, Nottingham, NG7 2WS
Printed by 1010 in China

games-workshop.com

THE FIRST LEGION

The Dark Angels make war with merciless determination. On the attack they are without remorse, striding unflinching through the fire of their foes; in defence they are utterly unyielding, the enemy dashing themselves to pieces against the Dark Angels' impenetrable lines. Where some Space Marine Chapters are given to grand speeches and ostentation, this insular brotherhood prefer to let their deeds speak for themselves. Where the Space Wolves or the Black Templars might give vent to wild war cries in the heat of battle, the Dark Angels intone solemn chants and battle-hymns as they hack apart their foes. Stony-faced and austere, the Dark Angels gun down their victims with frightening efficiency, never showing the slightest moment of weakness or unseemly pride.

When the Emperor first struck out upon the Great Crusade, he sought to unite Humanity in dominion over the stars. To aid him in this monumental task he created twenty Legions of post-human warriors known as Space Marines. Genetically engineered to be superior to Mankind in every way, these heroic warriors were the Emperor's ultimate weapon against a hostile galaxy. Of those Legions, the Dark Angels were the first and, arguably, the greatest. Led by their noble Primarch, Lion El'Jonson, the Dark Angels fought at the forefront of the Emperor's wars, and have continued to do so through the ten thousand years that have followed.

Since the destruction of their home world, Caliban, the Dark Angels have travelled the galaxy in a massive asteroid fortress known as the Rock. This vast edifice is the last remnant of Caliban itself, sundered by catastrophe and transformed through the addition of countless stone corridors, armoured gun turrets, strategic launch bays, force-field generators and gargantuan Warp engines. Aboard this monolithic battle station, the Dark Angels make their way through the void of space, following a winding path in pursuit of an agenda they will never reveal.

The Dark Angels are a stern gathering of heroes who fight an incessant war for Humanity's very survival. Yet they wrap themselves in archaic rites of battle, as though striving to distance themselves from those they protect. A sense of obsession lingers about this mysterious Chapter, a brooding menace that unsettles even those who fight alongside them. Beneath the Dark Angels' courage and nobility, behind the sinister veil of secrecy that hangs about their deeds, lies a darker motivation. The Dark Angels are seekers after redemption, a close-knit brotherhood whose shameful sins are hidden even from one another. They hunt those who betrayed them long ago, seeking to expunge a stain upon their honour that, were it ever brought to light, would see all they have striven for turn to ash upon the wind.

DARK HERITAGE

Ten millennia ago, the Imperium was almost annihilated by the calamitous galactic war known as the Horus Heresy. The Dark Angels and their Primarch, Lion El'Jonson, remained loyal to the Emperor throughout this terrible war, fighting heroically against their traitorous brothers. In the Heresy's aftermath, Jonson and his Legion returned to their home world of Caliban only to find that one last, terrible treachery awaited them. Consumed by his jealousy of the Lion's glories, the heroic knight Luther – formerly Jonson's closest friend and ally – had embraced the Dark Gods of Chaos. Worse, his impassioned oratory had led all the Dark Angels on Caliban into heresy.

The loyalist Dark Angels' grand homecoming was thus met not with jubilation, but by a sudden, shocking storm of laser-fire from Caliban's surface. Several Dark Angels ships were torn apart before Jonson's fleet could pull back into deep space, and once the Primarch pieced together what had occurred, his cold fury was terrible to behold. Determined to punish his once-brother – and to burn away the rot that had spread through his Legion – the Lion swiftly planned a devastating assault from space.

Moving into position, Jonson's ships began a massive orbital bombardment. They obliterated Caliban's defence lasers and drove the traitors back into their void-shielded fortress monasteries. At the same time, Jonson himself led a surgical drop assault against the greatest of these strongholds and the seat of Luther's power. As fire rained down from space, Jonson and Luther fought a furious duel, the violence of their clash tearing the fortress apart around them. Finally, as the intensity of the Dark Angels' bombardment cracked the very crust of the world, Luther stumbled. Yet Jonson was unable to strike down his old friend. Luther had no such compunction, and blasted the Primarch off his feet with a monstrously powerful psychic attack.

As Jonson fell, Luther realised at last what he had done. With a sorrowful scream, he fell to his knees at Jonson's side. Hearing this cry, the Dark Gods knew they had been denied their victory. Enraged, they engulfed Caliban in a vast Warp storm. Already mortally wounded, the home world of the First Legion disintegrated, much of it swallowed by the Warp along with the surviving traitors.

In the wake of this cataclysm, the loyalist Dark Angels descended to the surface of the last remnant of their world. Preserved by its mighty shields, Luther's ruined fortress stood atop that shattered rock. It was here that they found the arch-traitor himself, gibbering and insane. There was no sign of Jonson, though Luther swore the Primarch had been borne away by robed figures. Perhaps worse, the renegade Dark Angels were also gone, bearing with them the dire tale of their Legion's shame. Thus began the terrible, endless quest by the Lion's sons to find and silence those who would become known as the Fallen, to secure their repentance and finally wash away the stain upon their Chapter's soul.

THE HUNT FOR THE FALLEN

In the wake of Caliban's fall, the Dark Angels' leaders concealed their terrible shame, forming a small, secretive group known as the Inner Circle. Hidden even from their own brothers, this organisation dedicates itself completely to the hunt for the Fallen, and to finally securing absolution for the Chapter.

Since the inception of the Inner Circle, the Dark Angels have been fighting a secret war. They pursue a veiled agenda of which even the majority of their own brethren are ignorant. Most Dark Angels know nothing of their Chapter's shadowed past, and are instead indoctrinated to unquestioningly obey the commands of their masters. Only those who demonstrate their total devotion to the Chapter can join the Inner Circle, and even then they must pass numerous, dangerous tests to prove their worth.

Those who fail these trials vanish without a word, never to be seen again. The rest are sworn to absolute secrecy before being told of Luther's betrayal and the existence of the Fallen. Even then, though a Dark Angel will believe that he now knows the whole truth of his Chapter's history, there are circles within circles, and always more dark secrets to be revealed. But it is enough for him to know that it is the Fallen that move the Dark Angels to true fury, and it is these ancient traitors that the Inner Circle hunt, no matter the cost.

The Fallen themselves are deadly foes – warriors of a bygone age whose strength and cunning are beyond anything the galaxy has seen in millennia. While some regret their actions during the fall of Caliban, most are unrepentant renegades who surround themselves with whole armies of fanatical worshippers. To slay these heretics is hard enough, but simply killing them will not suffice. The Fallen must be defeated and taken alive. For this the Dark Angels have their fearsome 1st Company: the Deathwing. Armoured in absolute dedication to their Chapter, deaf to the lies of traitors and heretics, the Deathwing hunt down the Fallen, eradicate their followers, and subdue them for capture. The traitors are then borne back to the Rock in secret, where they are handed over to the skull-helmed Interrogator-Chaplains. It is these grim figures who are charged with extracting the confessions of the ancient traitors by any means necessary. Only through the repentance of the Fallen can the Dark Angels be absolved, and the Inner Circle will do absolutely anything to achieve this end.

Even before the last flaring teleport energies had faded, Brother Arafael was already firing. His storm bolter thumped in his grip, pumping a stream of shells into the shocked Cultists that packed the moonlit clearing. Around him, Arafael's brothers were doing the same, loosing a cacophonous storm of fire that reduced their victims to sprays of blood and severed limbs. The Deathwing had taken their foes completely by surprise, and Arafael sneered in disgust as the cowardly heretics broke and ran. None of them got far, the last few fleeing figures blown off their feet by a thundering burst of fire from Brother Azriah's assault cannon. The Cultists were ripped to pieces by the blizzard of shots, their twitching remains scattered upon the muddy ground.

Arafael swept his gaze across the clearing. It was only a small break in the forest, a sward of damp grass around which the shadowed mass of the forest loomed close. A huge statue rose at the clearing's heart, dominating the space utterly. Arafael felt a stab of cold anger as he took in the crudely carved figure clad in its archaic power armour, arms raised in a posture that might have been beneficence, but looked more like menace. Arafael was Inner Circle, oathsworn and conversant with the secrets of his Chapter. He knew an idol of the Fallen when he saw it. The Deathwing's quarry was here, and Arafael vowed that they would run him to ground.

The Dark Angel's thoughts were broken by fresh gunfire from the clearing's edge. Shots sparked off his armour as a band of traitor Space Marines burst from the trees. They were chanting a name, over and over, one that filled Arafael with fury.

'Shadrechael! Shadrechael! Shadrechael!'

Ignoring the bolt rounds that ricocheted from their armour, the Deathwing turned and opened fire once again. Renegades fell, shredded by bolt and blast, and the Terminators marched forward over their ruined corpses. Arafael strode at their fore, checking his armour's internal auspex-link as he went. Shadrechael's temple should be just a hundred yards into the treeline. With the Strike Cruiser Absolution's Hymn *hanging in low orbit overhead, there was no way the Fallen could escape by aircraft, and the Deathwing were closing in from all directions. Shadrechael would either have to fight his way out, or wait for his attackers to come to him. Whichever, the Deathwing would be ready.*

Arafael grunted as chainsword teeth bit into his shoulder guard, then smashed the weapon's wielder out of his path. He drummed fire into another heretic as he strode into the gloom beneath the trees. He could sense the Fallen out there, and his twin hearts beat faster at the thought. Shadrechael would be captured, and he would confess. Arafael would make sure of it.

CHAPTER ORGANISATION

Though shrouded in secrecy, much of the Dark Angels' organisation is not dissimilar to that of a typical Codex Chapter. However, their hunt for the Fallen has led the Dark Angels to include several groups whose numbers, and in some cases very existence, is a carefully guarded secret – these are the Ravenwing, the Deathwing, and the Inner Circle.

Chapter Strength as of 999.M41

CHAPTER MASTER
Commander Azrael
Supreme Grand Master of the Dark Angels

APOTHECARION
Brother Razaek
Master Apothecary

10 Apothecaries

RECLUSIAM
High Interrogator Sapphon
Grand Master of Chaplains

30 Interrogator-Chaplains

Dark Angels Chapter Banner

KNIGHTS OF THE ROCK
Brother Apharan
Warden of the Rock

6 Venerable Dreadnoughts

LIBRARIUS
Chief Librarian Ezekiel
Keeper of the Keys

4 Epistolaries
8 Codiciers
8 Lexicaniums
4 Acolytum

FLEET COMMAND
Brother Nephalor
High Huntsman of the Void

16 Strike Cruisers
8 Battle Barges
21 Rapid Strike Vessels
31 Thunderhawk Gunships

LOGISTICIAM
Brother Sepharon
Warden of the Gates

1200 Servitors

ARMOURY
Brother Belaphor
Master of the Rock

22 Techmarines
113 Servitors
16 Predators
10 Vindicators
12 Whirlwinds
21 Land Raiders

1ST COMPANY
'The Deathwing'

VETERAN COMPANY
Master Belial
Grand Master of the Deathwing

Deathwing Knights
Command Squad
20 Deathwing Terminator Squads
9 Venerable Dreadnoughts

2ND COMPANY
'The Ravenwing'

RAPID ASSAULT COMPANY
Master Sammael
Grand Master of the Ravenwing

Chaplain
Black Knights
Command Squad
6 Attack Squadrons
4 Support Squadrons

3RD COMPANY
'The Unmerciful'

BATTLE COMPANY
Master Astoran
Master of the Arsenal

Chaplain
Command Squad
Company Veterans
6 Tactical Squads
2 Assault Squads
2 Devastator Squads
3 Dreadnoughts

4TH COMPANY
'The Feared'

BATTLE COMPANY
Master Korahael
Master of the Fleet

Chaplain
Command Squad
Company Veterans
6 Tactical Squads
2 Assault Squads
2 Devastator Squads
2 Dreadnoughts

5TH COMPANY
'The Unrelenting'

BATTLE COMPANY
Master Balthasar
Keeper of the Unseen Ritual

Chaplain
Command Squad
Company Veterans
6 Tactical Squads
2 Assault Squads
2 Devastator Squads
4 Dreadnoughts

6TH COMPANY
'The Resolute'

TACTICAL COMPANY
Master Araphil
Master of Rites

Chaplain
Command Squad
Company Veterans
10 Tactical Squads
1 Dreadnought

7TH COMPANY
'The Unbowed'

TACTICAL COMPANY
Master Ezekiah
Master of Watchers

Chaplain
Command Squad
Company Veterans
10 Tactical Squads
3 Dreadnoughts

8TH COMPANY
'The Wrathful'

ASSAULT COMPANY
Master Molochi
Master of Condemnation

Chaplain
Command Squad
Company Veterans
10 Assault Squads
2 Dreadnoughts

9TH COMPANY
'The Remorseless'

DEVASTATOR COMPANY
Master Xerophus
Master of Relics

Chaplain
Command Squad
Company Veterans
10 Devastator Squads
4 Dreadnoughts

10TH COMPANY
'The Redeemed'

SCOUT COMPANY
Master Ranaeus
Master of Recruits

Chaplain
10 Scout Squads
117 Unassigned Neophytes

THE BATTLE COMPANIES

At the forefront of the Dark Angels' many wars, the Battle Companies fight in the name of the Emperor, the Primarch and Humanity. Utterly dedicated to their Chapter, these warriors conduct themselves with conviction and heroism on battlefields all across the galaxy.

Like the foundations of some great keep, the Battle Companies of the Dark Angels bear the weight of their Chapter's combat duties. The 3rd, 4th and 5th Companies of the Dark Angels are designated as Battle Companies, each comprising one hundred battle-brothers, and kept as close to full strength as possible at all times.

Leading each Battle Company is a Master. Ostensibly, his duty is to lead his brothers in Humanity's defence. In truth the Company Master must be always alert for the Fallen, ready to take up the hunt at a moment's notice. Below the Company Master stand his battle-brothers. According to the Codex Astartes, a Battle Company should be based around six squads of Tactical Marines, two of Assault Marines, and two of Devastators. The Battle Companies of the Dark Angels cleave close to this model, with the exception that a hand-picked selection of their finest warriors will be elevated to fight as Company Veterans. To ensure mobility and support, each Battle Company maintains enough Rhino and Razorback APCs to transport all of their warriors into battle, while the Dark Angels fleet carries sufficient Drop Pods for them to execute a full atmospheric assault whenever required. Finally, each Battle Company is supported by elements of the Librarius, Apothecarion, Reclusiam and Armoury, and accompanied by their honoured Dreadnought brothers.

Should members of a Battle Company be slain, their loss is replenished with warriors from the Reserve Companies. For the Dark Angels, this transition is laden with ritual and meaning. Each Company maintains its own archaic rites of initiation, its own oaths and traditions to be observed before a brother can be accepted. Knowledge is densely stratified within the Chapter's ranks. Battle-brothers learn by rote the allegorical tales and pseudo-myths that strengthen their resolve, build their dedication, and harden their hearts against traitors and betrayers. Even within a single Battle Company these layers of information exist, so that a Devastator of the 4th Company will have learned less of his Chapter's mysteries than a Tactical brother of the same company, both of whom will know less than their counterparts in the 3rd. Every advancement within the Dark Angels brings new secrets, preparing the Chapter's warriors for the appalling revelations that await them should they ascend to the tight-knit brotherhood of the Inner Circle.

BATTLE COMPANY STRUCTURE

COMPANY MASTER

CHAPLAIN

COMMAND SQUAD

Company Standard Bearer
Apothecary
Company Champion
Veterans

COMPANY VETERANS

Veterans

6 TACTICAL SQUADS

Each comprises:

Sergeant
or Veteran Sergeant

Tactical Marine
with heavy weapon

Tactical Marine
with special weapon

7 Tactical Marines
with boltguns

2 ASSAULT SQUADS

Each comprises:

Sergeant
or Veteran Sergeant

2 Assault Marines
with special weapons

8 Assault Marines
with bolt pistols and chainswords

2 DEVASTATOR SQUADS

Each comprises:

Sergeant
or Veteran Sergeant

4 Devastator Marines
with heavy weapons

6 Devastator Marines
with boltguns

DREADNOUGHTS

ARMOURY ASSETS

Attached as required

Predators
Whirlwinds
Vindicators
Land Raiders

TRANSPORT POOL

Transports typically dedicated to a specific squad

Rhinos
Razorbacks
Drop Pods

THE RAVENWING

Black clad huntsmen and masters of the art of lightning warfare, the Ravenwing race before their Chapter like thunder before a storm. Prizing speed and mobility above all else, they are their Chapter's foremost weapon in the hunt for the Fallen, and nothing can slow their pursuit.

Engines roaring, the Ravenwing tear forward through the enemy's fire to carve into their ranks like a blade through a monster's throat. These are the warriors of the Dark Angels' 2nd Company, a highly specialised formation that fights from fast-moving attack vehicles. It has long proven difficult for the Adeptus Terra to accurately gauge the size of the Ravenwing, for while the Dark Angels claim it maintains company strength, they carefully obfuscate the details of its numbers and operations. What is known for sure is that the Ravenwing comprises the finest riders and pilots their Chapter has to offer, combined into a single force capable of running down any prey in the galaxy.

The majority of the Ravenwing fight from the saddles of Space Marine Bikes, supported by brothers piloting various marks of Land Speeder, or atmospheric assault fighters. The Ravenwing is ideal for fast assault missions, often acting as an outriding reconnaissance force for larger armies. Its far-ranging Land Speeders search for the telltale signs of the foe, voxing back information on enemy movements and dispositions. When the moment is right, the Ravenwing gun their engines and roar into the fight en masse, a hurtling gale of black armour, blazing guns and roaring chainswords that sweeps the enemy before it. With but a word, the Ravenwing can switch between countless, perfectly drilled attack patterns in order to encircle, flank, break apart or otherwise harass their foes. At all times they strive to avoid becoming bogged down, swiftly dissecting even the largest enemy force with their hit-and-run attacks.

Should a vital target present itself, the Ravenwing mount teleport homers upon their bikes that allow them to summon the might of the Deathwing to the battlefield. Not only does this all but guarantee victory, it also gives a clue to the true, veiled purpose of the Ravenwing. Known only to their Grand Master, and to the carefully selected Inner Circle members of his Black Knight elite, the mission of the Ravenwing is to hunt out and run to ground Fallen Dark Angels. This is why every member of the Ravenwing must be not only an expert rider or pilot, but also fervently dedicated to his Chapter. More than any other force, the brothers of the Ravenwing are likely to be exposed to the pernicious lies of the Fallen. They must therefore be unquestioning in their faith, and are monitored closely at all times by their Chaplain to ensure no chinks appear in their armour of indoctrination.

RAVENWING STRUCTURE

GRAND MASTER OF THE RAVENWING

RAVENWING CHAPLAIN

RAVENWING COMMAND SQUAD

Ravenwing Champion
Ravenwing Standard Bearer
Ravenwing Apothecary

RAVENWING BLACK KNIGHTS

Ravenwing Huntmaster
Ravenwing Black Knights

1ST SQUADRON Ravenwing Attack Squadron Bikes Attack Bikes Land Speeders	2ND SQUADRON Ravenwing Attack Squadron Bikes Attack Bikes Land Speeders	3RD SQUADRON Ravenwing Attack Squadron Bikes Attack Bikes Land Speeders	4TH SQUADRON Ravenwing Attack Squadron Bikes Attack Bikes Land Speeders	5TH SQUADRON Ravenwing Attack Squadron Bikes Attack Bikes Land Speeders
6TH SQUADRON Ravenwing Attack Squadron Bikes Attack Bikes Land Speeders	7TH SQUADRON Ravenwing Support Squadron Land Speeders	8TH SQUADRON Ravenwing Support Squadron Land Speeders	9TH SQUADRON Ravenwing Support Squadron Land Speeders	10TH SQUADRON Ravenwing Support Squadron Land Speeders

ATTACK SQUADRON

(standard operational strength in the field)

Ravenwing Biker Sergeant/Veteran Sergeant
5 Ravenwing Bikers
Ravenwing Attack Bike
Ravenwing Land Speeder/Land Speeder Vengeance

SUPPORT ELEMENTS

Attached as required, rarely en masse

Darkshrouds
Land Speeder Vengeances

THE DEATHWING

Renowned as one of the finest fighting forces in the Imperium, the Deathwing are their Chapter's mailed fist. No foe is too great for them to subdue, and no mission is too difficult or dangerous for them to complete. Their reputation is such that the mere sight of their bone white armour is enough to put many foes to flight.

The Deathwing are the Dark Angels' 1st Company. Unlike the elite battle-brothers of most Space Marine Chapters, they fight clad exclusively in ancient suits of Terminator armour. That the Dark Angels can equip all of their veterans this way speaks volumes of the wealth of relics hidden deep within the Rock, and is an indication of how seriously the Chapter takes the Deathwing's true mission. Unbeknownst even to many within the Deathwing itself, they are their Chapter's ultimate weapon against the Fallen, the warrior elite charged with hunting and capturing these renegades. As such, only those who have shown incredible skill at arms and total loyalty to their Chapter can undergo the exacting rites of initiation required to join the Deathwing. Those who survive the mental, physical and spiritual rigours of this ritual take their place amongst the ranks of their Chapter's elite.

The Deathwing is an assault force capable of marching unflinchingly into the heaviest enemy fire. They can teleport straight into the midst of battle, ripping the heart from the enemy army with a single, perfectly coordinated strike. In battles such as the Olthariad Cleansing, the Seventh Pinnacle Massacre, and the hellish forlorn hope that breached the Fortress of Blackened Flesh, the Deathwing has proven that no foe can withstand its overwhelming might.

To achieve such heroics requires courage and a boundless hatred of the foe: emotions that burn fiercely within the breasts of those brought into the Inner Circle. These warriors know of Luther's betrayal, and their fanaticism strengthens both their own resolve and that of their brothers. In battle they are beacons of righteous fury, leading their brothers to pound their enemies into bloody, unrecognisable pulp. All Deathwing are utterly devoted, following the commands of their superiors without question and willingly performing any act, no matter how heinous, in the name of the hunt. For this reason, very few Dark Angels strike forces go to war without at least one squad of Deathwing on hand, ready to respond to the more ruthless orders of Chapter command at a moment's notice.

DEATHWING STRUCTURE

- GRAND MASTER OF THE DEATHWING
  - LIBRARIANS
  - INTERROGATOR-CHAPLAINS
    - DEATHWING KNIGHTS
    - DEATHWING KNIGHTS
    - DEATHWING KNIGHTS

Deathwing Knight Masters and Terminator Sergeants may bear heraldic devices upon their armour in place of conventional squad numbers, their true meaning known only to the Inner Circle.

Deathwing Terminator Squad	Deathwing Terminator Squad	Deathwing Terminator Squad	Deathwing Terminator Squad	Deathwing Terminator Squad
Deathwing Terminator Squad	Deathwing Terminator Squad	Deathwing Terminator Squad	Deathwing Terminator Squad	Deathwing Terminator Squad
Deathwing Terminator Squad	Deathwing Terminator Squad	Deathwing Terminator Squad	Deathwing Terminator Squad	Deathwing Terminator Squad
Deathwing Terminator Squad	Deathwing Terminator Squad	Deathwing Terminator Squad	Deathwing Terminator Squad	Deathwing Terminator Squad

DEATHWING SUPPORT ASSETS

Deployed as required. As with Deathwing Squads, actual numbers are obfuscated to outsiders.

Venerable Dreadnoughts
Land Raiders
Land Raider Crusaders
Land Raider Redeemers

STRIKE FORCES

Across the galaxy, the Dark Angels fight in countless different war zones, against myriad foes. In order to best combat these threats, their strike forces combine different elements of their Chapter's strength into deadly armies that are greater than the sum of their parts.

The Lion's greatest legacy is his strategic genius – a quality passed on to his sons through the Chapter's gene-seed. This trait manifests exponentially as a Dark Angel ascends toward the rank of Company Master. Such officers can plan a campaign to the last detail, execute faultless assaults, and assemble impenetrable defences instinctively. Central to this ability is the deployment of the correct mix of squads, vehicles and support elements. To this end, the Dark Angels form strike forces – self-contained armies assembled to prosecute a specific campaign or defeat a particular foe.

Every Chapter keeps tomes within its Librarius that detail templates for different strike forces, each with its own specific battlefield strengths. For most Chapters, their main source of such lore is the Codex Astartes, and in this the Dark Angels are no exception. However, the secret agenda of the Lion's sons has forced them to adapt these formations to their needs. Over time, a number of scrolls have been penned by Supreme Grand Masters detailing strike forces unique to the Dark Angels. Collectively, these writings are known as the Hunter's Lore, and are stored in stasis-sealed armaglass cases deep within the lowest levels of the Rock.

Many specialist formations are detailed within the Hunter's Lore, from the monstrous sledgehammer that is the Beastslayer Strike Force, to the many-pronged assault force of the Scourge of Caliban. All share one common factor: though applicable against any number of foes, their doctrines and composition make them excellent tools with which to hunt the Fallen, ready in a heartbeat to hurl themselves against any defence the renegades might possess and counter any weapon they may deploy.

The strike force most frequently used by the Dark Angels – known as the Lion's Blade – is structured primarily around a Battle Demi-company supported by elements of the Deathwing and the Ravenwing. The force is often strengthened by squads drawn from the 10th Company for reconnaissance and ambush duties, and vehicles from the Armoury for heavy fire support. An extremely versatile and powerful weapon of war, the Lion's Blade possesses the killing power to crush whole armies of heretics, or safeguard entire hive cities from xenos predation. As with all Dark Angels strike forces, it is likewise always ready to deliver the killing blow should one of the Fallen be foolish enough to drop their guard.

LION'S BLADE STRIKE FORCE

The Lion's Blade strike force is one of the Chapter's most effective weapons in their hunt for absolution. While the brethren of the Battle Companies launch assaults and claim objectives, the agents of the Ravenwing race in to cut off lines of retreat, and the Deathwing wait to launch the decisive hammer-blow against more powerful foes.

INNER CIRCLE

Grand Masters
Company Masters
Interrogator-Chaplains
Librarians

The overall commander of a Lion's Blade strike force is invariably a member of the Inner Circle. Having fought in each company of the Chapter, he knows their individual strengths and how best to employ them on the field of battle.

DEATHWING

Interrogator-Chaplains
Librarians
Deathwing Command Squads
Deathwing Knights
Deathwing Terminator Squads
Venerable Dreadnoughts

The Lion's Blade strike force is built around a core of redoubtable warriors from one of the Chapter's Battle Companies. A Battle Company can be broken down into two Battle Demi-companies, each led by the Company Master or Chaplain.

BATTLE DEMI-COMPANIES

Company Masters
Chaplains
Command Squads
Company Veterans
Tactical Squads
Assault Squads
Devastator Squads
Dreadnoughts

The Lion's Blade is typified by supporting elements from the elite 1st and 2nd Companies. Even when they are not actively hunting the Fallen, they are always ready to respond to reports of their presence.

ARMOURY

Techmarines
Predators
Whirlwinds
Vindicators
Land Raiders
Land Raider Crusaders
Land Raider Redeemers

RAVENWING

Ravenwing Black Knights
Ravenwing Bike Squads
Ravenwing Attack Bike squads
Ravenwing Land Speeders
Ravenwing Vengeance
Land Speeders
Nephilim Jetfighters
Ravenwing Dark Talons

10TH COMPANY

Scout Squads

THE UNFORGIVEN

Amid the ashes of the Horus Heresy, distrust and accusation thickened the air. Roboute Guilliman, Primarch of the Ultramarines, initiated the Second Founding and, across the galaxy, the Space Marine Legions fragmented into the Chapters of the Adeptus Astartes. Each of the original Legions spawned a First Founding Chapter that retained its name and identity, along with successor Chapters responsible for becoming their own, entirely autonomous entities. The Dark Angels could hardly resist this motion, for the cataclysmic destruction of Caliban was fresh in their minds, and they could not risk drawing undue attention to themselves. Thus they created several successor Chapters, and so it appeared that they followed Guilliman's dictates to the letter.

As with their every deed since the fall of Caliban, however, the Dark Angels were following a hidden agenda. Their successors, who would collectively become known as the Unforgiven, formed their own Inner Circles to guard the knowledge of the Dark Angels' secret shame. Each one established companies concurrent with the Deathwing and Ravenwing, though named differently to maintain at least the veneer of individuality. Finally, though the Unforgiven claimed their own Chapter home worlds, heraldry and doctrines, their leaders attended clandestine meetings on the Rock with the Supreme Grand Master of the Dark Angels. These ritual-laden gatherings saw the Unforgiven take their orders from the master of the Dark Angels, so that the ongoing hunt for the Fallen could continue in utmost secrecy. The Lion's sons could not risk these meetings becoming common knowledge. Yet rumours persist of nepotism and legion building. Over time these have led to the Unforgiven being regarded with distrust.

Despite their impeccably pure gene-seed, the Dark Angels have been passed over for many of the Foundings that have created fresh Chapters to fight the Imperium's wars. Yet from time to time the Adeptus Terra have been forced to permit the Dark Angels another Founding, the records of which have mysteriously vanished shortly afterward. In this way, an uncertain number of Unforgiven Chapters have been created, each giving every outward appearance of fighting their own wars for the Imperium, while secretly aiding in the Dark Angels' hidden hunt.

Sergeant Kreshnov watched in awe as the Space Marines tore their way through the last few Chaos worshippers. His lasgun forgotten in his hands, the Valhallan stared wide-eyed while metal crumpled, blood fountained, and flesh and bone were torn asunder. Kreshnov had emptied whole clips into those renegade scum, had seen his men do the same and die screaming for their troubles. Yet against the roaring chainswords and merciless strength of the Angels of Redemption, even the traitors' baroque power armour could not protect them. Outnumbered and outfought, the last handful of Chaos Space Marines were hacked down by their chanting foes, until only a single, hulking figure remained.

This one was a monster – twelve feet tall and boasting a horned helm, a tattered cloak of flayed skin and a sword that could fell a Valhallan frostoak. Before the Space Marines had dropped in to join the fight, Kreshnov had seen that giant cut Commissar Draski in half with a single swing, and flip the platoon's command Chimera onto its roof with just his gauntleted hands. Now the Chaos Space Marine swung his mighty sword, only for the Angels of Redemption's leader to catch the blade against his own in a shower of sparks. Kreshnov cried out as the Space Marine ducked inside the traitor's guard and smashed the pommel of his weapon into the monster's chin, sending him reeling back. The Angels of Redemption surrounded their victim, battering at him from all sides. With a furious roar, the renegade slammed his sword through the chest of one Space Marine, then hacked the head from another. Yet blades, mauls and gun butts continued to hammer into him. Kreshnov's men cheered as the Chaos Space Marine was caught in the back of the skull by a blow from a power maul and finally toppled. Caught up in the moment, none of them wondered why the Adeptus Astartes had not simply butchered their monstrous opponent as they had his followers. Instead, Kreshnov started forward, his jubilant men close behind, yelling out thanks and praise to the Space Marines. The Valhallan sergeant saw his rescuers share a silent glance. Their leader shook his head, and his brothers responded to the curt gesture by turning toward the Valhallans with their bolt pistols raised. Sergeant Kreshnov's frown of incomprehension was still spreading across his face as the shooting began...

SUCCESSOR CHAPTERS

The Dark Angels Legion is recorded as having sired three successor Chapters in the aftermath of the Horus Heresy, and several other Chapters are believed to have descended from the Sons of the Lion in the millennia since. The true legacy of the Unforgiven is known only to the most senior members of the Dark Angels' Inner Circle.

ANGELS OF VENGEANCE

The Angels of Vengeance shun fame and laurels, instead concentrating on their duties to the exclusion of all else. They are a grim and dour organisation, and all of their companies wear jet black armour in tribute to the original Dark Angels Legion that departed Terra at the beginning of the Great Crusade.

The Angels of Vengeance embody one particular aspect of the Dark Angels' character above all others – a stubborn devotion to their cause that borders on fanaticism. The Chapter is wont to become embroiled in battles that other forces would have little hope of winning, and emerging bloodied but victorious. The Angels of Vengeance have willingly suffered horrific casualties in the name of victory – a result of their absolute refusal to retreat in the face of any foe. The Chapter's very future has been put in jeopardy more than once, beginning with their appalling depletion during the Forgotten Wars. More recently, in the aftermath of the Siege of San Apolis, their losses were so extreme that the Chapter was forced to spend almost a century rebuilding before it could do battle once more.

CONSECRATORS

The Consecrators' first appearance is noted during the Second Kuppukin Schism, where they are said to have deployed at Chapter strength with no warning whatsoever. At the height of this terrible war, loyalist forces were surrounded within the Sanctum of Silence by a screaming sea of renegades, mutants and traitors. It appeared that the Imperial forces had but hours to live, until the Consecrators plummeted from the heavens. All vox-hails were ignored, but the Unforgiven went to war on the defenders' behalf with a terrible fury. In just six hours, the Adeptus Astartes reduced the traitor horde to little more than broken, twisted corpses. Their task complete, the Chapter withdrew without a word. Other such heroic intercessions have been noted since, the Consecrators always remaining silent. One aspect of the mysterious Chapter has been commented on time and again; their brethren bear all manner of holy relics, and utilise ancient patterns of armour, weapons and vehicles. It is as though the Consecrators have inherited the most revered arms of the Dark Angels Legion, preserving them and bearing them down through the ages against the foes of the Lion.

'What is our quest? To purge our shame through the death of those who turned from the Lion.'

ANGELS OF REDEMPTION

Nothing can dissuade the Angels of Redemption from their mission to hunt down the Fallen. It has been noted that the Chapter has, on occasion, withdrawn from a campaign in order to pursue their own undisclosed ends. It was at the height of the Defence of Gaitlinghive, at the moment of the Orks' final assault, that the Angels of Redemption redeployed, leaving seven brigades of the Gaitlinghive militia to face a greenskin horde three million strong. The Unforgiven had embarked upon a hunt that led them to capture a Fallen Dark Angel. To them, this victory was well worth the lives of the Gaitlinghive militia, as well as the millions of civilians they had fought to protect. The Angels of Redemption were never called to account for this act, as there were no survivors to press any form of enquiry.

Thanks to dark rumours of this and many similar events, Imperial forces have begun to decline offers of aid from the Angels of Redemption. More serious repercussions of the Chapter's actions – or flagrant inaction – have yet to take place, but may well range from Inquisitorial censure to outright excommunication.

DISCIPLES OF CALIBAN

The Disciples of Caliban are a fleet-based Chapter that strikes with blistering speed and ferocity. Their record of deeds is impeccable, their conduct exemplary. Still, the Founding of this Chapter is shrouded in controversy. It is believed that Dark Angels Supreme Grand Master Anaziel made a request of the High Lords of Terra late in the 37th Millennium for this Chapter to be founded. It is highly unusual for a Chapter Master to make such a demand, and the reasons given by Anaziel for his petition were never shared. Still, dispensation was eventually granted, and the Disciples of Caliban created. The Chapter's Founding gene-seed was of the highest pedigree, and scrutinised to a standard far beyond even that required by the Adeptus Terra. To this day, the purity of the Chapter's gene-seed is constantly monitored for the slightest sign of corruption or degradation, and the Chapter has the most exacting standards of recruitment of any of the Unforgiven. There have been whispers that Anaziel had the Disciples of Caliban created for a specific purpose, often rumoured amongst the other Unforgiven to be for the single-minded pursuit of the renegade known as Cypher.

ANGELS OF ABSOLUTION

A force for vengeful destruction in the Emperor's name, the Angels of Absolution have been sighted throughout the known galaxy, most often seen fighting alongside the Dark Angels themselves. The two Chapters often launch joint operations, such as the crusade against the Arch-Arsonist of Charadon, the Battle at Archangel VII, or the bloody suppression of the Rasputin uprisings.

The doctrines of the Dark Angels and the Angels of Absolution are almost identical, though with one notable distinction. The Angels of Absolution consider their guilt expunged by the actions of their forefathers during the Fall of Caliban, and thus fear no spiritual damnation for the actions of the Fallen. However, they still consider themselves responsible for meting out punishment upon the traitors, and take pride in the fulfilment of this duty. The Angels of Absolution are characterised by a certain gallows humour that the rest of the Unforgiven do not share, but they are no less dedicated for all their sardonic banter and bleak irony.

GUARDIANS OF THE COVENANT

It is not known from what Founding the Guardians of the Covenant came, only that they are part of the Unforgiven. Their adopted home world, Mortikah VII, lies near to the western rim of the Imperium, and their mountaintop fortress monastery takes the form of a mighty cathedral whose spire pierces the clouds. The Guardians of the Covenant fight most of their wars within the Segmentum Pacificus, and are utterly merciless in their destruction of the Emperor's foes. They have spearheaded a number of crusades into the Halo Stars and the Veiled Region, enacting xenocidal purges in which billions of enemy warriors have been put to the sword. This Chapter is known for its exceptionally monastic character. True warrior-monks of the Emperor, they are assiduous in studying the teachings of the Emperor and their Primarch, and have penned several tomes that have been added to the Lore of the Lion over the millennia. Their banners, armour and the flanks of their vehicles are covered in spidery, hand-written text extracted from the pages of the Codex Astartes, the Requiem Angelis and many other tomes held sacred by the Space Marines.

IN THE NAME OF ABSOLUTION

Across the galaxy, the Dark Angels strike without warning and vanish without explanation. For millennia they have slaughtered the Imperium's foes and defended its citizens with grim efficiency. Yet for every noble act, another, darker deed lies hidden in the Chapter's annals. Always the hunt for the Fallen drives them onward, and each new hope for redemption hides damnation in its shadow.

FALL OF CALIBAN

Caliban is torn apart by betrayal, and the Fallen are scattered across the galaxy.

NEW BLOOD

With Caliban gone, the Dark Angels must establish a new recruiting world. They choose numerous planets, hiding their precise number and nature.

2ND MORTIS GATE CAMPAIGN

The entire Dark Angels Chapter takes up arms against the renegade forces of the Death Guard. Three months of storm-wracked warfare see the traitor forces driven from their strongholds, and the Dark Angels' standards raised in victory.

THE DEATHWING UNLEASHED

The Deathwing deploys to crush the traitor forces of Obidiah Hrakon. The Fallen Dark Angel is finally defeated in a duel with the Grand Master of the Deathwing.

THE REBULUS CLEANSING

The Dark Angels and Unforgiven fight a thirty-year war against the cults of the Rebulus System. Many lives are lost before the destruction of the traitor moons of Ixx.

GRYMM'S LANDING

The Dark Angels recruiting world of Grymm's Landing falls into civil war after the Alpha Legion and Night Lords incite rebellion there. The Angels of Vengeance respond, fighting through wave after wave of renegades, cultists and madmen. Finally, despite massive casualties, they exterminate every living thing on the surface of Grymm's Landing.

MASSACRE ON MINORIA

The Deathwing assault Minoria in the Periliac System, capturing or killing every inhabitant. This action raises protests from several other Chapters, who claim the Dark Angels' aid was needed to defend Periliac Prime against a massive Ork Waaagh!.

THE HUNDRED PLANET REBELLION

Pursuing the notorious Fallen known as Cypher, the Dark Angels become mired in a long and costly war with the heretic cults of the mad priest Alldric the Subverter.

CEGORACH'S DUE

The Dark Angels track the Fallen known as Neziek to the world of Vriedos. They run their quarry to ground just as he is about to escape through a webway portal. However, the Dark Angels' efforts at capture are foiled when a sizeable band of Harlequins bursts from the portal. Fighting furiously, the Harlequins hold the wrathful Space Marines at bay long enough to snatch Neziek and drag him into the labyrinth dimension.

M38

M40

M41

THE LOST HOPE OF PERDITION

A Dark Angels investigation of a space hulk newly materialised out of the Warp discovers strong elements of the renegades known as the Cleaved. The battle is won when cyclonic charges destroy the hulk's engine rooms, though at the cost of Supreme Grand Master Zakaron who manually triggers the blast.

THE FOURTH QUADRANT REBELLION

Over ten years, a series of incredibly destructive wars engulf a quarter of the Segmentum Solar. Mystery shrouds the architects of this catastrophe, but the Dark Angels fight alongside the Imperial Fists at such battles as the Rastabal Drop and the siege of Kaligar to end the threat once and for all.

THE MACHARIAN HERESY

Over three decades, the Dark Angels are tasked with suppressing the civil wars that are ongoing across many of the territories gained during the Macharian Conquests. The Ravenwing uncover several corrupt cults largely instigated by the Alpha Legion, and the unmistakable signs of Cypher's presence.

THE FORLEX RESCUE

A Necron stasis-crypt awakens beneath the Imperial colony of Forlex. Striking from orbit, the Guardians of the Covenant drive the xenos back below ground and, though the cost in lives is steep, well over one hundred thousand colonists are safely evacuated.

M41

BATTLE FOR STYX
Tau forces attempt to annex the Dark Angel recruitment world of Styx. The Rock itself arrives in orbit to defend the planet, and the Dark Angels' response is so violent that the xenos are wiped out in a single day.

SEPHLAGM
The Ravenwing hunt the possessed governor of the toxic world of Sephlagm. During a fierce battle in the gubernatorial palace, they summon the Deathwing to strike the killing blow.

THE DEATH OF NABERIUS
Hot on the trail of the ever-elusive Cypher, Commander Naberius – Supreme Grand Master of the Dark Angels – is led into an ambush and slain by Chaos Space Marines. Azrael leads the Deathwing to recover his body, bringing an end to the shadow-shrouded conflict now known as the Rhamiel Betrayal. For this and many other heroic deeds, Azrael is named Naberius' successor.

WAAAGH! GROBLINIK
The Dark Angels join the Imperial defence against the vast horde of Waaagh! Groblinik. It is through the Dark Angels' sheer remorseless determination that the Orks are defeated, though at great cost.

THE CANYONS OF KORIS
Azrael leads a strike force to purge the Orks of Waaagh! Gutgouger from Koris. Wings of Nephilim Jetfighters engage in furious dogfights through the planet's storm-lashed canyon maze, covering the Dark Angels' final push against Warboss Gutgouger's monstrous Killfort.

WYRMWOOD
Several squads of Deathwing board the space hulk *Wyrmwood*. None are ever seen again, and records of the action are erased.

TERROR ON DABASCUS

THE SHADOWSHRINE
A strike force under Chaplain Asmodai battle a Commorrite host in the shrine-city of Gothala. Thousands of Mandrakes fall upon the Space Marines from squirming portals of sentient shadow, and it seems the Dark Angels must be overrun. However, Asmodai holds his force together through sheer willpower, eventually leading an attack to collapse the Dark Eldar portals with explosives and end the nightmare.

DURGANION XIII
A distress call lures a Dark Angels strike force into a Genestealer ambush amid the hives of Durganion XIII. Only when Sammael himself leads a headlong charge to cut down the hulking xenos Broodlord are the Dark Angels able to hack and blast their way out of the trap.

THE RED HUNT

STORM OF VENGEANCE
The Dark Angels defeat Ghazghkull Thraka and Nazdreg on Piscina IV.

THE 3RD TYRANNIC WAR

Several Dark Angels strike forces join the battle against the far-reaching tendrils of Hive Fleet Leviathan as they spread deeper into the Imperium.

THE RICH PRIZE

A Deathwing assault smashes the renegade enclave of Darkenhel. Over two dozen Fallen are seized, and the cells of the Rock ring with agonised screams for many months.

THE 13TH BLACK CRUSADE

A vast tide of Chaos worshippers pours from the Eye of Terror into the Cadian Gate. Detecting many Fallen amongst the horde, the Dark Angels risk all by ordering the Unforgiven to join them in a headlong assault against the renegade forces.

TO CATCH CYPHER

The Black Templars fight alongside the Dark Angels on the world of Parabulus in an attempt to weaken the renegade pirates who use the world as their base. However, a dispute over a Black Templars prisoner causes both Chapters to briefly engage. The incident is reported, and an Inquisitorial enquiry commences.

DARK VENGEANCE

Seeking to avenge the death of Company Master Zadakiel on Stern's Remembrance – and to strike down a foe who appear to know their darkest secret – the Dark Angels 5th Company engage the Crimson Slaughter on the world of Bane's Landing. The fight is a desperate one, and only an act of supreme self-sacrifice prevents the Chaos worshippers from achieving their aims.

COMPANY MASTERS

With solemn determination, the Company Masters of the Dark Angels lead their warriors into battle. Foes pinioned by their steely gaze lose the will to fight, for no amount of aggression is a match for the Masters' cold fury. Veterans of centuries of warfare, inheritors of their Primarch's skills at both bladesmanship and grand strategy, the Dark Angels' Masters are mighty warriors and compelling commanders.

More than this, the Company Masters are amongst the foremost hunters of the Fallen. They bear a terrible burden upon their shoulders, for they must wage two wars – the Imperium's galaxy-wide fight for survival, and the Dark Angels' ongoing battle for redemption. The secrets to which they are privy strengthen the Company Masters' resolve, yet they also distance them from their battle-brothers. Though they fight to protect Humanity, and seek always to preserve the lives of the heroic warriors they lead, the Company Masters must be ready at a moment's notice to abandon both of these closely held principles should the hunt demand it. Nothing is more important than capturing the Fallen, and if the lives of every one of a Company Master's followers must be spent to see another Fallen Dark Angel seized, then he must make that trade without the slightest hesitation. Small wonder, then, that these devoted leaders are quiet, sombre individuals; their secrets weigh heavy, and it is a testament to the Company Masters' heroism that they continue to discharge their duties regardless.

THE LION AND THE WOLF

Perhaps the most famous rivalry in the Imperium is between the Dark Angels and the Space Wolves. During the Great Crusade, on the world of Dulan, the Space Wolves and Dark Angels fought side by side. After receiving a personal insult from the world's tyrant ruler, Durath, Leman Russ vowed to cut off the man's head and demanded the Dark Angels stand down. However, Jonson had already planned his assault and, disinterested in pandering to Russ' ego, swept into Durath's palace. The Dark Angels' victory was so swift that the Space Wolves were caught flat-footed, and Russ could only howl in frustration when told that Jonson had slain Durath. After the battle, Russ struck Jonson a blow. Jonson rose to his feet and struck back. A space was cleared, and the two Primarchs wrestled while their assembled men cheered. The Primarchs were matched in strength, speed and cunning, and their duel went on for a day and a night. Finally Russ, quick to anger but also to mirth, stepped back with a laugh. Jonson, however, was silent; dour and resentful, he saw Russ' first blow as treacherous. As Russ laughed, Jonson knocked him unconscious. By the time the Space Wolf Primarch woke, the Dark Angels had departed. Russ vowed vengeance, and so began a feud that lasts to this day. Even now, when Dark Angels and Space Wolves meet in the field, a champion from each Chapter is called upon to refight that ancient duel.

CHAPLAINS

Few beings have greater presence upon the field of battle than a Chaplain of the Dark Angels; he sunders foes with the very symbol of Imperial authority, every strike of his crozius arcanum a devastating hammerblow. He bellows Liturgies of Battle, damning his enemies and inspiring his brothers with words like thunder. He sermonises upon the righteousness of his cause, even as the fires of war rage all around him and the blows of the foe glance from the crackling nimbus of his rosarius.

The Chaplains of the Adeptus Astartes are the spiritual guardians of their Chapter, stern figures of authority who watch their brothers' every thought, word and deed for the slightest signs of corruption. Nowhere is this truer than amongst the Chaplains of the Dark Angels. To them falls the duty of seeing that the Chapter's apocryphal lessons are fully understood by their battle-brothers, that the timeless rituals are observed and the proper rites maintained to guarantee unquestioning devotion by all to their leaders. As with all Space Marine Chapters, the Chaplains of the Dark Angels are the keepers of the Reclusiam. For the Dark Angels this is a vast colonnaded shrine deep beneath the surface of the Rock. It is here that many of the Chapter's most precious relics are kept, and all of its most sacred ceremonies undertaken. It is the Chaplains who lead these rites, who ensure that they are remembered and passed down through each generation of the Chapter, so that they might never be forgotten.

THE DARK ORACLE

Near the heart of the Rock resides a single cell, where only the Supreme Grand Master and those called the Watchers in the Dark are allowed to venture. There, past dozens of locked gates, is an oubliette. Its walls are inscribed with potent runes of warding meant both to keep hostile entities out, and something dreadful in. There, sustained for ten thousand years by a stasis field, languishes the ruined thing once known as Luther.

Down the ages, the Supreme Grand Masters have had some success in using Luther as an oracle. Although his Warp-contaminated mind wanders or tries to deceive, during moments of lucidity the traitor speaks of events that will be, or might be, or drops hints at what is hidden and where.

Since the Fall of Caliban, each Supreme Grand Master has tried to extract a confession from the thing that was, and may still be, Luther. Though the creature has divulged many secrets – from the names and locations of the Fallen, to the whereabouts of Legion relics hidden deep within the bowels of the Rock – it has never sought absolution. Mostly, all that comes from Luther are mad ravings; over and over again he repeats that he need not repent, for one day Lion El'Jonson will return and absolve him of his sins. He claims that day is near, and that he can feel the Lion already close at hand...

COMPANY VETERANS SQUAD

Clad in swirling monastic robes, faces shadowed by deep cowls, squads of Dark Angels Company Veterans are a sinister sight upon the field of battle. Masters of both long-ranged firefights and vicious, close-quarters combat, the Company Veterans are in their element no matter what the enemy throws at them. The Veterans fight wordlessly, the bark of their guns and the crunch of their blades through flesh and bone all the forms of expression they require. Coupled with the single-minded way in which these warriors pursue their objectives upon the battlefield, Company Veterans make for frightening foes.

The Dark Angels are a solemn Chapter, not given to grandiose displays or acts of self-aggrandisement. This does not mean, however, that deeds of sufficient heroism are not recognised or rewarded. Those who fall valorously in battle will be honoured with sombre battlefield ceremonies, providing duty permits time. Meanwhile, those who distinguish themselves and live often find themselves elevated to the rank of Company Veteran.

To be acknowledged before the assembled might of the Dark Angels is a proud and humbling moment, for each battle-brother is a hero in his own right. Their leaders, hooded and robed, are living legends whose names provoke awe amongst even the most powerful men in the galaxy. It is one of the highest honours that a Dark Angel can attain to be officially recognised for their deeds by such an assemblage, and one that they will fight to be worthy of ever after.

Each company from the 3rd to the 9th has a complement of Veterans. These experienced warriors often form into elite squads for single missions, or for the duration of specific campaigns, but while so assembled they fight with complete surety and mutual trust. It is from such close-knit brotherhoods that the warriors of the Deathwing are chosen, their deeds of heroism earning them ever greater – if sternly delivered – accolades.

'Forget your past life. From this day on you are simply a Dark Angel – nothing else is of consequence. The Chapter is all that matters.'

- Supreme Grand Master Azrael, addressing the Dutysworn

THE ROCK

Following the destruction of Caliban, the Dark Angels made the Rock their new home. Although only a fraction of what was once a planet, the Rock is larger than even the heaviest class of starship, and it bears truly staggering firepower. The sheer sides of its mass are studded with gun turrets, lance batteries, torpedo tubes, observation blisters, and comm-relays. Its cavernous docking bays, built with the aid of the Tech-Priests of Mars, can accommodate many hundreds of smaller craft, including Thunderhawk Gunships, Nephilim Jetfighters and escort frigates. Finally, the Rock is outfitted with Warp engines, allowing the Dark Angels' headquarters to travel across the galaxy at will.

When the Dark Angels first claimed the Rock, a massive labour force carved out deeper and deeper catacombs in the asteroid's bedrock, excavating room for an entire Legion. In the halls and dungeons beneath the ancient, ruined fortress monastery, the Dark Angels found a hoard of machinery that had sat untouched since the Age of Technology. Many of the devices – like the Rock's arcane shield generator – still worked, though their mechanisms were now unfathomable.

While the artisans did marvellous work transforming this remnant of Caliban, crafting halls full of clustered columns rising to arched vaults, and much-decorated ceremonial crypts to hold the Legion's sacred items, the Rock remains a grim place, full of echoes and cold stone.

Although the Warp storm that scoured Caliban could not penetrate the Rock's ancient shields, they did leave an indelible mark. To this day, there exists a disturbance within the force field that protects the asteroid, as if part of that tempest still rages within. Great chain-lightnings arc across the artificial atmosphere, briefly outlining the ruins. No effort was made to rebuild the ruined Tower of Angels atop the Rock, and even now it remains undisturbed and eerily silent as the storm crackles above.

Although attempts have been made to mask it, an unusual energy signature emanates outward from the Rock, portending of some great power hidden within. Beneath the shattered ruins, many dark secrets lie cloistered from sight, and the deeper into the Rock's labyrinth dungeons one goes, the closer one comes to the truth.

The highest ranking Dark Angels believe that they know all of the Rock's many secrets, yet even they remain ignorant of their stronghold's greatest revelation. Hidden inside a secluded chamber, unreachable by all save the small, robed figures of the Watchers in the Dark, the mighty Primarch Lion El'Jonson lies sleeping. His wounds long healed, he waits for that time when he will be needed once again. When the clarion call of battle sounds for the last time, Jonson will be summoned forth from his millennial rest to defend the Imperium of Mankind from its enemies. Then shall all traitors quake in fear, for the Lion's vengeance will be terrible indeed.

COMMAND SQUADS

Defenders of their Company's honour and bodyguards to their Chapter's greatest heroes, the Veterans of the Command Squad form a steadfast rallying point for their brothers in even the most chaotic battle. Each is an expert in his field, whether it be lethal marksmanship, restorative field-surgery or one-on-one combat. For this reason, Command Squads are often employed by the Dark Angels in roles of great strategic importance, such as seizing key objectives or stiffening the resolve of defensive lines against overwhelming enemy attacks. While the Company Standard Bearer inspires all around him, the Company Champion engages the heroes of the foe in duels, cutting them down for his Company's honour.

Many Command Squads include an Apothecary amongst their number. Working in the front lines, an Apothecary uses his narthecium – a field kit that contains all the tech, stim-packs and sacred unguents needed to heal wounds – to patch up his wounded brethren and return them to battle. Should he find a warrior who is past saving, the Apothecary calms the dying brother, perhaps mercifully helping them on their way with a deft cut, before taking out his reductor. This special device is used to remove the progenoids – the glands that contain a battle-brother's gene-seed, and from which new Space Marine organs can be cultured. In this way, Apothecaries safeguard the future of their Chapter, ensuring further generations of warriors will be created to avenge those who have been lost.

THE BLADES OF CALIBAN

Each Blade of Caliban is a longsword enfolded in a power-field that emits a spine-chilling moan – known as the Angels' Lament – as it cuts the air. A single dolorous blow with one of these weapons is enough to lop the head from the mightiest traitor champion or hack down a rampaging xenos war-leader. Yet the Blades of Caliban are more than just potent weapons. Each is a precious relic that dates back to the days before the Great Crusade, when the Knights of old Caliban rode out on quests to scour the Chaos-tainted monsters from their world's vast forests. As such, each Blade of Caliban is a piece of the Dark Angels' heritage, a noble and inspiring heirloom from a time before betrayal stained their souls. It is only fitting that such weapons should be wielded by the most honourable warriors amongst the Dark Angels' ranks, and it for this reason that they are given to the Company Champions to wield. When a Company Champion first takes up his mantle, he is presented his Company's Blade of Caliban in a long and solemn ritual that takes a full two days to conclude. During these proceedings, the name of the previous bearer is engraved upon the weapon's grip, and the powered-down blade used by the Chaplains to cut the new wielder's palm. The freshly instated Champion then grasps the weapon, symbolically binding himself with blood to the previous wielder, and to all those who have gone before.

TACTICAL SQUADS

The iron resolve of the Dark Angels Tactical Marines is the stuff of legend, and they are renowned throughout the Imperium. Humourless, merciless and murderously efficient, these skilled warriors form the adamantium backbone of their Chapter's fighting forces.

Adaptability is the hallmark of all Tactical Squads. Their battle-brothers are versed in the arts of fighting with blade and pistol, heavy weapons such as missile launchers and plasma cannons, and special weapons like the flamer, meltagun or grav-gun. It is this versatility that makes Tactical Squads so indispensable. They can be tasked with holding ground, with providing fire support, or with charging headlong into the bloody storm of close combat – often all in the course of a single battle – and will fulfil each new command with speed and skill.

When circumstances demand, Tactical squads can even split into smaller units known as Combat Squads, dividing their strength and armaments to further increase their versatility. This will often be done when a particular objective needs to be seized; one Combat Squad, led by the Sergeant, advances with the squad's special weapon to make a close-quarters assault, while the other sits back in cover, using their boltguns and heavy weapon to provide fire support for their brothers. This has proven an effective model on countless battlefields through the ages, and has secured victory for the Dark Angels time and again.

Though not privy to the secrets of the Inner Circle, Dark Angels Tactical Marines are thoroughly indoctrinated in such a way as to make them ideal weapons for hunting the Fallen. They never question the teachings of their Chapter or the orders of their superiors, and frown upon the sort of improvisation and free thought that characterises such brotherhoods as the Blood Angels or Space Wolves. Furthermore, they prize self-sacrifice above all other virtues, ensuring that they will lay down their lives at the command of their Masters without any hesitation.

ASSAULT SQUADS

With chainswords roaring and bolt pistols at the ready, the Assault Squads of the Dark Angels charge into battle as the vanguard of their brothers' attack. They are the tip of the spear, the first-strike weapon of the Battle Companies. Their violent onset punches holes in the enemy lines, paving the way for those who come behind. Unlike the bellicose hot-heads of many Chapters' Assault Squads, Dark Angels Assault Marines are reserved, and grimly serious. In place of howled battle-cries, they maintain a constant chant, a mantra of hatred and repugnance every bit as terrifying as the vox-amplified bellows of their counterparts in other Chapters. Droning over the screams of the dying and the thunder of gunfire, this sinister sound spreads a pall of dread over the enemy ranks, shattering the enemy's resolve as surely as the Assault Marines' onslaught.

Dark Angels Assault Marines embody the selfless creed of their Chapter, and are honoured accordingly. Often using jump packs to bound ahead or to drop directly into the midst of the foe, the Assault Squads are usually first to the fight. They dive headlong into enemy strongpoints, suffering the worst of their foe's firepower in order to carve the heart from their defences. Artillery emplacements are blown sky high by well-placed krak grenades, enemy officers are cut down where they stand. Wherever the Assault Squads strike they sow devastation, depriving the foe of key strategic assets and leaving the enemy battle plan in tatters.

Brother Naphirim fell through dense black cloud. For long seconds it was as though he plunged alone through some strange hell, with only the steady thud of his twin hearts for company. Then his helm-vox pipped twice, Sergeant Balophor signalling readiness. Seconds later, Naphirim burst from the underside of the cloud bank and saw the Ork fortress directly below, hurtling up toward him at incredible speed. Calmly, the Assault Marine thumbed his jump pack's activation trigger, his fall suddenly arrested as jets of flame roared from its exhausts. Around him, Naphirim saw his brothers do the same, and as one the Dark Angels fell upon their foes. Ceramite boots crunched down onto riveted metal as the Assault Marines hit the fort's north rampart. Bellowing greenskins poured in from all directions, their momentary surprise forgotten at the sight of worthy opponents. The xenos were met with a hail of bolt pistol fire, torsos and heads bursting in wet sprays as the mass reactive bolts did their work. Naphirim lobbed a frag grenade over the heads of the foe, the explosive arcing down into a tight press of greenskins where it detonated in a sudden blizzard of green flesh and dark red blood. Crude slugs clanged from the Assault Marines' armour, a lucky shot blowing Brother Raziel off his feet. Calmly, Naphirim gunned down the greenskin that had shot his comrade, before beginning the third chant of Scornful Repugnance. Turning west along the rampart, Naphirim and his squad-mates began to hack a path toward the fort's heavily defended gatehouse. They had a mission to complete, and they would see their duty done, no matter the cost.

DEVASTATOR SQUADS

The very air shakes with fury as the heavy weapons of the Dark Angels Devastators cut loose. Enemy battle tanks and aircraft are reduced to blazing wrecks, while infantry squads are churned to bloody mulch or blasted into drifting ash by the overwhelming firestorm. Many warriors would be moved to vent cheers of exhilaration or bellowed invective while unleashing such incredible destruction; not so the Devastator brethren of the Dark Angels. The most these stubbornly reserved battle-brothers offer is the occasional curt nod of satisfaction as their fire sees some particularly troublesome target blown to pieces.

Not all the members of a Devastator squad tote heavy weapons. A battle-brother's first posting upon advancing from the ranks of the 10th Company will be as a member of a Devastator Squad. After observing all the proper rites of ascension, advancement and obeisance to their new brethren, the first duty of a new Devastator Marine is to prove their worth with bolter, blade and grenade. Such battle-brothers provide covering fire for their more experienced comrades, act as spotters for their squad's heavy weapons, and are on hand to hack down any foe who might think to neutralise the Devastators at close quarters. Under the stern tutelage of their squad's Sergeant, each Devastator Marine works to prove their worth, absorbing all of the strategic and spiritual teachings necessary to become one with the wrathful machine spirit of a heavy weapon.

It is during their time in the Devastator Squads that Dark Angels battle-brothers truly learn the intractable ways of their Chapter. Feet planted and guns blazing, Dark Angels Devastators are expected to hold their ground no matter the odds stacked against them. The cool and efficient prioritisation of targets is key to this style of warfare. At the direction of their Sergeant, the Devastators eliminate enemy threats in the optimal order to prevent themselves from being overrun or wiped out by enemy fire. They ensure the correct weapon is deployed at precisely the right moment, and that not a single shot is wasted. After all, self-sacrifice is to be respected, but the careless expenditure of lives and material is an unforgivable sin.

'IN WARFARE, PREPARATION IS KEY. DETERMINE THAT WHICH YOUR FOE PRIZES MOST, THEN SITE YOUR HEAVY WEAPONS SO THAT THEY OVERLOOK IT. IN THIS WAY, YOU MAY BE QUITE SURE THAT YOU SHALL NEVER WANT FOR TARGETS.'

- Lion El'Jonson, 'Tenets of Strategy and Supremacy'

TRANSPORTS

Whether advancing upon the foes of Mankind with guns blazing, or snatching up a member of the Fallen before he can flee their closing net, the Dark Angels make extensive use of armoured transports. The Adeptus Astartes' way of war emphasises speed and manoeuvrability and – while the Dark Angels may be more restrained and methodical than some Chapters – they still prize the ability to swiftly redeploy their forces, or to rapidly storm their foe's positions. To ensure that infantry assets such as Tactical and Devastator Squads can keep pace with these sort of advances, Rhinos, Razorbacks and Drop Pods are deployed.

For many millennia, the Rhino APC has served as the Dark Angels' most reliable and widespread armoured transport. This pugnacious tank boasts resilient armour, a modicum of anti-personnel firepower, and transport space for ten fully armoured battle-brothers and all of their wargear. Furthermore, the Rhino's systems are so straightforward that – between the efforts of the vehicle's crew and its machine spirit – battlefield repairs can be effected upon the tank without the need for a Techmarine in attendance.

By comparison, the Razorback is a strategically versatile half-way house between armoured transport and dedicated battle-tank. It sacrifices part of its transportation space in order to accommodate the power capacitors, heat-sinks and ammunition hoppers for a turret mounted, twin-linked heavy weapon. This modification allows the Razorback to provide covering fire for its passengers, both while they are embarked and once deployed into the enemy's midst.

The Drop Pod is an effective terror weapon. Deployed in invasion waves from the launch bays of Dark Angels space craft, Drop Pods carry their passengers safely through a planet's atmosphere. They rain down upon enemy positions, their retro-rockets arresting their hurtling descent at the last moment and bringing the pod in for a crunching landing amongst the shocked foe. A full squad of Dark Angels or – with minor modifications – a Dreadnought can ride inside each Drop Pod, allowing the deployment of overwhelming force in a matter of seconds.

BATTLE TANKS

The battle tanks of the Dark Angels rumble across the field with enemy fire rattling from their armoured hulls. Crewed by adept and determined battle-brothers, the tanks plough undaunted through the firestorm, weapons swivelling and tracking as they acquire their targets. With cool, methodical skill the Dark Angels gunners line up their shots, refusing to be rushed by the attacks of the foe. Finally, the gunners hit their firing runes, their tanks' guns lighting up in a storm of vengeance as they hammer killing shots into their victims. Heretic war engines explode in balls of dirty flame, their armour pierced at its weakest points. Lumbering monsters roar their last as they crash to the ground, bodies rent and torn by deadly accurate fire. Enemy infantry scream in terror as explosions engulf them, leaving nothing but a fire-lit abattoir of carnage where deadly warriors once stood. Ever mindful of the teachings of their Primarch, Dark Angels tank crews are steady and precise, dissecting their foes with withering fire patterns and ensuring they are never outmanoeuvred or outgunned.

The most common and by far the most versatile of Dark Angels battle tank formations are the Predator squadrons. Able to vary its loadout between anti-tank or anti-infantry weaponry as required, the Predator's firepower and resilience make it a dependable favourite with Company Masters. Indeed, it is a rare Dark Angels strike force that takes to the field without at least one squadron of these potent vehicles to lend armoured support. Only those battle-brothers well versed in armoured warfare are permitted the honour of crewing the Chapter's Predators, meaning that each of these sturdy tanks is driven into battle by an experienced veteran.

The Whirlwind is very much an artillery support vehicle. Usually deployed in positions behind the main Dark Angels battle line, Whirlwind squadrons can rain explosive or incendiary rockets on the foe from great distances. Thanks to their advanced augur systems, Whirlwinds are able to maintain impressive accuracy even against targets they cannot see. Meanwhile, their crashing bombardments are the ideal weapon to scour dug-in foes from their trenches, or disrupt massed enemy infantry prior to a major Dark Angels assault.

Vindicators are the most unsubtle of the Dark Angels' battle tanks. Mounting massive demolisher siege cannons and clad in dense adamantium armour, the tanks of the Vindicator squadrons are often held back by Dark Angels commanders until a decisive moment is reached. They are then deployed, tasked with the absolute annihilation of a single, crucial target or fortified enemy strongpoint. The sheer destructive potential of these tanks proves useful when all evidence of a Fallen's presence must be swiftly expunged; more than one traitor has been atomised by a coordinated bombardment from a squadron of Vindicators when their capture proved impossible.

LAND RAIDERS

No main-line Imperial tank is the equal of the mighty Land Raider. The vehicle's slab-armoured bulk is enormous, looming over even the other battle tanks of the Adeptus Astartes. Its weapon systems are devastatingly potent, able to lay down a storm of firepower that few foes can long endure. Even its machine spirit is a bold and bellicose presence far greater than that of most other Imperial vehicles, possessing a warlike sentience closer to those of the god-machines of the Collegia Titanica. It is therefore a great boon to Dark Angels commanders that the armouries of the Rock still house an impressive number of these ancient, mighty war engines.

Once, the Legiones Astartes could field whole armies of warriors mounted in Land Raiders. Now, the methods of their manufacture have been all but lost, with only a few forge worlds clinging jealously to the requisite lore. It is whispered that the Dark Angels must maintain close ties with at least one such world – this would certainly explain their continued ability to field substantial numbers of Land Raiders. But, like all other matters, the Chapter keeps any such relationship strictly secret. Still, though their Land Raiders are not in as short supply as those of many Chapters, the Dark Angels revere every single one of these noble battle tanks. Their Land Raiders' hulls are decorated by the Chapter's finest artisans, and whole squads of battle-brothers willingly lay down their lives to protect them.

Alongside the standard Land Raider, two alternative marks of this potent battle tank see regular service among Dark Angels forces. The first of these is the Land Raider Crusader, whose weapon fit is adapted to facilitate close infantry assault. Its racks of hurricane bolters and pintle-mounted multi-melta can generate a storm of point-blank covering fire, while its sizeable transport bay can bear up to sixteen fully armoured warriors into battle.

Perhaps the most feared Land Raider variant is the Redeemer. Excelling amid dense environments such as urban cityscapes or tangled jungle, the Redeemer is designed to flush enemy infantry from even the most defensible positions. To this end, lascannons are replaced by massive flamestorm cannons, allowing the Redeemer to engulf the foe in great torrents of blazing promethium.

DREADNOUGHTS

Heroism has its cost. Even the greatest warriors of the Dark Angels will eventually meet their death in battle. Yet there are those who cling tenaciously to life despite the most horrific wounds. Such heroes refuse to let death take them while even a single foe remains to threaten Humanity. If they can be recovered from the battlefield in time, these brothers are interred within the armoured sarcophagi of Dreadnoughts, exchanging the finality of death for an eternity of battle in their Chapter's name.

Each Dreadnought is an armoured walker, roughly humanoid in shape but massive in comparison to even the largest Space Marine. Each limb is a bulky arrangement of layered ceramite plating, electrofibre bundles and heavy hydraulic pistons that lend the Dreadnought enormous strength and resilience. A thrumming power plant is fitted to the walker's back, providing sufficient motive force for the Dreadnought to march across the battlefield, smash a path through any obstacle that bars its advance, and even effect a lumbering run when circumstance demands. Meanwhile, the Dreadnought sarcophagus itself is a sizeable armoured coffin that cocoons the pilot's biological remains. Safe within, the deathless hero is linked to countless motive systems, sensorium arrays, voxponder hook-ups, targeting augurs and the like, that allow them to move their mighty, armoured body as though it was their own flesh-and-blood. It is this that makes Dreadnoughts such incredibly potent weapons; they fuse the might of a battle tank with the boundless combat experience and absolute determination of one of the Lion's greatest sons.

'I AM VENGEANCE. I AM RETRIBUTION.
FEAR ME, HERETIC, FOR I AM YOUR DEATH.'

- Dreadnought Brother Zakiel at the Battle of Shadowmarch

Unless their sarcophagi suffer irreparable damage in battle, Dreadnought pilots are rendered functionally immortal by their incarceration. They feel no regret at this purgatorial fate, for it allows them to continue their fight against the heretics and traitors of the galaxy for hundreds, often thousands of years before their final destruction in battle. Between conflicts, the Dreadnought sarcophagi are removed from their armoured bodies and placed at rest within the Hall of Silence. There, amid the echoes of that vast, vaulted cavern, the ancients dream of days long past, until the time comes for them to be awoken and called to war once again in the Primarch's name.

TECHMARINES

The war engines of the Dark Angels are every bit as tenacious as the Chapter's battle-brothers, grimly able to soak up tremendous amounts of enemy fire and keep on fighting. They are not invincible, however, and over the duration of a campaign they must be repaired numerous times, often amid the most furious of battlefield conditions. This is the task of the Dark Angels Techmarines – a noble brotherhood of warrior mechanics and artisans who have been trained in the mysteries of the Machine God by the Priests of Mars themselves.

Without the Techmarines, the Dark Angels' vast armoury would soon degrade, leaving the Chapter unable to wage war. Thus, these specialists and their lumbering Servitor assistants perform a crucial function within the Dark Angels Chapter. For this they are honoured, yet they are also viewed with mistrust and suspicion by many among their own Chapter. The reason for this enmity is the dual loyalty of the Techmarines, who must be inducted into the Cult Mechanicus as part of their sojourn to Mars. Even those Dark Angels not invited to join the Inner Circle are insular and mistrustful of outside influences, meaning that, once a battle-brother has taken his first, fateful step on the path to becoming a Techmarine, he will forever stand apart from the majority of his brothers. This stigma is borne without complaint by the Techmarines, however, for they understand that their self-sacrifice is necessary to ensure the survival of their Chapter.

THE MASTER OF THE ROCK

Most Space Marine Chapters have a Master of the Forge, who is their most senior Techmarine. With deep understanding of the arcane sciences refined over many years of experience, the Master of the Forge is comparable to a Tech-Priest of the Adeptus Mechanicus. The Dark Angels have a similar role, known as the Master of the Rock, although there is an ominous difference. Upon ascending to this honoured position, the Master of the Rock is permanently wired into the control nave of machine banks located deep within the asteroid base. It is his solemn duty to placate the most important machine spirits, directing the maintenance of the engines and the Warp drive that allow the enormous asteroid to travel the galaxy. It is his mind alone that perceives the workings of the force field that still shields the Rock from the void. His augur senses watch every inch of the asteroid's outer shell, from the ruined Tower of Angels to the vast gun-decks that stud its flanks, and reach deep into space in search of potential threats. The previous Masters, whose fleshly bodies have withered, are left in place, their mechanical upgrades still working while their bones fall in dusty heaps below. Because of his allegiance to both the Chapter and the Adeptus Mechanicus, the Master of the Rock is never allowed to join the Inner Circle. Instead, he is the keeper of the Rock itself, and of its vast hoard of ancient, secret technology.

SCOUT SQUADS

Swift and subtle, the Scout Squads of the Dark Angels 10th Company use guerilla tactics to take the fight to their foes. Scouts are neophyte battle-brothers – newly created Space Marines still in the process of mastering their own augmented bodies. They are new to the ways of the Dark Angels, still immersed in the first round of doctrinal learnings, trials and rituals that will prove them worthy of advancement. Their tutelage is harsh, overseen by Veteran Sergeants whose duty it is to teach the new recruits the skills necessary to survive and prevail on the battlefields of the 41st Millennium.

Not all Scouts will pass the exacting tests they must undergo at each stage of their development. Those who fail are removed to become Chapter Thralls or lobotomised Servitors – others are simply never seen again. However, those who reach the fifth stage of their Scout training are formed into squads, equipped for battle, and permitted to join Dark Angels strike forces in full battlefield operations.

Though Scouts in the field are still comparatively inexperienced, no allowances are made for them by their grizzled Sergeants. After all, these warriors represent the future of their Chapter, and must therefore be tempered in the fires of war lest weakness creep into the ranks. Thus they learn to master their new wargear while raiding the foe's camps, severing supply lines, and harassing enemy forces alongside their more experienced brothers.

VETERAN SERGEANT NAAMAN

In 997.M41, a desperate war was fought on the recruiting world of Piscina IV. The conflict pitted a small Dark Angels force against the greenskin hordes of Ghazghkull Thraka and Nazdreg. One name stood out as a paragon of honour and dedication throughout the campaign: that of courageous Veteran Sergeant Naaman. When the Orks attacked Piscina IV they used high-powered tellyportas to beam straight to the planet's surface. The Dark Angels responded, Company Master Belial attempting to block the Ork attack on the planet's capital, Kadillus Harbour. After a crushing defeat, the surviving Dark Angels forces fell back to Koth Ridge, determined to hold there or die in the attempt. During the nightmarish hours that followed, Veteran Sergeant Naaman was unremitting. He and his brothers held the slopes on the 63rd Parallel against overwhelming Ork forces until reinforcements could move up. It was he who, alongside Belial, led the counter-attack around the Ork flank and guided the Deathwing to destroy the greenskin tellyporta arrays. Finally, it was Naaman who, to save the rest of his squad, detonated his own krak grenades and destroyed a rampaging Ork Deff Dread. Naaman is believed to have died in the ensuing fireball, though no body was ever recovered. Still, he is held up by the Dark Angels as a modern-day paragon of self-sacrifice, and his tale is told to all neophytes as an example of how best to serve the Chapter.

RAVENWING BIKE SQUADS

Aliens, heretics and witches alike fear the avenging huntsmen of the Ravenwing Bike Squads. Bearing down upon their prey with a roar of powerful engines, these speeding bands of warriors are swift and deadly in the extreme.

Ravenwing Bikers and Attack Bikes form the greater part of the company's strength, and are commonly fielded together as Attack Squadrons. Often, these squadrons are further augmented by the inclusion of a lightning-fast Land Speeder that skims above their heads on anti-gravity repulsor engines. Working in concert, these elements combine to make a deadly, lightning-fast force. They possess the speed to outflank their enemies, to surround them or run them to ground should they try to flee. Between the Attack Bikes and the Land Speeder, each Attack Squadron can muster a surprising amount of firepower, often enhanced by special weapons wielded by the Bikers themselves. This allows them to cripple enemy transport vehicles, eliminate armoured threats and mow down ranks of bodyguards surrounding their true prey. Meanwhile, the Ravenwing Bikers who form the squadron's armoured core are highly effective assault troops, able to tear their way through the heart of the foe's forces, then break away once more before the enemy can retaliate.

It is these Attack Squadrons that make up the bulk of the Dark Angels' 2nd Company. Their warriors are drawn from the finest riders and assault troops of the 3rd to 9th Companies, hand-picked by the Grand Master of the Ravenwing based on field reports from Sergeants, Company Masters and Chaplains. Only the most incorruptible battle-brothers will be given this chance, for the Ravenwing demands not only skill in battle, but unquestioning loyalty from its warriors.

Once formed, an Attack Squadron begins a remorseless training regime intended to forge it into a single, perfectly coordinated fighting force. The battle-brothers of the squadron kneel together in contemplation, compete against one another in trials of strength and will, and commit to memory every detail of one another's combat histories and personalities. Most importantly, they undergo endless, exacting combat drills, perfecting dozens of formations and manoeuvres. Eventually, the brothers of a Ravenwing Attack Squadron can predict one another's actions and intentions faultlessly, even while hurtling at breakneck pace through the maelstrom of battle. They are the perfect hunters, a single pack of lethal predators that moves with unified, undeniable purpose and will not rest until its mission is complete.

RAVENWING LAND SPEEDERS

Screaming down from storm-wracked skies, Ravenwing Land Speeders hurtle low over the enemy battle-lines with their guns blazing. Foes cower as the storm descends, just more fodder for the Land Speeders' guns. The Land Speeder is an ancient and revered form of anti-grav attack vehicle that dates back to the days of the Great Crusade. Though they have changed somewhat in the ten millennia since, these light skimmers still see frequent use by the Chapters of the Adeptus Astartes. Most Chapters employ these vehicles for long-range reconnaissance, or use them as fast-moving reserves. Few have mastered their deployment like the Dark Angels, however.

Several variants of Land Speeder are commonly used by the Ravenwing, mixed freely into squadrons where their different weapon loadouts can provide greater combat versatility. Alongside the standard models fly Land Speeder Tornados, their firepower augmented by nose-mounted heavy weapons. In addition, many squadrons will include one or more Land Speeder Typhoons – a vehicle whose multiple missile launchers can be employed to blast enemy tanks to pieces or shred infantry with bombardments of fragmentation warheads.

Where it is the role of the Attack Squadrons to run the Ravenwing's prey to ground, it is the duty of the Support Squadrons to provide covering fire and annihilate urgent threats as they arise. To this end, Support Squadron crews comprise those battle-brothers who display a true hunter's instinct, coupled with a thorough grasp of wider strategy. In battle, each Support Squadron normally hangs high above the battlefield as it scans for threats. The moment incoming reinforcements are detected, artillery positions sighted, or some other danger rears its head, the Support Squadron dives from the clouds. The lethal strafing run that follows sees their targets obliterated wholesale, torn apart by a salvo of shells and missiles that come screaming down from the skies.

RAVENWING VENGEANCE LAND SPEEDERS

Both the Land Speeder Vengeance and the Ravenwing Darkshroud are adaptations of an STC design unearthed in M36 from the ruined, crumbling chasm-cities of ancient Cortolos. Blessed with a larger chassis, heavy lift-engines and powerful – if slightly sinister – machine spirits, these new marks of Land Speeder were immediately appropriated by the Ravenwing, and have been utilised by them ever since as highly mobile platforms for some of their most potent and esoteric weapons.

The Vengeance variant was the first of these Ravenwing Land Speeders to appear within the Dark Angels' ranks, and it proved an immediate success. For long centuries, the Chapter had possessed the ancient relic weapons known as plasma storm batteries, but had lacked the appropriate vehicles to properly deploy them. They found this platform in the Vengeance, which provided a hard-hitting edge to those Ravenwing formations it fought alongside. The plasma storm battery is a much sought-after weapon, its deployment limited only by the Dark Angels' inability to manufacture replacements for those units lost in battle. It is a terrifying armament, capable of blasting almost any target to ash with a single salvo and wreaking untold destruction and devastation as swathes of foes are blasted to glowing ash.

The Darkshroud is a far more mysterious war engine. Soon after the fall of Caliban, the Dark Angels explored the ruined Tower of Angels atop the Rock. Though much of that ancient fortress had been ruined, they did find certain relics still standing proud amid the devastation, including a series of statues from a past age, old even by Caliban's standards. The statues had been bathed in the strange radiation of the Rock's crackling force field, and now glowed with an energy all of their own. Mounted in reliquaries at the rear of Ravenwing Land Speeders, these eerie statues, known as the Ten Brothers of the Order, emanate an unsettling barrier of rippling darkness that veils friendly troops and shields them from harm.

RAVENWING BLACK KNIGHTS

Few warriors in the galaxy are as tenacious and merciless as the Black Knights of the Ravenwing. Styling themselves after the monster-hunting knights of old Caliban, these elite warriors fall upon the mightiest of foes with their corvus hammers swinging in bone-crushing arcs. Mounted upon Mark IV Raven-pattern bikes, the Black Knights are a swift and utterly lethal assault force. The impact of their headlong charge is matched only by the devastation they can cause with a howling volley from their plasma talons – indeed, few foes will survive either. The Black Knights are the ultimate weapon of the Grand Master of the Ravenwing, deployed wherever their might is needed most.

To rise to the ranks of the Black Knights is a massive honour for any member of the Ravenwing, for the invitation can only be issued by one who is already a member of the elite brotherhood. If the offer is accepted the candidate must pass a series of deadly trials known as the Seven Rites of the Raven. Those who live through these tests are sworn into the Black Knights in a long and solemn ritual that culminates in the Vow of the Beastslayer. With this vow, the newly elevated Black Knight swears to seek out evil and heresy wherever it may lurk, to stalk it to its lair and there smite it with righteous fury until its threat to the Imperium is ended forever.

It is from the Black Knights that the Grand Master of the Ravenwing selects his Inner Circle, imparting to them the terrible revelations of their Chapter's history and revealing the true purpose of their never-ending hunt.

It is also from amongst the Black Knights that the warriors of the Ravenwing Command Squad will be drawn. Much as in a typical Command Squad, this unit includes the Ravenwing Company Standard Bearer, Apothecary and Champion among their number, and are tasked as bodyguards to whichever officer they accompany. Racing into battle at the head of their mounted brotherhood, Ravenwing Black Knights form the tip of the spear, leading their comrades' thunderbolt charge into the foe.

'If our quarry stands? We lay them low.
If our quarry flees? We run them down.
If our quarry pleads? We listen not.'

- Ravenwing Catechism of the Hunt, 3rd Passage

NEPHILIM JETFIGHTERS

Sleek air-to-air interceptors, Nephilim Jetfighters are hunting craft perfectly in keeping with the Dark Angels' secret mission. The oversized 2nd and 3rd Squads of the Ravenwing provide the pilots for these craft, their skills at performing lightning manoeuvres in high-speed warfare making them the ideal candidates for the role. The combination of such skilled pilots with the heavy armaments, impressive speed and stalwart resilience of the Nephilim has proved a truly potent one and, since their inception in late M40, these craft have served as the foremost combat aircraft of their Chapter.

The Dark Angels are a conservative Chapter, highly resistant to change or innovation. Freedom of thought is, after all, the first step upon a dangerous path that leads to questions that should never be asked. Yet for all this, Nephilim pilots are something of a breed apart. While they revere the ancient relics that have been used in combat since the days of the Great Crusade, they continually push their Chapter's Techmarines for enhancements, modifications or newer marks of craft – anything that can boost the speed with which they can take the fight to those who would deny the Emperor's will. Such enthusiasm is looked upon with tolerance by the Company Masters, for the results it produces are substantial.

THE SILVER TALON

The Dark Angels can claim a significant number of skilled combat pilots amongst their ranks. Of those talented individuals, only a handful have ever achieved sufficiently spectacular deeds to be awarded the order of the Silver Talon. This is the greatest honour that a Dark Angels pilot can earn, and is given only to those battle-brothers who have achieved seemingly impossible feats of heroism. Previous incumbents of the order include Brother Azaziel, who single-handedly defended the skies above Neuvenport in his Nephilim Jetfighter for six hours against successive waves of Necron Doom Scythes, and Brother Raphaenus of the Ravenwing, whose airborne capture of the Fallen known as Ghuldarkk is legendary within the Inner Circle. Recipients of this award have their names graven into the Gate of Angels, the huge stone arch that gives access to the Rock's largest launch bay. Furthermore, they are permitted to wear a simple silver pendant in the shape of a Raven's talon, and to have the same device painted onto the hull of their Nephilim or Dark Talon. This is an unusual – if understated – decorative honour that shows how greatly the Dark Angels value their ace pilots.

RAVENWING DARK TALONS

Sweeping from the ash-filled skies, the ominous form of the Ravenwing Dark Talon descends to snatch up the 2nd Company's prey. This archaic-looking craft bears sepulchral flourishes across its hull – a gothic facade well in keeping with its grim purpose. It is the carrion bird that descends upon the Fallen when the chase is run. It is the shadowed angel of death that gathers them up to its cold, dark bosom. Those that the Ravenwing hunt have learned to fear the sinister silhouette of this craft, for they know that it brings with it a fate far worse than death.

The Dark Talon is equipped with wing-mounted hurricane bolters ideal for mowing down any foolish enough to stand in its way. However, the craft's main armaments are far stranger – prohibited weapons from the Age of Technology which the Dark Angels have repeatedly denied having in their possession. The most deadly of these, the rift cannon, is a weapon of absolute annihilation intended to obliterate the darkest devices and mightiest protectors of the Fallen. Many of the renegades possess the ability to summon forth Daemons of the Warp to fight in their stead. The rift cannon provides the Ravenwing with the means to simply hurl such entities straight back where they came from. Should the Fallen prove impossible to capture, or another agency of the Imperium threaten to discover the nature of the Dark Angels' hunt, it is also an excellent weapon with which to remove all evidence – or indeed he who was about to discover it – in the most permanent of ways.

The most terrifying feature of the Dark Talon is not a weapon at all, however. Concealed within the craft's hull is a small chamber – little more than a lightless metal tomb that echoes with sinister, whispering voices – into which a captured Fallen can be loaded for transport back to the Rock. This holding cell has the capacity to engage a stasis field to pacify especially troublesome cargo, though if the pilot is feeling vindictive they may neglect to activate this function. Spending days trapped in a void-dark coffin with the voices of the lost gnawing at their minds prepares the Fallen for questioning quite effectively...

'You are ours now, heretic. Whatever you have done, whatever you have been, all that is over now. From this moment on you have but one purpose, and one hope: Repent.'

- Brother Zerekian, Ravenwing Dark Talon pilot

DEATHWING TERMINATORS

The battle-brothers of the Deathwing take no pride in their exceptional reputation. They know that their physical and mental fortitude is merely what is necessary to discharge their duties, prizing humble, monastic asceticism and selflessness above all else. Clad in the pale, hulking plates of their Tactical Dreadnought armour, the veteran warriors of the Deathwing march unflinching into the fires of war. They feel no compassion, no remorse and no fear. Their absolute devotion to the Chapter leaves no room for anything but a cold and steely fanaticism, and they would advance willingly into the very maw of the Warp itself were they ordered to do so. Whether fighting in a Deathwing Terminator Squad, or advancing at the side of a Chapter hero as part of his Deathwing Command Squad, these warriors are amongst the greatest in the Imperium.

The constant regime of ritual, contemplation and self-denial undergone by the Deathwing scours their souls clean of impurities. They are mentally and spiritually armoured against the temptations of the Daemon and the heretic, deaf to their lies and blandishments just as they are to pleas of innocence or cries for mercy. The battle-brothers of the Deathwing – whether indoctrinated into the Inner Circle or not – fight in the full knowledge that they are weapons, extensions of their masters' will, and indeed the Imperium has few weapons greater; the 1st Company of the First Legion might not bask in their terrifying, glorious reputation, but they always live up to it.

APOCRYPHAL TALES

The Terminators of the Dark Angels originally wore black armour, but it was painted bone white in honour of a battle fought long ago. Legends state that a band of Deathwing returned to the recruiting world of their birth only to find their people enslaved to Genestealer invaders. The brethren repainted their armour, symbolising that they were dead men walking. Fighting hordes of Genestealers, they penetrated the alien lair and, though the battle claimed many of the Terminators' lives, ultimately the world was freed. Since that day, the Deathwing have kept their armour white, in remembrance of the sacrifice of their predecessors. This instructional tale is told by a hooded Sergeant to every Dark Angels Scout upon his elevation to battle-brother. Other oft-repeated tales in the Dark Angels' lore are 'The Fall of House Perivigilium', 'The Scouring of the Space Hulk *Place of Fears*', the 'Vengeance of Beleaguerest', 'The Lion and the Snake of Caliban', and 'Whisper in the Gloom'. All such Dark Angel legends are told at specific points in a brother's progress through the Chapter's ranks. Some tell of heroes returned from war to find their brothers corrupted. Others speak of self-sacrifice or the refusal to accept surrender. No few touch upon those seeking redemption from dishonourable deeds. Such tales instil in every Dark Angel a zealous drive to right wrongs and seek out enemies, no matter where they might hide.

DEATHWING KNIGHTS

The very pinnacle of an already elite fighting force, the Deathwing Knights are a shock assault force without equal. Robed and cowled, they embody the silent nobility and brooding threat of the Lion himself, while in battle they sweep their enemies before them with contemptuous ease.

When a member of the Deathwing is deemed worthy, he is brought into the Chamber of Judgements to face a series of challenges that test his strength, resolve and loyalty to the Chapter past any breaking point he may have. Should he prevail, the warrior is granted the title of Knight and passes beneath the shadowed arch. At this time, if he is not already privy to the secrets of the Inner Circle, the Knight will gain revelation, learning of the terrible history of his Chapter and its quest for absolution. The Watchers in the Dark present each new Knight with his mace of absolution and a finely wrought storm shield – heirlooms of the Great Crusade that sing with barely suppressed power.

It is from amongst the Deathwing Knights that new Company Masters are selected, for there is no finer proving ground than this august brotherhood. The Knights are utterly devoted to the hunt for the Fallen, and it is in the pursuance of this quest that they truly learn its cost. By the time a Deathwing Knight is promoted to the rank of Master, he understands implicitly that no life – even his own – is more important than the Dark Angels' never-ending quest for forgiveness.

CYPHER

Of all the Fallen, none is as hated or feared as the enigmatic and deeply sinister individual known as Cypher. He appears as if from nowhere, bringing death and destruction with him, and then vanishes as abruptly as he arrived. Cypher displays a supernatural ability to evade capture; he has been surrounded by the Dark Angels many times, yet has always eluded them. It is as if Cypher is watched over by dark forces that whisk him away from harm, though some among the Inner Circle have claimed that perhaps it is a higher power that protects him. Whatever the truth, it is possible that Cypher represents the Dark Angels' only true chance of redemption. It has been suggested that the seemingly random appearances of this mysterious, cowled figure hide a pattern that has not yet been discerned. There is a theory, most commonly espoused by the Inner Circle of the Disciples of Caliban, that Cypher moves slowly across the galaxy towards Terra and the Emperor himself. Many have pointed to the fact that Cypher carries a sword which he never draws in combat, and that this could be the fabled Lion Sword, the blade once wielded by Lion El'Jonson himself and thought lost forever with his disappearance. Whatever the truth, it is certainly the case that when Cypher appears, he attracts other Fallen. Because of this, the Inner Circle seek Cypher more than any other. No price is too high, and no deed too heinous, to ensure his capture.

VENERABLE DREADNOUGHTS

THE WARDENS IN WHITE

Below the Rock's vaulted galleries, beyond the Corridors of Shadows and the Portal of Penumbral Sorrow, is the Chamber of Passageways. It is to this domed and mysterious space that each prospective Supreme Grand Master is led by the Keeper of the Keys. As the greatest heroes of the Chapter perform the rituals to send the aspirant on into darkness alone, they are watched over by a pair of silent, ancient guardians. These are the Wardens in White, the two eldest Venerable Dreadnought brothers of the Deathwing.

The sarcophagi of these timeless gatekeepers are heavy with oath papers and ornate decoration, and their power plants rumble softly as they loom motionless in the dark. The identities and names they possessed in life are now completely subsumed by secrets. Were any foe to penetrate the Rock's countless defences, it would be the duty of the Wardens in White to form the last line, and to destroy him without hesitation. For this reason, these Dreadnoughts are only taken to war in the very greatest need, and even then only one may leave his post and his duty at any given time.

With their armoured hulls decorated by the Chapter's finest artisans, the Venerable Dreadnoughts of the Dark Angels exude sombre nobility. All were once members of the Deathwing, and their hulls are still painted in the ritual bone white borne by those elite warriors. The Venerable Dreadnoughts of the Dark Angels have fought for many centuries and sometimes longer, in their Chapter's name and they are, without exception, oath-sworn members of the Inner Circle.

It is rare, but not unknown, for a battle-brother to learn the secrets of his Chapter only after his interment in a Dreadnought sarcophagus, and the sorrow and wrath of such enlightened revenants is terrible to behold. The dedication of the Dark Angels' Venerable Dreadnoughts to the hunt for the Fallen is fervent in the extreme. After all, where a typical battle-brother may live to see a handful of the Fallen brought to justice, with their exceptionally long lifespans the Venerable Dreadnoughts see hundreds hunted down and captured. Furthermore, over time, the pilots of the Venerable Dreadnoughts accumulate a wealth of wisdom concerning the Fallen – their habits, their ploys, and the best ways to hunt them. Thus do the leaders of the Chapter come to these ancients for advice on such matters, and perfect the art of the hunt under their guidance.

DEATHWING LAND RAIDERS

Like great hunting beasts, the Land Raiders of the Deathwing bear down upon their prey with lethal intent. Painted in white and bearing the insignia of the Deathwing upon their armoured flanks, these mighty tanks are elite specialists in their own right. Only the eldest Land Raiders are selected to serve the Deathwing, vehicles with indefatigable machine spirits that detest the works of traitors and heretics. So potent are these mechanised presences that they can effect rudimentary repairs upon their own structures as battle proceeds, shrugging off damage and rerouting power around compromised systems. In this way, enemies who see their shots strike home against weapons or motive units have their cries of triumph cut short as the Land Raider rolls from the blast, scorched but undaunted and with its offensive capabilities still intact.

The Deathwing make full use of both the Crusader and Redeemer variant marks of Land Raider, and benefit enormously from the specialist abilities of these armoured behemoths. The Dark Angels' annals are full of accounts of Deathwing Squads delivered into the heart of the foe by thundering Crusaders, or supported against overwhelming hordes of xenos or heretics by the sweeping firestorms of the Redeemers. Whoever the foe, the Land Raiders of the Deathwing face them with murderous determination.

RITUALS OF THE DARK ANGELS

The Dark Angels hold to a bewildering array of ancient rites and traditions, from the Feast of Malediction and the Rite of Sins Renounced to the three day Mindchant of the Iron Penance. Most sacraments are led by the Dark Angels Chaplains, often accompanied by Company Masters. Many of these rites and rituals involve only small groups of robed and hooded figures, but others are delivered to whole companies or even, very rarely, the entire Chapter. Some are instructional, some involve oath-taking, while others are mysterious, leaving the neophytes in awe at the unusual proceedings.

All, however, are cold and solemn ceremonies, for the Sons of the Lion are a serious-minded Chapter who believe in a singularity of purpose – that of absolute devotion to battling the Imperium's foes. Though they seem prosaic, none of the Dark Angels' ceremonies are without meaning; whether or not the participants understand it is another matter. Through devotion to these traditions, the Masters strive to make their Dark Angel brethren stronger – in mind, body and spirit – for in the wars to come, only the most resolute will survive.

LIBRARIANS

The etheric energies of the Warp taint and ultimately destroy anything they touch. Yet for one with sufficient willpower, they can be mastered and turned into a potent weapon. This is the purview of the Librarians – battle-brothers whose unique mutation allows them to sense and wield the energies of the Warp in Humanity's defence.

Few prospective Librarians survive the hellish training regime they must undergo to prove their worth to the Dark Angels. Were a corrupting Warp entity to possess one of these psychically gifted Space Marines, the Dark Angels' grim secrets might be exposed to all. As such, they cannot countenance even the slightest crack in their Librarians' mental armour, and have tested to destruction numerous talented candidates whom other Chapters might have accepted and tutored. While this extreme intolerance makes the Dark Angels slow to replace losses within their Librarius, it also ensures that those battle-brothers who do earn their place are utterly incorruptible, and completely trustworthy. As such, every single Dark Angels Librarian is a member of the Inner Circle. This position of knowledge allows the Librarians to discharge their duties to the fullest; alongside the normal tasks of record keeping, psychic warfare and interstellar communication, these powerful psykers are expected to assist in the interrogation of the Fallen. It is for this reason that the Dark Angels Librarians have developed their own, sinister branch of telepathy, a discipline that allows them to burrow into the minds of their victims and lay their darkest secrets bare.

THE WATCHERS IN THE DARK

Perhaps the strangest facet of the Dark Angels Chapter is the presence of the Watchers in the Dark. These diminutive, hooded attendants cluster around the highest-ranking warriors of the Chapter, often forming eerie processions behind them during their archaic rites, or bearing ancient artefacts into battle at their side. None can say for certain what manner of creature lies beneath the robes of these strange figures, but whatever they are they never speak a word. Their presence is solemnly accepted, if never acknowledged, by the Dark Angels; they simply linger, like some omnipresent manifestation of guilt clad in cowled monastic robes.

The Watchers are able to access areas of the Rock that even the Dark Angels cannot. They come and go as they please, and from their first days as novitiates all Dark Angels are warned not to interfere with or obstruct the Watchers in any way. Cautionary tales persist, whispered by Scout brothers, of those who ignored these warnings and soon disappeared, never to be seen again. The air of mystique and menace that surrounds these strange beings is only heightened by their propensity to haunt the winding passages and dusty scroll-chambers of the Rock's Librarius, though what strange business they have there is a mystery to all.

INTERROGATOR-CHAPLAINS

Menacing figures of fear, the Interrogator-Chaplains of the Dark Angels unsettle even their own battle-brothers with their silent scrutiny. Sworn to the Inner Circle during a convoluted ceremony in the Hall of Secrets, every Interrogator-Chaplain has passed the Test of Faith and learned the grim secrets of his Chapter's history. Henceforth they become shadowed mirrors of their previous selves; where most Chaplains are bellowing firebrands who inspire their brothers, Interrogator-Chaplains are silent and intense, watching always for the slightest hint of heresy or weakness.

The cause of this shift in demeanour is not simply the revelations of the Inner Circle, though certainly these discoveries assail a Chaplain's faith in the incorruptibility of his brethren. Rather, it is the dread duties that come with promotion that turn Interrogator-Chaplains into such grim and brooding figures. When the Fallen are captured and brought back to the dark cells deep within the Rock, it is the Interrogator-Chaplains who must secure their confessions by any means necessary. This requires a will of unbreakable adamant, as the horrific acts of forcing repentance are not an easy burden to bear. Interrogator-Chaplains must weather heretical ranting and lies, discern insincere bleating and remain steadfast in their commitment to compel contrition from the lips of traitors. Ever more drastic agonies must be administered by the Interrogator-Chaplain, and over time their own souls are soured by the vile acts required to save those of the Fallen.

THE BLACK PEARLS

An Interrogator-Chaplain is permitted to add a single black pearl to his rosarius for each one of the Fallen that he convinces to repent. Confessions are as hard-won as they are rare, and most Interrogator-Chaplains meet their end with only a handful of black pearls to their name. Master Molocia – inarguably the greatest of his grim profession – died after over three hundred years of service with only ten black pearls, and to this day no other has been able to emulate his achievement. Still, every Interrogator-Chaplain strives to do just that, not for personal glory but because every pearl acquired represents a tiny shred of their Chapter's honour stitched back into that once-proud tapestry.

The black pearls themselves can only be found on the planet of Malmar, a watery death world on the edge of the Eye of Terror. Upon promotion to his role, each Interrogator-Chaplain must travel to Malmar to retrieve a black pearl from amongst the razor-reefs. This treasure is stored within the Reclusiam, in the hope that one day it will be returned. Malmar's global oceans are swept by storms of incredible ferocity, their churning waves thick with arthropod super-predators the size of Strike Cruisers. Worse, it is said that on Malmar one must face his own darkest temptations, a test of will that makes all other threats pale in comparison.

BATTLE & RESERVE COMPANIES

Brother Arakiel, Tactical Marine, 3rd Company, 4th Squad. Azakiel's left knee displays his company's colours.

Brother Nezekh, Company Veteran. The left shoulder guard shows the Chapter icon with 3rd Company markings.

Brother Zendek is a member of the 8th Company's 3rd Assault Squad, under the command of Master Molochi.

Devastator Marine Borias, 9th Company, 2nd Squad, bears his company's colours on a roundel upon his greave.

Dark Angels display their squad designation and number upon their right shoulder guard. Shown above are the traditional markings of Dark Angels Tactical Marines, who comprise the first six squads in each of the Chapter's Battle Companies.

Master Ezekiah. His left shoulder guard shows the Chapter icon, while his right bears Terminator Honours.

Chaplain Azazel. His left shoulder guard shows the Chapter icon, while his right displays the insignia of the Reclusiam.

Brother Zacharius, Company Champion. The gold-plated shoulder guards are a clear indicator of his status.

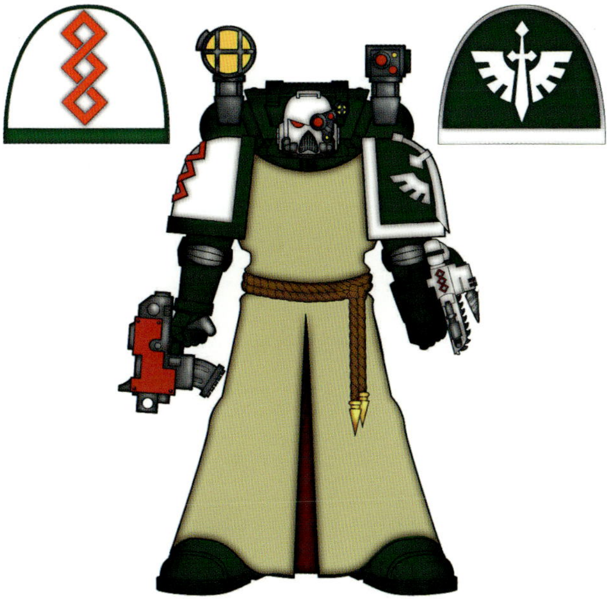

Apothecary Nephriel. His right shoulder guard bears the Prime Helix upon the white of the Apothecarion.

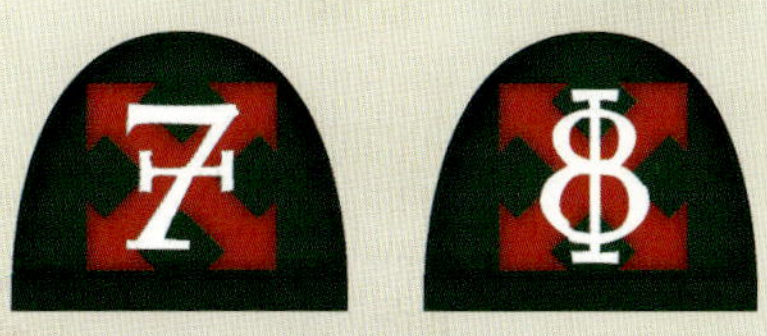

Assault Squad markings

Devastator Squad markings

Company Veteran marking

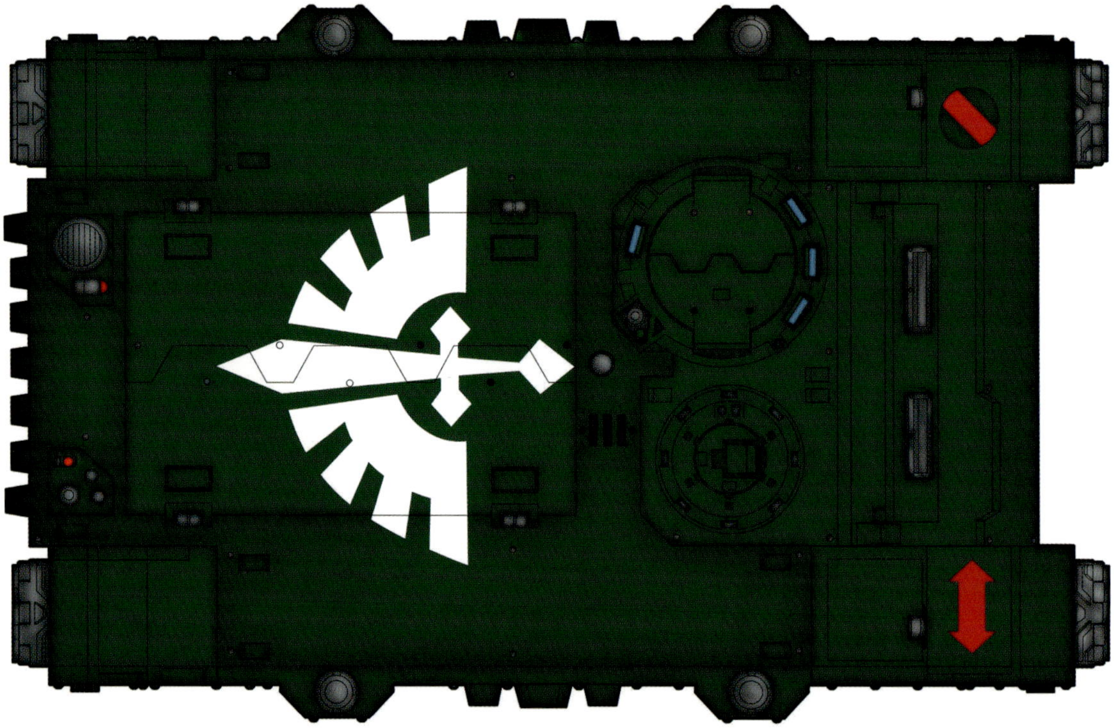

Dark Angels Rhino *Lionheart* is attached to a Tactical Squad of the 3rd Company.

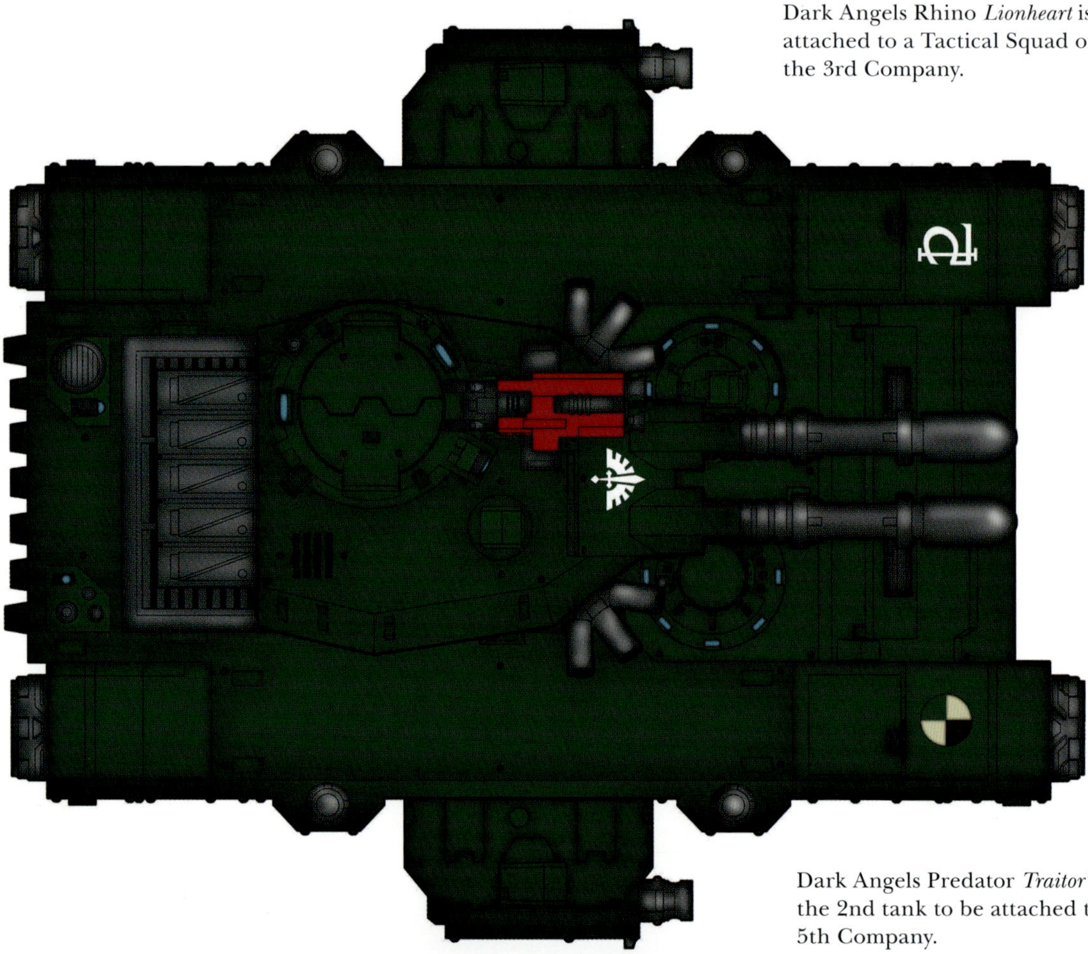

Dark Angels Predator *Traitor's End* is the 2nd tank to be attached to the 5th Company.

The Dark Angels Chapter icon

Squad designations borne by transport vehicles

Brother Azmodor. The markings on his hull indicate that he is the 2nd Dreadnought of the Dark Angels 5th Company.

3rd Company

4th Company

5th Company

6th Company

7th Company

8th Company

9th Company

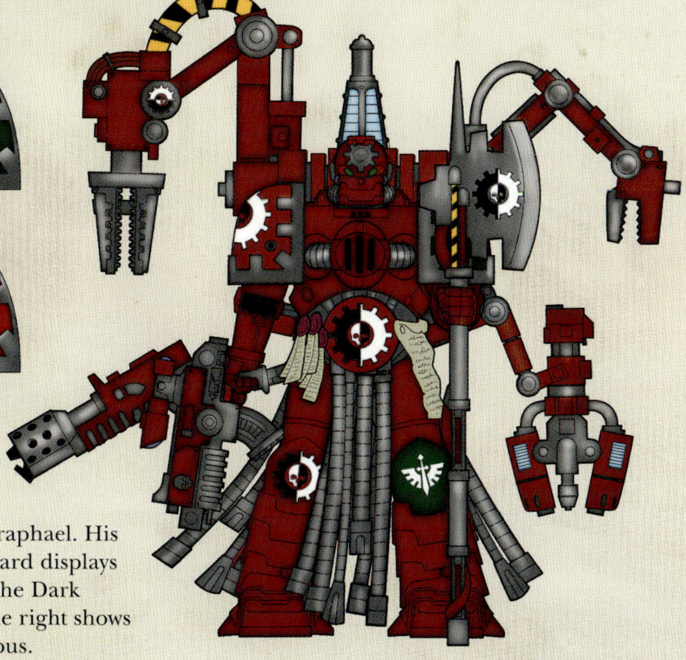

Techmarine Loraphael. His left shoulder guard displays the insignia of the Dark Angels, while the right shows the Machina Opus.

DEATHWING

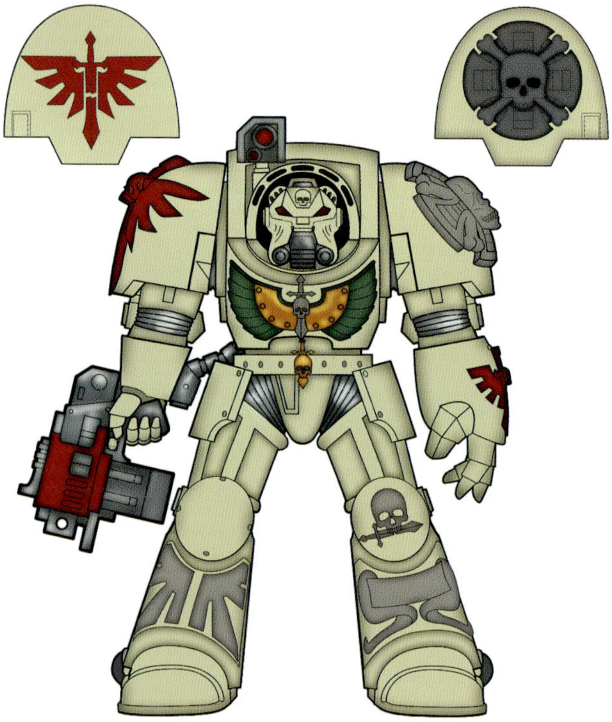

Brother Depheros, Deathwing Terminator. The left shoulder guard bears the Crux Terminatus, while the right shows the broken-sword insignia of the Deathwing.

Deathwing Terminator Sergeant Isiah. Both shoulder guards are embellished with devotional scrolls, while his left knee carries a heraldic device to identify his squad.

Brother Nephoros, Deathwing Knight. The left shoulder guard bears the Crux Terminatus, while the right shows an icon of the Deathwing Knights.

Deathwing Knight Master Achrabael. Both shoulder guards feature the green trim that distinguishes Deathwing Knights from Terminator Squads.

Codicier Turmiel, Dark Angels Librarian. The left shoulder guard shows an ornate Chapter insignia, while the right displays the horned skull icon of the Librarius.

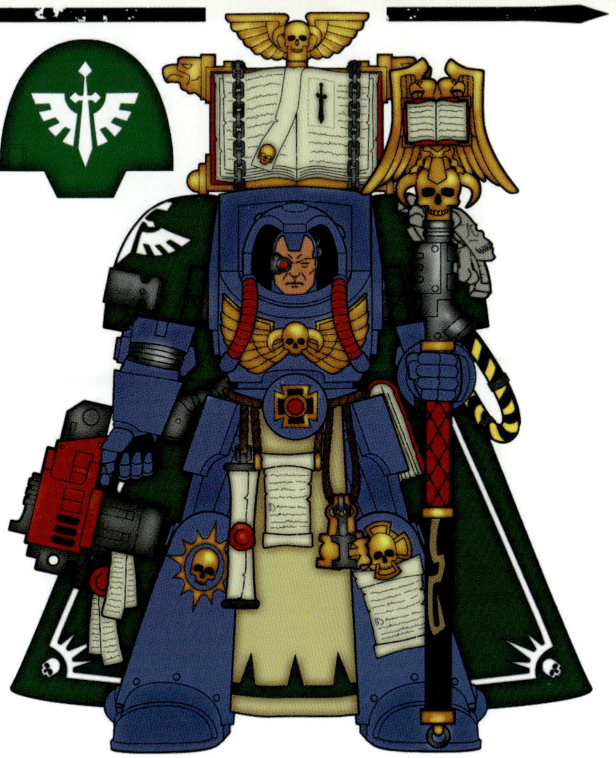

Lexicanium Aspholon, Dark Angels Librarian. Hidden in ancient scrolls and tomes secured about his person, Aspholon bears to war the dark secrets of interromancy.

Interrogator-Chaplain Dakarus. His left shoulder features both Chapter insignia and Inner Circle markings, while the right shows a skull icon of the Interrogator-Chaplains.

Interrogator-Chaplain Ephrek. The left shoulder bears the Crux Terminatus, while the right combines a symbol of the Interrogator-Chaplains with the Chapter icon.

DEATHWING

Venerable Dreadnought Rakaziel. The inscriptions on Rakaziel's hull list some of the many campaigns he has fought in over the millennia.

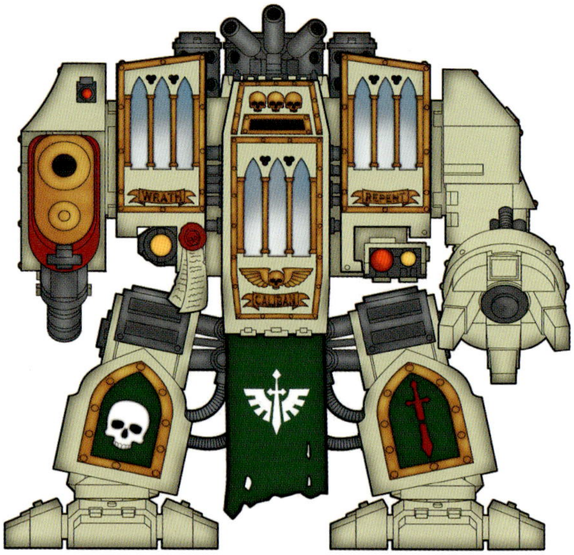

Venerable Dreadnought Hammael. Hammael bears a number of devotional scrolls and personal honour badges on the hull of his Venerable Dreadnought.

Deathwing company insignia

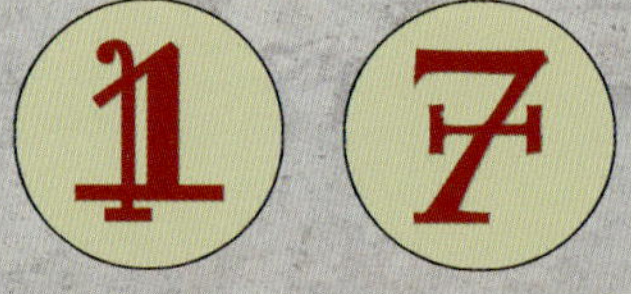

Roundels indicating the 1st and 7th vehicles of the company.

Deathwing heraldic devices

The Company Banner of the Deathwing, above, is carried into battle by the Company Standard Bearer.

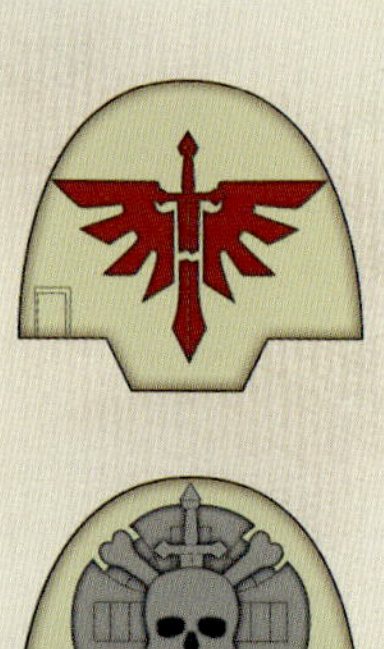

Deathwing Apothecary Vandriel, left, bears the Prime Helix of the Apothecarion upon the Crux Terminatus on his left shoulder.

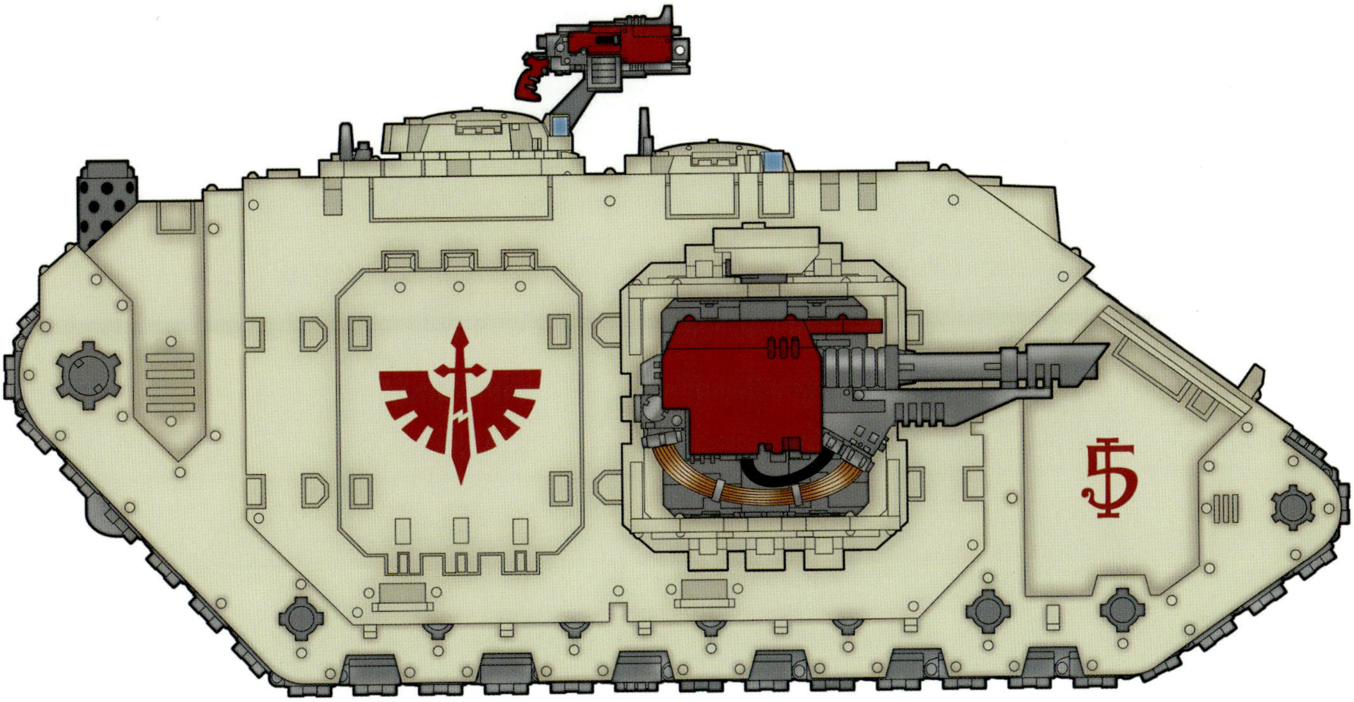

Deathwing Land Raider *Indefatigable*, identified as the 5th tank of the 1st Company.

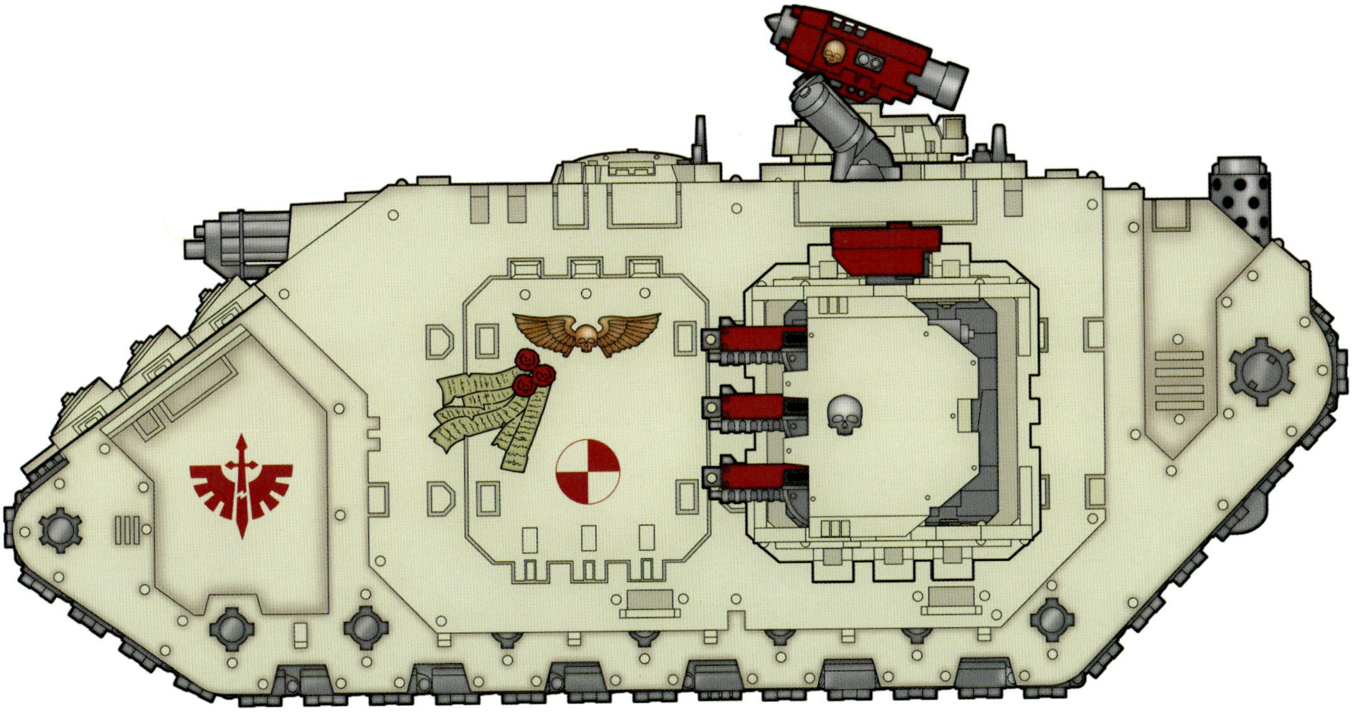

Deathwing Land Raider Crusader *Final Sanction*. Instead of conventional numbering, this vehicle displays the heraldic device adopted by its passengers.

RAVENWING

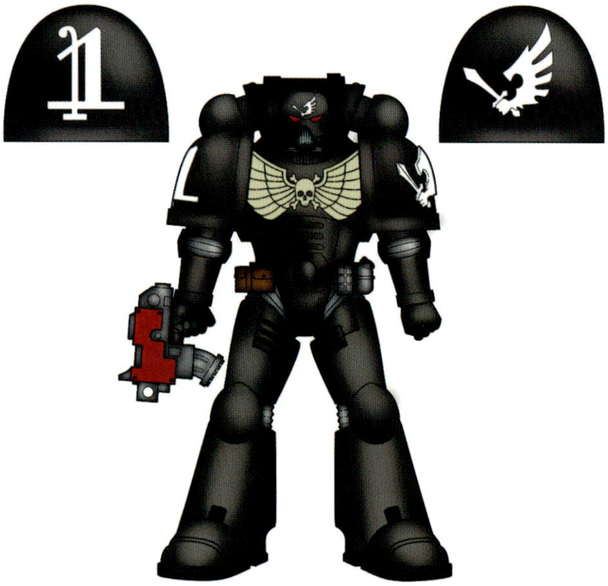

Brother Zephrael, Ravenwing Biker, 1st Squad. The Ravenwing company insignia is worn on the left shoulder.

Sergeant Rithiel, Ravenwing Sergeant, 2nd Squad. The squad number is displayed on the right shoulder.

Ravenwing helmets tend to feature Dark Angels iconography, as well as hardened vox aerials. The emblem of the Ravenwing is always depicted in white.

Ravenwing Marines display their squad number on their right shoulder guard, as shown above.

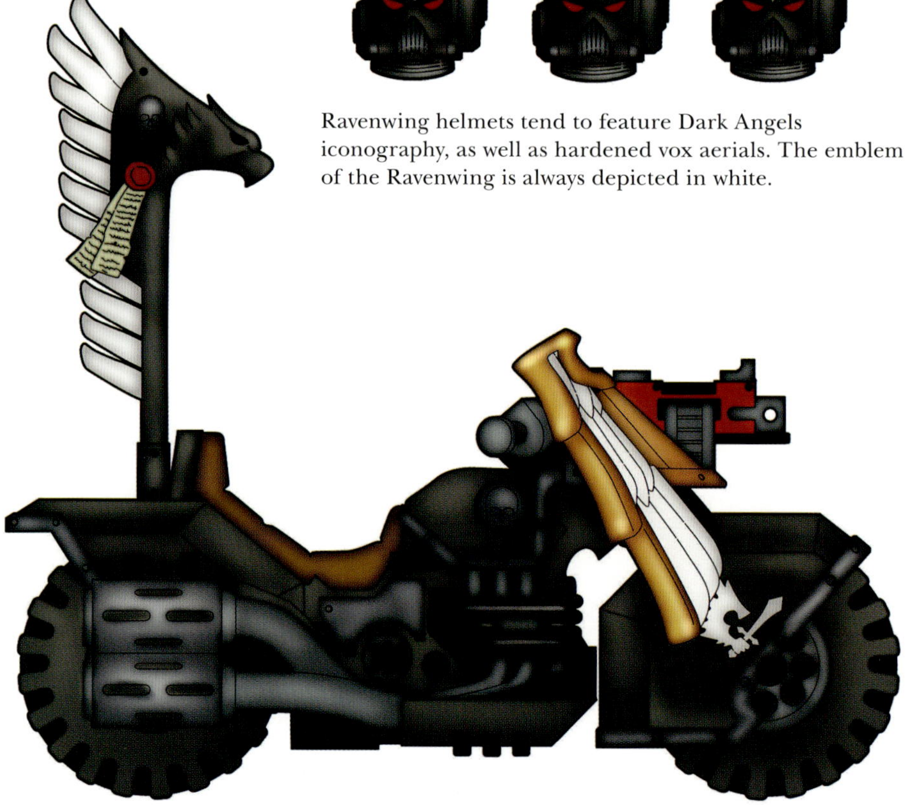

The Space Marine bikes of the Ravenwing are instantly recognisable by the stylised banners fitted to their chassis.

Brother Zaelion, Ravenwing Company Champion, is armed with the Blade of Caliban that signifies his rank.

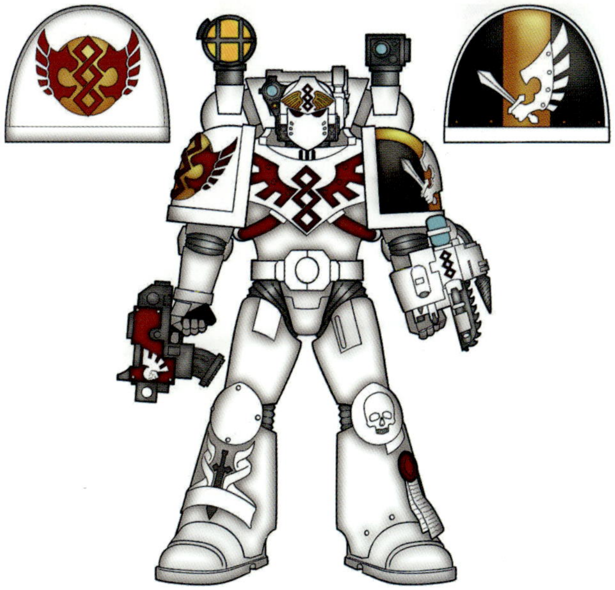

Ravenwing Apothecary Ekrophan. His right shoulder guard carries the insignia of the Ravenwing Apothecary.

Ravenwing Company Banner

Members of the Ravenwing Inner Circle can be identified by vertical gold bars on their shoulder pads.

Ravenwing Black Knight 'Raven' pattern bikes are armed with the fearsome plasma talon, and often feature ornate honour markings reflective of their riders' veteran status.

RAVENWING

Land Speeder Tornado *Stormlash*. This vehicle's hull shows its squadron number and the icon of the Ravenwing.

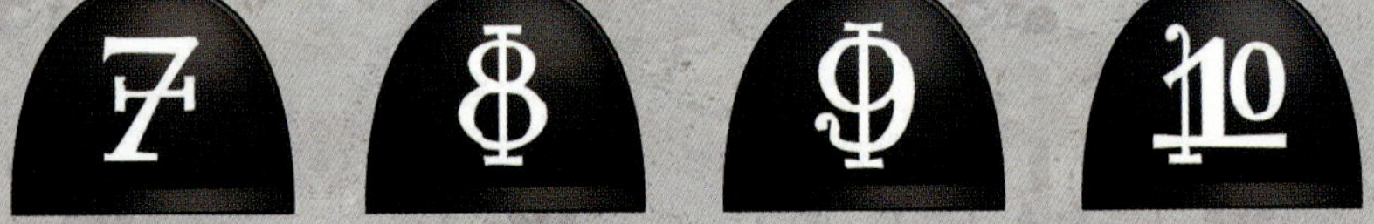

Ravenwing shoulder guards for squads seven to ten, from which Support Squadron crews are often drawn.

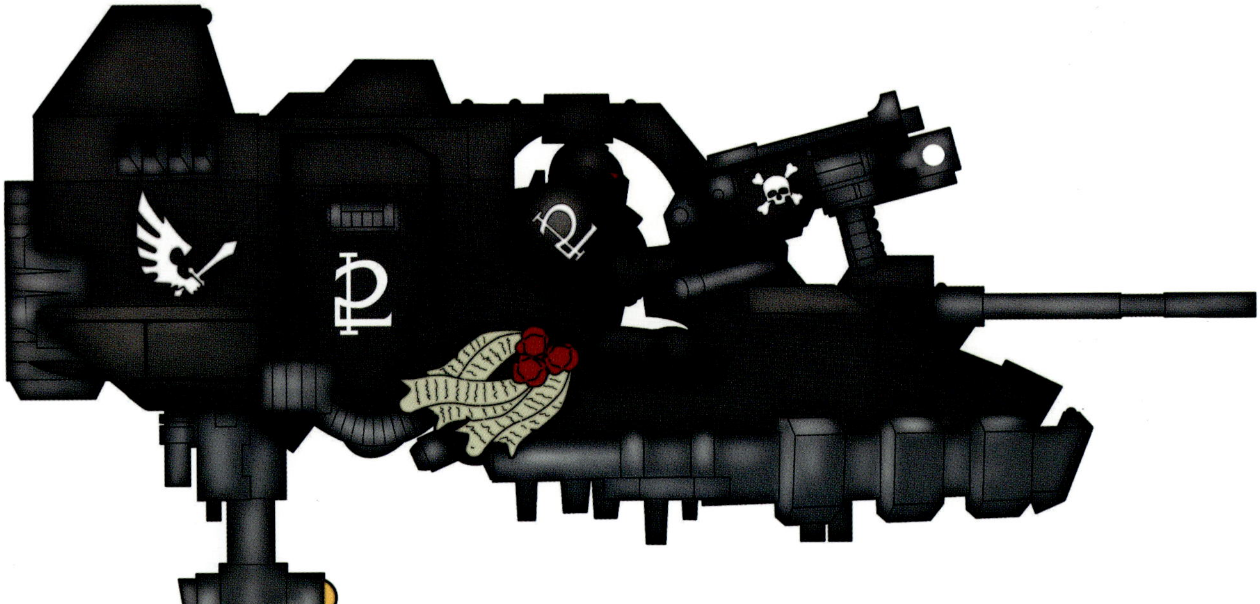

Ravenwing Land Speeder *Heresy's End*, displaying its squadron number and purity seals.

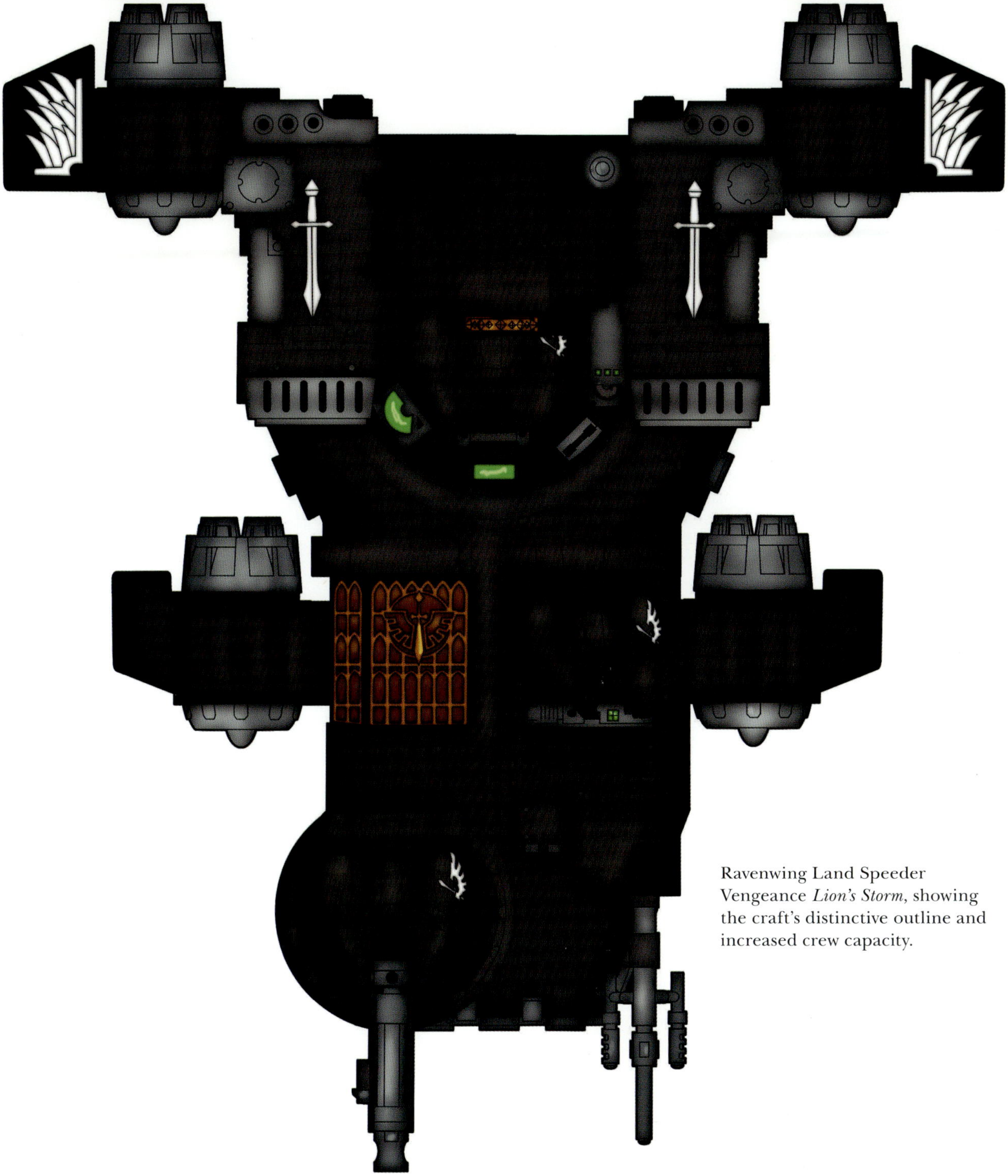

Ravenwing Land Speeder Vengeance *Lion's Storm*, showing the craft's distinctive outline and increased crew capacity.

This Ravenwing gunner's shoulder guard incorporates a marksman's honour.

RAVENWING

Ravenwing Dark Talon *Deathshroud*. The craft's hull displays the Ravenwing insignia and its squadron number.

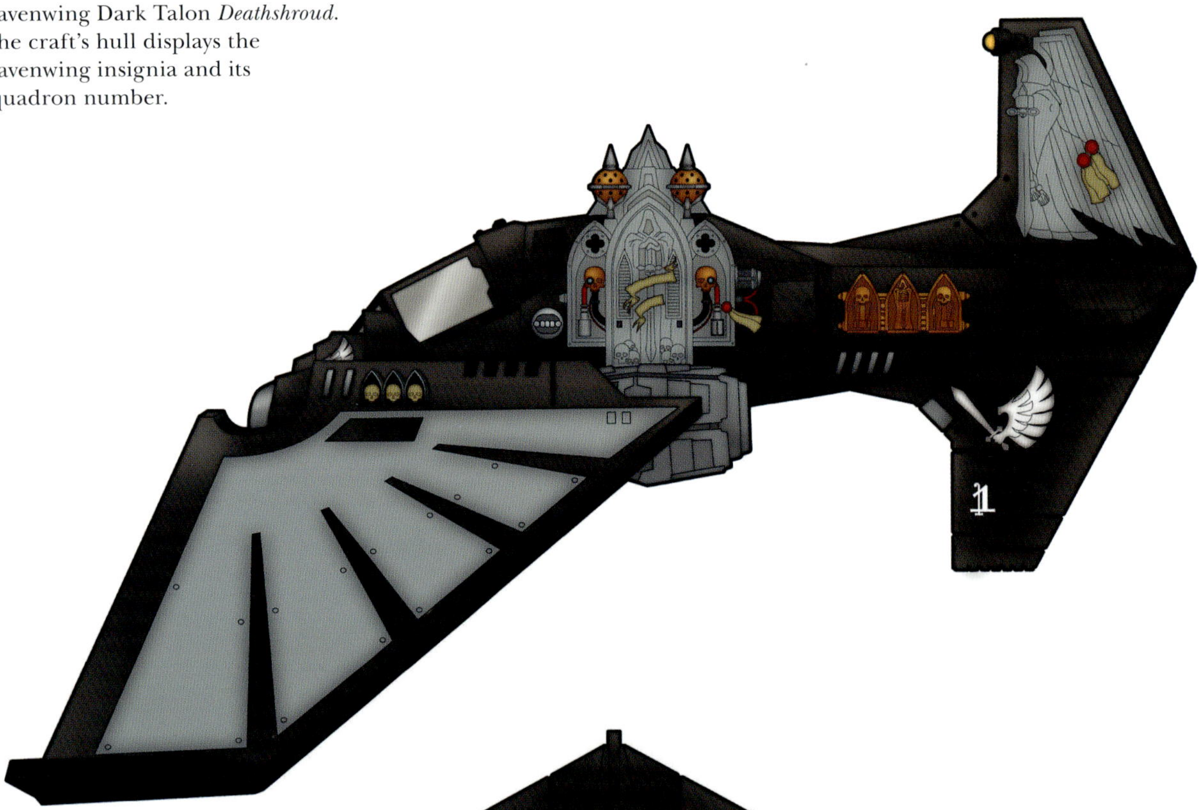

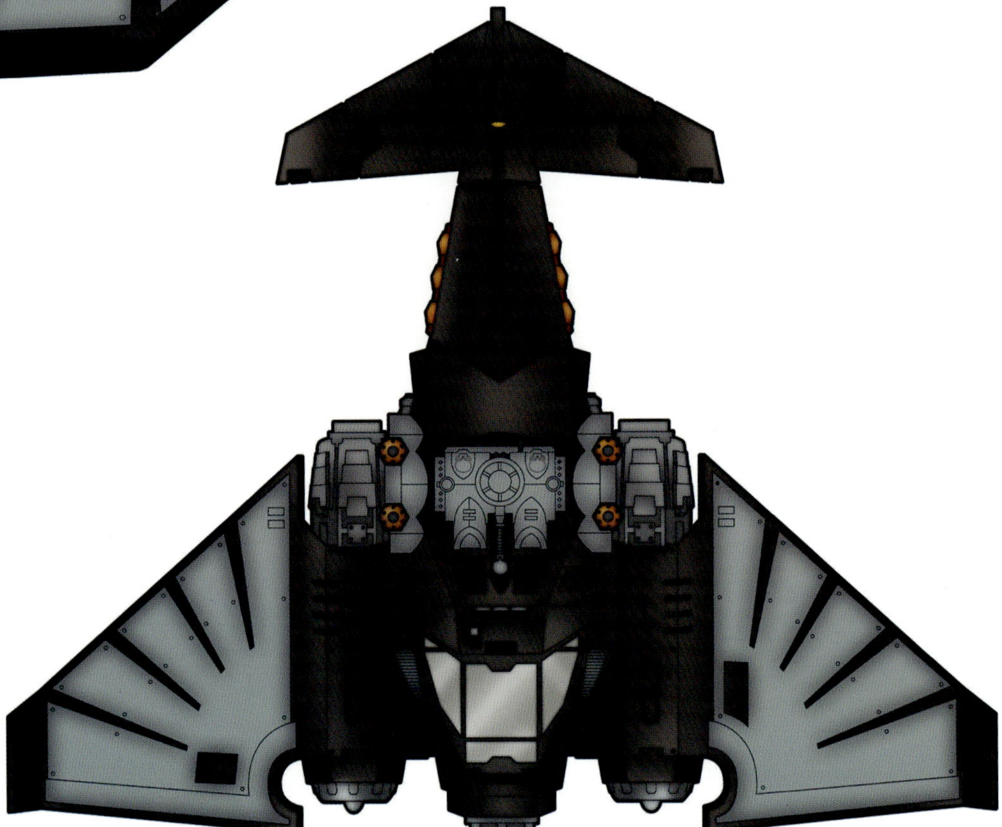

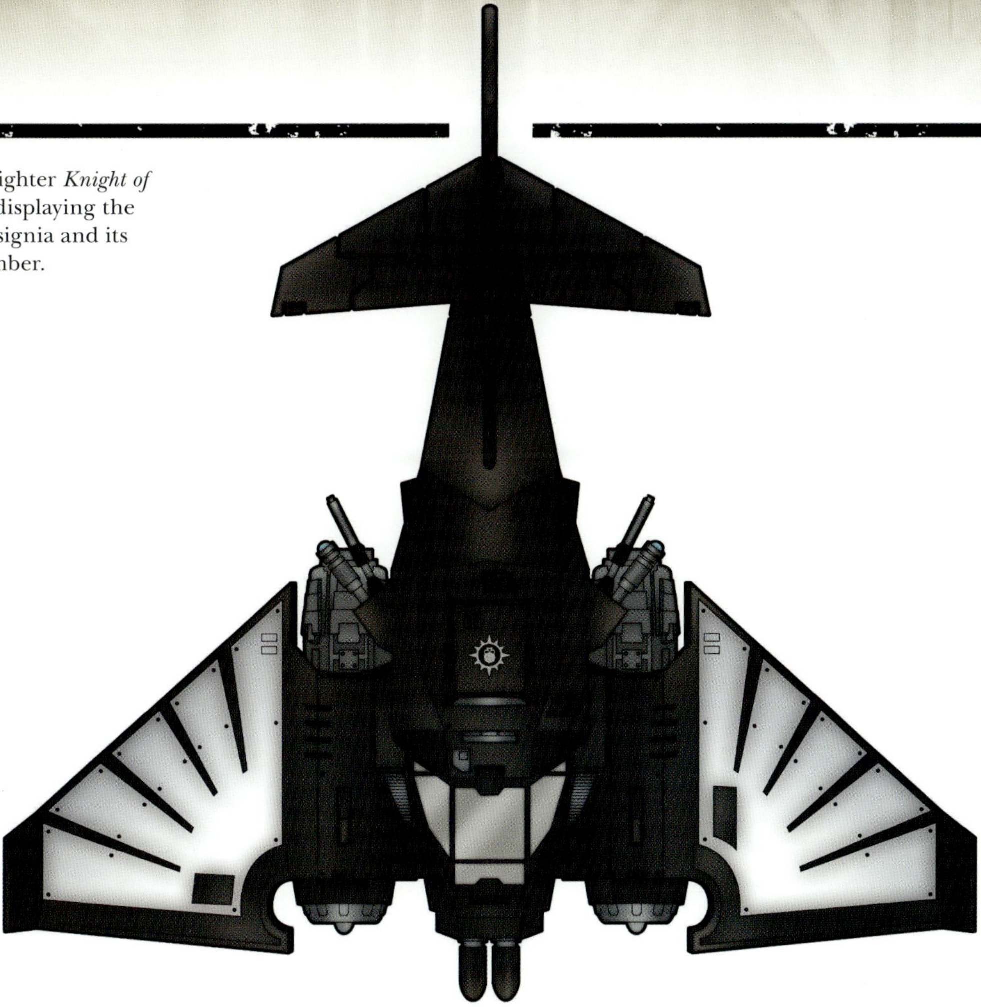

Nephilim Jetfighter *Knight of the Gloaming*, displaying the Ravenwing insignia and its squadron number.

Ravenwing Marines bear honour markings such as the one shown here, which can be applied to the hulls of their craft.

SUCCESSOR CHAPTERS

ANGELS OF VENGEANCE

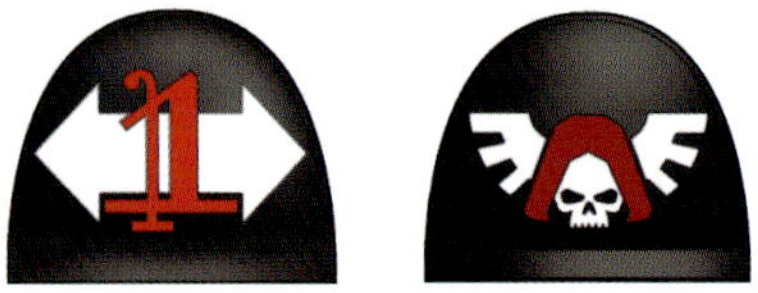

The Angels of Vengeance retain the original black armour of the Dark Angels Legion, and the members of their Inner Circle are robed in the same grim colour.

Brother Scylo and Brother-Sergeant Shaddrach, Angels of Vengeance 3rd Company, 1st Tactical Squad

CONSECRATORS

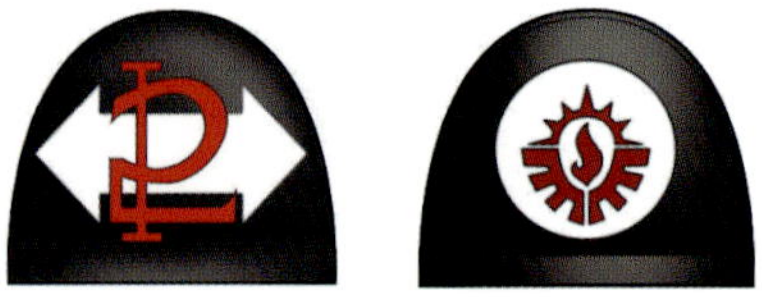

The Consecrators Chapter are known to favour older patterns of power armour and wargear. On occasion, this may compel them to display squad numbers and designations elsewhere upon their armour.

Brother Vand and Brother-Sergeant V'draes, Consecrators 6th Company, 2nd Tactical Squad

ANGELS OF REDEMPTION

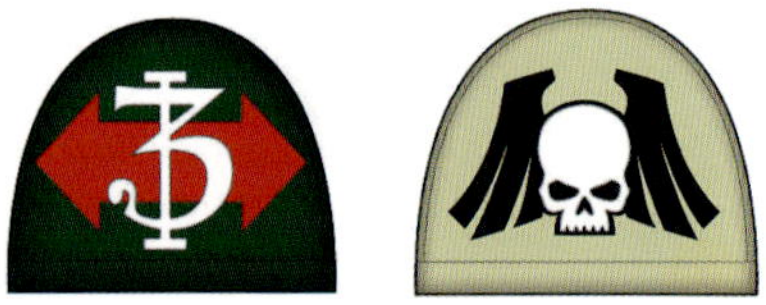

The Angels of Redemption's halved colour scheme is complemented by the red robes of their senior officers.

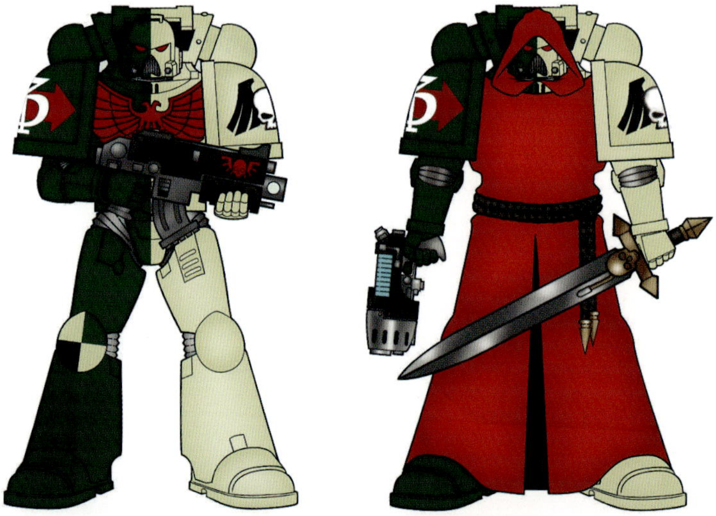

Brother Z'chael and Brother-Sergeant Tol, Angels of Redemption 5th Company, 3rd Tactical Squad

DISCIPLES OF CALIBAN

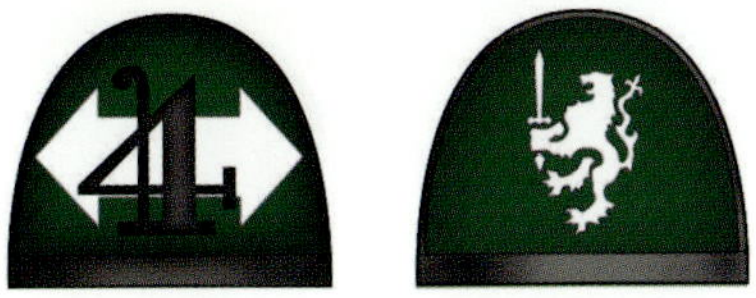

The black and dark green of the Disciples of Caliban is similar to the livery of the Dark Angels, with squad designations picked out in white.

Brother Alaron and Brother-Sergeant Ramiel, Disciples of Caliban 7th Company, 4th Tactical Squad

ANGELS OF ABSOLUTION

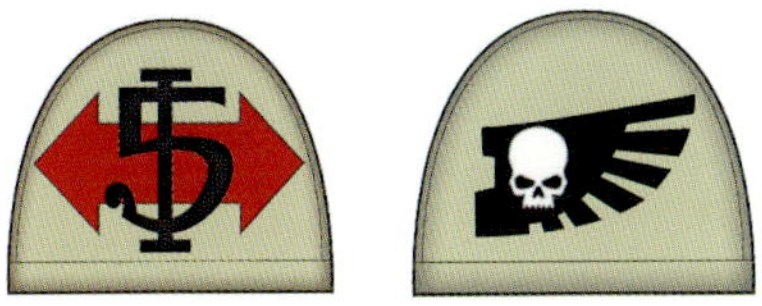

Armoured in bone white and dressed in robes of deep green, the Angels of Absolution invert the company markings of their parent Chapter.

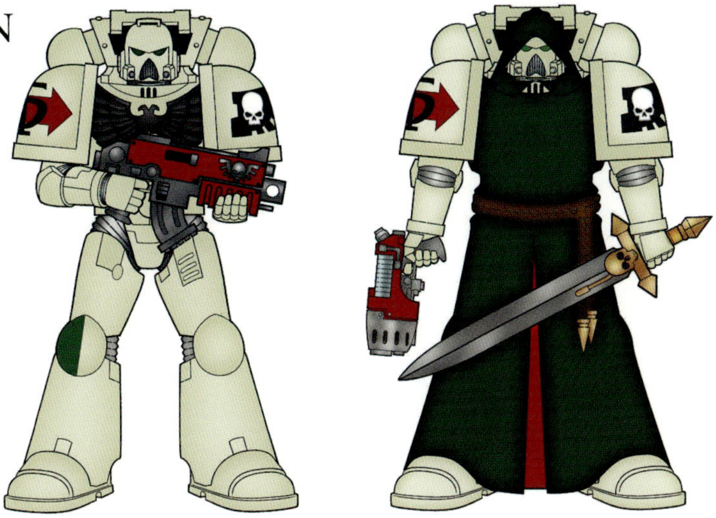

Brother Calen and Brother-Sergeant Cafael, Angels of Absolution 6th Company, 5th Tactical Squad

GUARDIANS OF THE COVENANT

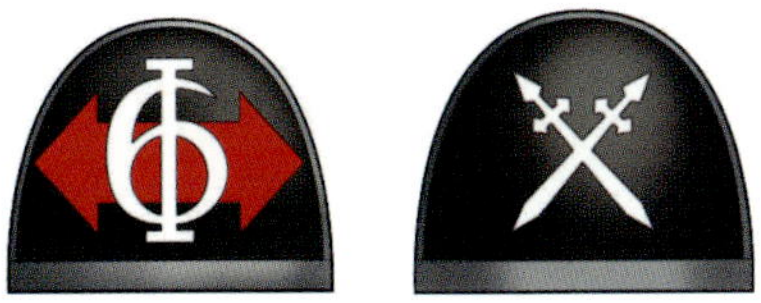

The gunmetal armour of the Guardians of the Covenant is often covered in lines of painstakingly engraved script copied from the pages of revered texts.

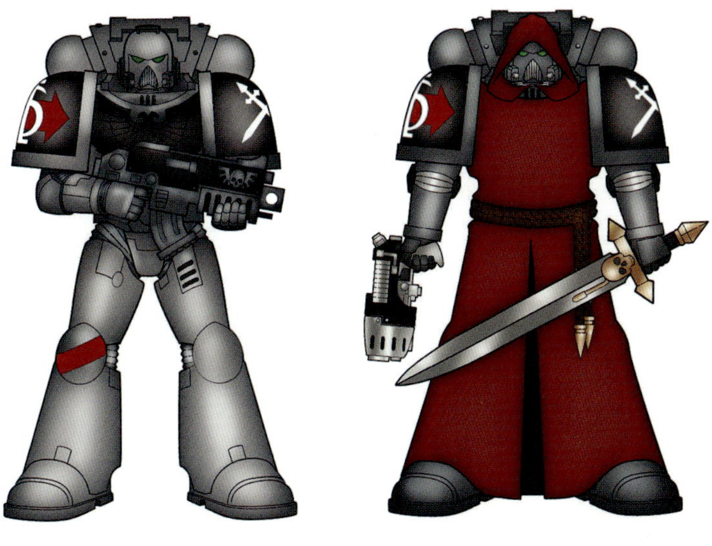

Brother Boros and Brother-Sergeant Nyphas, Guardians of the Covenant 3rd Company, 6th Tactical Squad

SONS OF THE LION

The Dark Angels radiate stern nobility as they march into battle, their ornate banners and graven reliquaries a sombre but inspiring sight. The dark green of their warriors' power armour contrasts with the bone white and midnight black of the Deathwing and Ravenwing, creating a striking panoply of war that is unmistakable upon the field of battle.

INTERROGATOR-CHAPLAIN

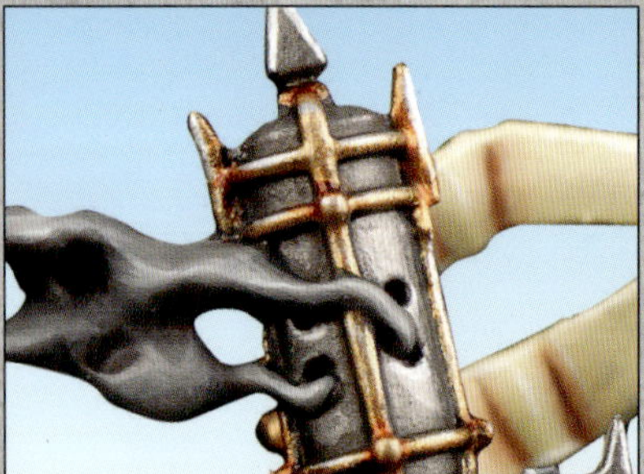

COMPANY MASTER

BELIAL

DEATHWING TERMINATOR SQUAD

DEATHWING COMMAND SQUAD

FORCES OF THE DARK ANGELS

The following section details background and rules information that describe the forces used by the Dark Angels – their warriors, their vehicles and the characters that lead them to battle. This section will enable you to forge your collection of Dark Angels miniatures into an army ready to fight battles in your games of Warhammer 40,000.

CHOOSING AN ARMY

When choosing an army to play a game of Warhammer 40,000, there are two main ways of organising your collection. These are the Unbound method, which means taking whichever units you like, and the Battle-forged method, which is more rigid but has extra benefits. Both are described fully in *Warhammer 40,000: The Rules.*

If you are using the Unbound method, simply use the datasheets later in this section that correspond to the models in your collection. If you are using the Battle-forged method, you will instead need to organise the models in your collection into Detachments. This is a fun process in its own right. The most common of these are the Combined Arms and Allied Detachments. Note that you can also include any of the Formations presented in this section as part of a Battle-forged army.

The Lion's Blade Strike Force is a special type of Detachment that can be included in any Battle-forged army. Unlike the Detachments shown in *Warhammer 40,000: The Rules*, it has a Force Organisation Chart whose slots are a combination of specific Formations and Army List Entries instead of Battlefield Roles. However, it still has compulsory and optional elements, as well as Restrictions and Command Benefits, just like any other Detachment.

Although units cannot normally belong to more than one Detachment, units from a Formation that is part of a Lion's Blade Strike Force are an exception. They count as part of both their Formation and the Detachment, and have all associated Command Benefits and special rules. If your Warlord is part of a Formation or an Army List Entry that makes up part of a Lion's Blade Strike Force, that entire Strike Force is your Primary Detachment.

BATTLE DEMI-COMPANY (pg 140)

- 1 Company Master or Chaplain
- 0-1 Command Squad
- 0-1 Company Veterans Squad
- 3 Tactical Squads
- 1 Assault Squad
- 1 Devastator Squad
- 0-1 units of Dreadnoughts

INNER CIRCLE (0-1 PER BATTLE DEMI-COMPANY)

- 1 Azrael, Belial, Sammael [1], Company Master, Interrogator-Chaplain [2] or Librarian [3]

RAVENWING ATTACK SQUADRON (pg 142)

- 1 Ravenwing Bike Squad or 1 Ravenwing Attack Bike Squad
- 1 Ravenwing Land Speeder or Land Speeder Vengeance

RAVENWING SUPPORT SQUADRON (pg 143)

- 1 unit of Ravenwing Land Speeders
- 1 Ravenwing Darkshroud or Land Speeder Vengeance

RAVENWING SILENCE SQUADRON (pg 144)

- 2 Nephilim Jetfighters
- 1 Ravenwing Dark Talon

RESTRICTIONS:

This Detachment must include a minimum of one Core choice and one Auxiliary choice. It can optionally include any number of additional Core or Auxiliary choices, in any combination, and up to one Command choice for each Core choice. Only the datasheets listed above can be included in this Detachment, and all units in the Detachment must have the Dark Angels Faction.

[1] *Sableclaw may be taken in place of Sammael.*
[2] *Asmodai may be taken in place of an Interrogator-Chaplain.*
[3] *Ezekiel may be taken in place of a Librarian.*

LION'S BLADE STRIKE FORCE

The Lion's Blade Strike Force allows you to represent the typical structure of a Dark Angels army on the Warhammer 40,000 battlefield. Whether you wish to field a full Battle Company with support elements to cleanse an entire star system of foes, or a force assembled to tackle a specific threat, the choices below offer a great way to pick your army.

For example, Adam's Dark Angels collection consists of Azrael, Belial, a Company Master, an Interrogator-Chaplain, four Tactical Squads, a Scout Squad, two units of Deathwing Terminators, a Ravenwing Bike Squad, an Assault Squad, a Ravenwing Land Speeder, a Nephilim Jetfighter, a Devastator Squad and a Land Raider.

If Adam wishes to organise his collection using the Battle-forged method – as described in Warhammer 40,000: The Rules *– all of his units need to be part of a Detachment or a Formation. Adam achieves this by choosing one Lion's Blade Strike Force and one Combined Arms Detachment from* Warhammer 40,000: The Rules.

The Lion's Blade Strike Force in Adam's army consists of one Core choice, one Command choice and two Auxiliary choices. Specifically, it consists of an Inner Circle (Azrael), a Battle Demi-company (the Company Master, three Tactical Squads, the Assault Squad and the Devastator Squad), a Ravenwing Attack Squadron (the Ravenwing Bike Squad and the Land Speeder) and a Deathwing Redemption Force (Belial and both of the Deathwing Terminator Squads).

Adam's last Tactical Squad (Troops), his Scout Squad (Troops), his Interrogator-Chaplain (HQ), his Nephilim Jetfighter (Fast Attack) and his Land Raider (Heavy Support) form a Combined Arms Detachment. As all of his units belong to a Detachment or a Formation, Adam's army is a Battle-forged army. The units that are part of the Lion's Blade Strike Force therefore have the Supreme Fire Discipline Command Benefit, whilst those that are part of the Combined Arms Detachment have the Objective Secured Command Benefit. Finally, Adam chooses Azrael to be his Warlord – the Lion's Blade Strike Force is therefore his army's Primary Detachment.

Core 1+ Auxiliary 1+ Command 0-1 per Core

THE HAMMER OF CALIBAN (pg 145)

- 1 Techmarine
- 1 Land Raider, Land Raider Crusader or Land Raider Redeemer
- 1 unit of Predators, Whirlwinds or Vindicators

10TH COMPANY SUPPORT

- 1-5 units of Scouts

DEATHWING REDEMPTION FORCE (pg 141)

- 1 Belial, Company Master, Interrogator-Chaplain or Librarian
- 2-5 Deathwing Terminator Squads
- 0-1 Deathwing Command Squad
- 0-1 units of Deathwing Knights
- 0-1 unit of Venerable Dreadnoughts

COMMAND BENEFITS:

Company Support: If a Lion's Blade Strike Force includes two Battle Demi-companies, one including a Company Master and the other including a Chaplain, then together they form a Battle Company. Any unit from the Battle Company that has the option to take a Rhino (pg 120), Razorback (pg 121) or Drop Pod (pg 122) as a Dedicated Transport may take one at no points cost (though they must pay for any additional upgrades and options as normal).

Supreme Fire Discipline: Unless Jinking, all models in this Formation that have the Grim Resolve special rule fire Overwatch using their normal Ballistic Skill characteristic.

DATASHEETS

Each Dark Angels unit in this book has a datasheet. These detail either Army List Entries or Formations, providing all the rules information that you will need to use your models in your games of Warhammer 40,000.

Army List Entries

Each Army List Entry contains the following information:

(1) **Faction:** *The unit's Faction is shown here by a symbol. All units that have this symbol, which includes all the units described in this book, have the Dark Angels Faction.*

(2) **Battlefield Role:** *The unit's Battlefield Role is shown here by a symbol. Units in this book have one of the following Battlefield Roles: HQ, Troops, Elites, Fast Attack, Heavy Support or Lords of War. The symbols for these Battlefield Roles are defined in* Warhammer 40,000: The Rules.

(3) **Unit Name:** *Here you will find the name of the unit.*

(4) **Unit Description:** *This section provides a background description of the unit, detailing their particular strengths and weaknesses along with the tactics and methods they employ to wage war in the grim darkness of the 41st Millennium.*

(5) **Points Cost:** *This is the points cost of the unit without any upgrades, used if you are choosing an army to a points value.*

(6) **Unit Profile:** *This section will show the profiles of any models the unit can include.*

(7) **Unit Type:** *This refers to the unit type rules in* Warhammer 40,000: The Rules. *For example, a unit may be classed as Infantry, Bike or Vehicle, which will subject it to a number of rules regarding movement, shooting, assaults, etc.*

(8) **Unit Composition:** *This section will show the number and type of models that make up the basic unit, before any upgrades are taken.*

(9) **Wargear:** *This section details the weapons and equipment the models in the unit are armed with, many of which are described in more detail in the Appendix of this book. The cost for all the unit's basic equipment is included in its points cost.*

(10) **Special Rules:** *Any special rules that apply to models in the unit are listed here. Special rules that are unique to models in that unit are described in full here, whilst others are detailed either in the Appendix of this book (pg 148) or in the Special Rules section of* Warhammer 40,000: The Rules.

(11) **Options:** *This section lists all of the upgrades you may add to the unit if you wish to do so, alongside the associated points cost for each. Where an option states that you may exchange one weapon 'and/or' another, you may replace either or both, provided you pay the points cost for each. The abbreviation 'pts' stands for 'points' and 'pts/model' stands for 'points per model'. Where applicable, this section also refers to any Transports the unit may take. These have their own datasheets. Dedicated Transports do not use up any slots on a Force Organisation Chart, but otherwise function as separate units. The Detachments section of* Warhammer 40,000: The Rules *explains how Dedicated Transports work.*

(12) **Warlord Traits:** *Sometimes a character's datasheet will have a specific Warlord Trait, in which case it will be listed here.*

(13) **Relics of Caliban:** *Some entries have unique items of wargear, the description and rules for which will be listed here.*

Formations

Formation datasheets are identified by this symbol. The rules for Formations can be found in *Warhammer 40,000: The Rules.* A Formation datasheet will list the Army List Entries which make up the Formation, any restrictions upon what it may include, and any special rules the Formation's units gain.

DARK ANGELS WARGEAR LIST

These lists detail the points values of various items of wargear available to units in your army. Many unit entries in the datasheets that follow may include wargear options from one or more of these lists – in each instance, the datasheet will tell you (in bold text) exactly which of these lists you may use. Rules for these items can be found in the Appendix.

Ranged Weapons...pg 149
A model may replace its boltgun, bolt pistol and/or Melee weapon with one of the following:
- Boltgun ... *free*
- Storm bolter ... *5 pts*
- Combi-flamer, -grav, -melta or -plasma ... *10 pts*
- Grav-pistol or plasma pistol ... *15 pts*

Melee Weapons...pg 150
A model may replace its boltgun, bolt pistol and/or Melee weapon with one of the following:
- Chainsword ... *free*
- Lightning claw ... *15 pts*
- Power weapon ... *15 pts*
- Power fist ... *25 pts*
- Thunder hammer ... *30 pts*

Terminator Weapons
A model wearing Terminator armour may replace its storm bolter with one of the following:
- Combi-flamer, -melta or -plasma ... *5 pts*
- Lightning claw ... *10 pts*
- Thunder hammer ... *25 pts*

A model wearing Terminator armour may replace its power weapon with one of the following:
- Lightning claw ... *5 pts*
- Storm shield ... *5 pts*
- Power fist ... *10 pts*
- Chainfist or thunder hammer ... *15 pts*

Terminator Heavy Weapons
A model wearing Terminator armour may replace its storm bolter with one of the following:
- Heavy flamer ... *10 pts*
- Plasma cannon ... *15 pts*
- Assault cannon ... *20 pts*
- Cyclone missile launcher [1] ... *25 pts*

Heavy Weapons
A model may replace its boltgun with one of the following:
- Heavy bolter or multi-melta ... *10 pts*
- Missile launcher (with frag and krak missiles) ... *15 pts*
  May also take flakk missiles ... *10 pts*
- Plasma cannon ... *15 pts*
- Lascannon ... *20 pts*
- Grav-cannon with grav-amp ... *35 pts*

Special Weapons
A model may replace its Melee weapon or boltgun with one of the following:
- Flamer ... *5 pts*
- Meltagun ... *10 pts*
- Grav-gun or plasma gun ... *15 pts*

Special Issue Wargear...pg 151
A model may take up to one of each of the following:
- Auspex ... *5 pts*
- Combat shield ... *5 pts*
- Melta bombs ... *5 pts*
- Digital weapons ... *10 pts*
- Jump pack [2] ... *15 pts*
- Conversion field ... *20 pts*

Dreadnought Weapons
A model may replace its multi-melta with one of the following:
- Twin-linked autocannon ... *5 pts*
- Twin-linked heavy bolter ... *5 pts*
- Twin-linked heavy flamer ... *5 pts*
- Plasma cannon ... *5 pts*
- Assault cannon ... *10 pts*
- Twin-linked lascannon ... *15 pts*

Dark Angels Standards
A model may take up to one of the following:
- Company standard ... *15 pts*
- Chapter banner (one per army) ... *25 pts*
- Sacred standard ... *35 pts*

Relics of Caliban...pg 155
Only one of each relic may be taken per army. A model may replace one weapon with one of the following:
- Shroud of Heroes [3] ... *10 pts*
- Foe-smiter ... *15 pts*
- Lion's Roar ... *20 pts*
- Mace of Redemption ... *30 pts*
- Monster Slayer of Caliban ... *40 pts*
- The Eye of the Unseen [3] ... *40 pts*

Dark Angels Vehicle Equipment...pg 154
A model may take up to one of each of the following:
- Dozer blade [4] ... *5 pts*
- Storm bolter ... *5 pts*
- Extra armour ... *10 pts*
- Hunter-killer missile ... *10 pts*

[1] *Does not replace the model's storm bolter.*
[2] *May not be taken by a Techmarine, or a model equipped with Terminator armour or a Space Marine bike.*
[3] *Does not replace one of the character's weapons.*
[4] *May not be taken by a Land Raider of any type.*

LION

BELIAL

190 POINTS

GRAND MASTER OF THE DEATHWING

Blade in hand, Grand Master Belial advances implacably upon his foes. No greater swordsman exists within the ranks of the Dark Angels, for Belial's expertise with a blade is as instinctive as it is lethal. It makes no difference whether his foe is a bellowing Ork warlord, a towering Tyranid bio-horror, or a daemonically empowered heretic; Belial's onslaught soon sees them cut to ribbons, their blood slicking the gloaming blade of the Sword of Silence. Belial takes no joy in his victories, or his heroic accomplishments. Rather, the Grand Master expects nothing but perfection from himself in every sword-blow and shot, treating even the slightest failure as cause for censure. He demands no less of the warriors who march at his side, his Deathwing brethren fighting their way through impossible odds beneath the glare of their exacting master. Belial has good reason for his stern style of leadership. He knows that, with every chance missed and battle-brother lost, the task of hunting down the Fallen becomes harder. No matter what miracles he and his brethren achieve, absolution will always require more...

	WS	BS	S	T	W	I	A	Ld	Sv	Unit Type	Unit Composition
Belial	6	5	4	4	3	5	4	10	2+	Infantry (Character)	1 (Unique)

WARGEAR:
- **Terminator armour** (pg 154)
- **Storm bolter**
- **Iron halo** (pg 152)
- **Teleport homer** (pg 153)

WARLORD TRAIT:
- **The Hunt** (pg 148)

SPECIAL RULES:
- **Deathwing** (pg 148)
- **Grim Resolve** (pg 148)
- **Independent Character**

Marked for Retribution: Belial re-rolls all failed To Hit rolls when fighting in a challenge.

Tactical Precision: Belial and his unit do not scatter when arriving by Deep Strike.

OPTIONS:
- May replace storm bolter and Sword of Silence with two lightning claws or a thunder hammer and storm shield (pg 153).....*free*

RELIC OF CALIBAN

Sword of Silence: *A power weapon crafted from the same meteorite as the Sword of Secrets, the Sword of Silence has traditionally been gifted to the most lethal close-quarters combatant in the Dark Angels. The Sword of Silence seems to swallow nearby light and sound, absorbing them into its glowing obsidian blade.*

Range	S	AP	Type
-	User	3	Melee, Fleshbane, Master-crafted

SAMMAEL

200 POINTS

GRAND MASTER OF THE RAVENWING

Screaming over the heads of his foes upon the ancient jetbike Corvex, *Grand Master Sammael strikes like the Lion's own blade. Courageous to the point of madness, the master of the Ravenwing weaves low over the battlefield, hurtling between the striding legs of Titans or hammering through the ranks of the foe with the Raven Sword flashing brightly. Sammael's cloak streams behind him as he arcs through the skies, resembling the dark wings of some vast raven as he sweeps ahead of the warriors under his command. Of course, the Grand Master and his jetbike are far more than a figurehead; the ferocious blasts of* Corvex*'s plasma cannon reduce even the mightiest foes to vitrified ash, while Sammael's every sword blow leaves contrails of blood streaming through the air behind it.*

	WS	BS	S	T	W	I	A	Ld	Sv	Unit Type	Unit Composition
Sammael	6	5	4	5	3	5	3	10	3+	Jetbike (Character)	1 (Unique*)

* *You may not include Sammael and Sableclaw in the same army.*

WARGEAR:
- **Bolt pistol**
- **Plasma cannon**
- **Twin-linked storm bolter**
- **Frag grenades**
- **Krak grenades**
- **Iron halo** (pg 152)
- **Teleport homer** (pg 153)

WARLORD TRAIT:
- **Rapid Manoeuvre** (pg 148)

SPECIAL RULES:
- **Eternal Warrior**
- **Fearless**
- **Grim Resolve** (pg 148)
- **Hatred (Chaos Space Marines)**
- **Hit & Run**
- **Independent Character**
- **Ravenwing** (pg 148)
- **Scout**
- **Skilled Rider**

Swift Vengeance: Sammael can fire up to two ranged weapons in the Shooting phase.

RELIC OF CALIBAN

Raven Sword: *This sword is one of a number of blades fabricated out of a meteorite that struck the Rock at Al Baradad, shortly after the fall of Caliban. It was named the Raven Sword, for it is traditionally the weapon of the Grand Master of the Ravenwing. Like the other relics whose origin it shares, the Raven Sword has a razor-sharp edge that has never dulled. Alone amongst its brothers, however, it makes a low keening sound when swung that few foes have heard and lived to speak of.*

Range	S	AP	Type
-	User	2	Melee, Master-crafted

SABLECLAW

200 POINTS

GRAND MASTER OF THE RAVENWING'S LAND SPEEDER

A dark shadow falls across the foe as Sammael's personal Land Speeder, Sableclaw, *sweeps overhead. This is followed moments later by a vicious barrage of explosions – a withering hail of assault cannon and heavy bolter fire churning through the enemy ranks and leaving trails of torn corpses in its wake. Where return fire lashes skyward, it is unable to penetrate* Sableclaw*'s mysterious defences and bursts into harmless blossoms of smoke. So protected, Grand Master Sammael is able to lead his Ravenwing into the deadliest of firestorms, directing his pilot's shots to hit key targets, and reaching down with his Raven Sword to strike the heads from the foe as* Sableclaw *speeds past.*

		Armour					
	BS	F	S	R	HP	Unit Type	Unit Composition
Sableclaw	5	14	14	10	2	Vehicle (Fast, Skimmer, Character)	1 (Unique*)

* *You may not include Sammael and Sableclaw in the same army.*

WARGEAR:
- **Twin-linked assault cannon**
- **Twin-linked heavy bolter**
- **Iron halo** (pg 152)

WARLORD TRAIT:
- **Rapid Manoeuvre** (pg 148)

SPECIAL RULES:
- **Deep Strike**
- **Grim Resolve** (pg 148)
- **Ravenwing** (pg 148)
- **Scout**
- **Skilled Rider**

RELIC OF CALIBAN

Raven Sword: *The keening of the Raven Sword rises to a shriek as Sammael swings it from his seat aboard* Sableclaw.

At the end of the Movement phase, nominate one enemy unit not locked in combat that this model has moved over that turn. That unit takes D3+1 hits resolved at Strength 4 AP2, using Random Allocation. These hits have the Ignores Cover special rule, but do not benefit from any of the model's other special rules. Against vehicles, these hits are resolved against the target's rear armour.

INTERROGATOR-CHAPLAIN

110 POINTS

The sinister, hooded forms of the Interrogator-Chaplains stalk the battlefield, ever ready to dispense violent and bloody absolution. Where the enemy resists, the Interrogator-Chaplains cut deep like scalpels slicing into flesh, leading their brothers in the pitiless dissection of the foe. Privy to the secrets of the Inner Circle, these menacing warrior-priests are charged with securing the confessions of the Fallen. This is a dark and terrible task, for the subjects of their interrogations are ancient and powerful beings with wills of iron. An Interrogator-Chaplain must therefore be capable of any deed – no matter how cruel or horrific – if it will break his victim's resolve. This readiness to inflict sanity-flaying horrors upon their victims extends beyond the torture chambers of the Rock; an Interrogator-Chaplain in battle knows precisely where to strike his victims for maximum effect. With every swing of his crozius, an Interrogator-Chaplain elicits piteous wails of agony from his foes. Thus does a wave of terror spread before this skull-helmed figure, the enemy sure in the knowledge that death itself comes to claim them.

	WS	BS	S	T	W	I	A	Ld	Sv	Unit Type	Unit Composition
Interrogator-Chaplain	5	5	4	4	3	5	3	10	3+	Infantry (Character)	1 Interrogator-Chaplain

WARGEAR:
- **Bolt pistol**
- **Crozius arcanum** (pg 150)
- **Frag grenades**
- **Krak grenades**
- **Rosarius** (pg 153)

SPECIAL RULES:
- **Deathwing** (pg 148)
- **Fear**
- **Grim Resolve** (pg 148)
- **Independent Character**
- **Preferred Enemy (Chaos Space Marines)**
- **Zealot**

OPTIONS:
- May take items from the **Melee Weapons**, **Ranged Weapons**, **Special Issue Wargear** and/or **Relics of Caliban** lists.
- May take a power fist .... *25 pts*
- May take a Space Marine bike (pg 153) .... *20 pts*
- If neither a power fist or Space Marine bike is taken, an Interrogator-Chaplain may replace his bolt pistol, frag and krak grenades with Terminator armour (pg 154) and storm bolter .... *30 pts*
- An Interrogator-Chaplain in Terminator armour may take items from the **Terminator Weapons**, **Special Issue Wargear** and/or **Relics of Caliban** lists.
- An Interrogator-Chaplain in Terminator armour may replace his storm bolter with a combi-flamer, -melta or -plasma .... *5 pts*

ASMODAI

MASTER INTERROGATOR-CHAPLAIN

140 POINTS

The ends justify the means. No member of the Dark Angels' Inner Circle personifies this concept as completely as Asmodai, whose spectacularly violent excesses make him a figure of fear to friend and foe alike. Whether upon the field of battle, or within the firelit gloom of the Rock's dungeons, Asmodai's wicked blades are ever red with the blood of his victims. In the eyes of the Master Interrogator-Chaplain, guilt is as insidious as it is widespread, and his self-appointed duty is to root it out no matter where it lies.

Asmodai is a zealous exemplar in whose sight enemies quail and allies fight all the harder. His sonorous hymnals and rousing bellows of hatred are amplified through his vox grill, their impact all the greater for their contrast to the usual quiet stoicism of the Dark Angels. Whether holding together a defence line, as was his duty upon the Daemon world of Amity, or leading a forlorn hope through the blazing breach of an enemy fortress, as he did against the palace of the Traitor of Rhun, Asmodai stokes his brothers' righteous hatred into an inferno.

	WS	BS	S	T	W	I	A	Ld	Sv	Unit Type	Unit Composition
Asmodai	6	5	4	4	3	5	3	10	3+	Infantry (Character)	1 (Unique)

WARGEAR:
- **Bolt pistol**
- **Crozius arcanum** (pg 150)
- **Frag grenades**
- **Krak grenades**
- **Rosarius** (pg 153)

WARLORD TRAIT:
- **The Hunt** (pg 148)

SPECIAL RULES:
- **Deathwing** (pg 148)
- **Fear**
- **Grim Resolve** (pg 148)
- **Independent Character**
- **Preferred Enemy (Chaos Space Marines)**
- **Zealot**

Master of Repentance: If Asmodai slays the enemy Warlord in a challenge, you immediately score D3 extra Victory Points.

RELIC OF CALIBAN

Blades of Reason: *This is an ancient and horrific device, saturated with arcane cruelty and the sorrow of Mankind. Its many sharply honed and well-polished blades are etched with scriptures of repentance, and criss-crossing the weapon's head are cables and fine neural-wires powered by a mystic science that amplifies pain to agonies beyond endurance.*

Range	S	AP	Type
-	User	-	Melee, Instant Death, Specialist Weapon

LIBRARIAN

65 POINTS

Enemies fall to the ground screaming in agony and terror as the Dark Angels Librarian advances upon them. An insidious, fear-inducing cloud emanates from him, called into being by his sinister psychic powers. The Librarian's eyes glow and his lips move in silent mantras, armoured fingers forked into arcane symbols as he cuts and thrusts with the blade of his mind. The Librarian's powers wind like razored tendrils through his foes' psyches, shredding sanity and excising knowledge with a surgeon's skill. Against his interromantic powers, even the most heavily armoured warriors are all but defenceless. One after another, they clutch their skulls with shaking hands, crumple to the floor as their life-force is extinguished, or turn their guns upon themselves in a desperate effort to block out the horror. Disruption ripples outward from the Librarian, panic and confusion leaving the enemy as easy prey for the battle-brothers that march at his back with bolters thundering and flamers roaring. So perish all who seek to stand against the Dark Angels – cowering on their knees, begging for the benediction of a swift death.

	WS	BS	S	T	W	I	A	Ld	Sv	Unit Type	Unit Composition
Librarian	5	4	4	4	2	4	2	10	3+	Infantry (Character)	1 Librarian

WARGEAR:
- **Bolt pistol**
- **Force weapon**
- **Frag grenades**
- **Krak grenades**
- **Psychic hood**

SPECIAL RULES:
- **Deathwing** (pg 148)
- **Grim Resolve** (pg 148)
- **Independent Character**
- **Psyker (Mastery Level 1)**

PSYKER:
A Librarian generates his powers from the **Daemonology**, **Divination**, **Interromancy** (pg 156), **Pyromancy**, **Telekinesis** and **Telepathy** disciplines.

OPTIONS:
- May upgrade to Psyker (Mastery Level 2) .... *25 pts*
- May take items from the **Ranged Weapons**, **Special Issue Wargear** and/or **Relics of Caliban** lists.
- May take a Space Marine bike (pg 153) .... *20 pts*
- If a Space Marine bike is not taken, a Librarian may replace his bolt pistol, frag and krak grenades with Terminator armour (pg 154) .... *25 pts*
- A Librarian in Terminator armour may take one of the following:
  - Storm bolter .... *5 pts*
  - Combi-flamer, -melta or -plasma .... *10 pts*
- A Librarian in Terminator armour may take items from the **Special Issue Wargear** and/or **Relics of Caliban** lists.

EZEKIEL

GRAND MASTER OF LIBRARIANS

145 POINTS

Like an angel of death, Ezekiel strides fearlessly through the ranks of the foe and leaves naught but pain-twisted corpses in his wake. Those not slain outright by the barbed thought-worms of Ezekiel's mind meet their end beneath the killing edge of his force sword. It is said that many simply throw down their weapons and plead for mercy beneath Ezekiel's icy gaze, for a single glance reveals the look of one who has stared deeply into the soul of Man, and found something lacking. Yet the Grand Master of the Dark Angels' Librarius has no mercy to give, as the headless corpses of countless battlefields can attest. As one of the key members of the Dark Angels' Inner Circle, Ezekiel is the bearer of the Book of Salvation. This potent artefact is a precious icon to the Chapter's battle-brothers, who are taught from their earliest days as Scouts that its secrets must never, ever fall into enemy hands. Thus do the brothers under Ezekiel's command fight all the harder, chanting the sonorous hymnal of the Sacred Secret as they slay with extreme prejudice any enemy foolish enough to threaten Ezekiel and the tome he bears.

	WS	BS	S	T	W	I	A	Ld	Sv	Unit Type	Unit Composition
Ezekiel	5	5	4	4	3	5	3	10	2+	Infantry (Character)	1 (Unique)

WARGEAR:
- **Master-crafted bolt pistol**
- **Master-crafted force sword**
- **Frag grenades**
- **Krak grenades**
- **Psychic hood**

WARLORD TRAIT:
- **Courage of the First Legion** (pg 148)

SPECIAL RULES:
- **Deathwing** (pg 148)
- **Grim Resolve** (pg 148)
- **Independent Character**
- **Psyker (Mastery Level 3)**

PSYKER: Ezekiel generates his powers from the **Daemonology**, **Divination**, **Interromancy** (pg 156), **Pyromancy**, **Telekinesis** and **Telepathy** disciplines.

RELIC OF CALIBAN

Book of Salvation: *This renowned tome lists the names of all the Fallen who have been captured by the Dark Angels. Only the Inner Circle knows the contents of this book, but the whole Chapter understands that its protection is paramount.*

All friendly models with the Dark Angels Faction within 6" of Ezekiel at the start of the Fight sub-phase have +1 Attack until the end of the phase.

COMPANY MASTER

90 POINTS

Blades held ready, the Company Masters lead their brothers into battle with grim determination. They are supreme warriors, but unforgiving and coldly distant figures whose strategic brilliance echoes that of the Lion himself. Brooding and reserved, the Masters of the Dark Angels are not given to the inspirational theatrics common amongst their counterparts in some other Chapters. Rather, they devote all of their attention to the complete annihilation of the enemy, and in this duty they are never found lacking. Advancing at a steady pace, Company Masters place every blade-thrust with precision, embodying the meticulous lethality for which their Chapter is known. All the while, they show consummate tactical mastery, maintaining an awareness of troop dispositions and grand-scale battlefield manoeuvres that would put the most skilled strategium adept to shame. Strategic brilliance is a fundamental requirement of Company Masters, for they must be ever mindful of their Chapter's hidden agenda, ready to shift their focus to the hunt for the Fallen at any moment and swiftly redeploy their forces no matter the cost.

	WS	BS	S	T	W	I	A	Ld	Sv	Unit Type	Unit Composition
Company Master	6	5	4	4	3	5	3	10	3+	Infantry (Character)	1 Company Master

WARGEAR:
- **Bolt pistol**
- **Chainsword**
- **Frag grenades**
- **Krak grenades**
- **Iron halo** (pg 152)

SPECIAL RULES:
- **Deathwing** (pg 148)
- **Grim Resolve** (pg 148)
- **Independent Character**

OPTIONS:
- May replace chainsword with a relic blade (pg 151) .... *25 pts*
- May take a storm shield (pg 153) .... *15 pts*
- May take artificer armour (pg 154) .... *20 pts*
- May take items from the **Melee Weapons**, **Ranged Weapons**, **Special Issue Wargear** and/or **Relics of Caliban** lists.
- May replace bolt pistol, chainsword, frag and krak grenades with Terminator armour (pg 154), storm bolter and power sword .... *30 pts*
- A Company Master in Terminator armour may replace his power sword with a relic blade .... *10 pts*
- A Company Master in Terminator armour may take items from the **Terminator Weapons**, **Special Issue Wargear** and/or **Relics of Caliban** lists.

CHAPLAIN

90 POINTS

The Chaplains of the Dark Angels are stern war-priests whose rhetoric stirs the solemn hearts of their battle-brothers. Clad in night-black armour and wearing skull helms whose eye lenses blaze with inner light, Dark Angels Chaplains are grim and frightening figures. They maintain a steady stream of chanted catechisms and exhortations as battle rages around them, armouring their brothers in faith and conviction. Ignoring the shots and shrapnel that rebound from their protective force fields, the Chaplains call upon their comrades to let their righteous hatred flow, stoking their just revulsion toward heretic, xenos and witch alike. As battle is joined, the Chaplains stride to the fore, brandishing aloft their iconic weapons of office and spitting words of detestation into the faces of the foe. Their every blow is calamitous, crushing bone and buckling armour plate amid crackling blasts of energy. The Dark Angels battle-brothers fight ever harder, driven on by the selfless example of their Chaplains. All the while, the Chaplains watch the warriors at their side with a seasoned eye, alert for weakness and quick to stamp it out.

	WS	BS	S	T	W	I	A	Ld	Sv	Unit Type	Unit Composition
Chaplain	5	4	4	4	2	4	2	10	3+	Infantry (Character)	1 Chaplain

WARGEAR:
- **Bolt pistol**
- **Crozius arcanum** (pg 150)
- **Frag grenades**
- **Krak grenades**
- **Rosarius** (pg 153)

SPECIAL RULES:
- **Grim Resolve** (pg 148)
- **Independent Character**
- **Zealot**

OPTIONS:
- May take items from the **Melee Weapons**, **Ranged Weapons** and/or **Special Issue Wargear** lists.
- May take a Space Marine bike (pg 153) .... *20 pts*

TECHMARINE

65 POINTS

Amid the fury of battle, even the mightiest engines of war can be crippled, reduced to smoking wrecks by the heretical works of the foe. It is the task of the Techmarines to repair this damage, to shepherd their mechanised flock through the horrors of one war zone after another and sustain their machine spirits through the sorest tests of faith. In this duty, the Techmarines of the Dark Angels Armoury are both fearless and selfless, braving the most murderous cauldrons of enemy fire to reach damaged vehicles in need of aid. Under the covering fire of gun Servitors and fellow battle-brothers, and often taking up their own formidable weapons to keep the foe at bay, the Techmarines work with icy calm to re-route power flows, spot-weld repairs to armour plating, and coax motive actuators and weapon systems back into life.

	WS	BS	S	T	W	I	A	Ld	Sv	Unit Type	Unit Composition
Techmarine	4	5	4	4	2	4	2	9	2+	Infantry (Character)	1 Techmarine
Servitor	3	3	3	3	1	3	1	8	4+	Infantry	

WARGEAR:

Techmarine

- **Bolt pistol**
- **Power axe**
- **Frag grenades**
- **Krak grenades**
- **Servo-arm** (pg 151)

Servitor

- **Servo-arm**

SPECIAL RULES:

Techmarine

- **And They Shall Know No Fear**
- **Grim Resolve** (pg 148)
- **Independent Character**

Blessing of the Omnissiah: In each of your Shooting phases, instead of firing his weapons, a Techmarine can choose to repair a single friendly vehicle that he is in base contact with or embarked upon. To repair a vehicle, roll a D6 and add 1 for each Servitor with a servo-arm in his unit, and an additional 1 if the Techmarine has a servo-harness. If the result is a 5 or more, you may either restore a Hull Point lost earlier in the battle, or repair a Weapon Destroyed or Immobilised result suffered earlier in the battle; this is effective immediately.

'Be slow to anger, quick to action. The patient warrior knows that one well-placed shot can end a war.'

- from the teachings of Lion El'Jonson

Bolster Defences: After deployment, but before Scout redeployments and Infiltrate deployments, nominate one piece of terrain in your deployment zone (this cannot be one you have purchased as part of your army). The terrain piece's cover save is increased by 1 for the duration of the game (to a maximum of 3+). Note that a piece of terrain can only be bolstered once.

Servitor

Mindlock: If it does not contain a Techmarine, an unengaged unit that contains at least one model with this special rule must roll a D6 at the start of its turn. On a 4+, this special rule has no effect this turn. On a 1, 2 or 3, the unit is mindlocked until the start of its following turn. A mindlocked unit may not voluntarily move, shoot or charge, but must still complete compulsory moves, such as Pile In and Fall Back moves.

OPTIONS:

Techmarine

- May take a Space Marine bike (pg 153) .... *20 pts*
- May replace servo-arm with a servo-harness (pg 153) .. *25 pts*
- May take items from the **Melee Weapons**, **Ranged Weapons**, and/or **Special Issue Wargear** lists.
- May take up to five Servitors .... *10 pts each*

Servitor

- Up to two Servitors may replace their servo-arm with one of the following:
  - Heavy bolter .... *10 pts/model*
  - Multi-melta .... *10 pts/model*
  - Plasma cannon .... *20 pts/model*

TACTICAL SQUAD

70 POINTS

As the Tactical Squad's volleys ring out across the battlefield, enemy warriors are blown from their feet, heads and limbs blasted apart and torsos torn to ribbons by drumming boltgun fire. Through this devastation the Dark Angels Tactical Marines advance, chanting their hymnals of loathing and fortitude. Whether pressing forward on the attack or standing stubborn and immovable in defence, these heavily armoured, highly skilled warriors are the bane of their foes and a mighty boon to their comrades. They can be relied upon to complete their mission regardless of the cost and no matter the odds – a trait much prized by the commanders of the Dark Angels in their secret war for the redemption of their Chapter.

	WS	BS	S	T	W	I	A	Ld	Sv	Unit Type	Unit Composition
Space Marine	4	4	4	4	1	4	1	8	3+	Infantry	4 Space Marines
Space Marine Sergeant	4	4	4	4	1	4	1	8	3+	Infantry (Character)	1 Space Marine Sergeant
Veteran Sergeant	4	4	4	4	1	4	2	9	3+	Infantry (Character)	

WARGEAR:
- **Boltgun**
- **Bolt pistol**
- **Frag grenades**
- **Krak grenades**

SPECIAL RULES:
- **And They Shall Know No Fear**
- **Combat Squads** (pg 148)
- **Grim Resolve** (pg 148)

OPTIONS:
- May include up to five additional Space Marines .... *14 pts/model*
- If the squad numbers less than ten models, one Space Marine may take one item from either the **Special Weapons** or **Heavy Weapons** list.
- If the squad numbers ten models, one Space Marine may take one item from the **Special Weapons** list, and one other Space Marine may take one item from the **Heavy Weapons** list.
- May upgrade the Space Marine Sergeant to a Veteran Sergeant .... *10 pts*
- The Space Marine Sergeant or Veteran Sergeant may take items from the **Melee Weapons** and/or **Ranged Weapons** lists.
- The Space Marine Sergeant or Veteran Sergeant may take melta bombs .... *5 pts*
- The unit may select a Drop Pod (pg 122), Rhino (pg 120) or Razorback (pg 121) as a Dedicated Transport.

SCOUT SQUAD

55 POINTS

Slipping through the tangled terrain of the battlefield with their weapons held ready, Dark Angels Scouts shadow their foes like a hunter stalks his prey. Conscious of their Sergeants' stern glares, these novitiate warriors whisper newly-learned hymnals of righteous detestation as they slide into firing positions and stare down their weapons' sights. Only when the moment is perfect do they squeeze their triggers, sniper rifles and bolters spitting death into the midst of the unsuspecting foe. Enemy warriors spin from their feet in sprays of blood, even as the Scouts advance, weapons blazing, to finish off the shocked survivors. The battlefield is the proving ground of the Dark Angels Scouts, the theatre in which they can show their worthiness to progress through the ranks and learn the mysteries of their noble Chapter.

	WS	BS	S	T	W	I	A	Ld	Sv	Unit Type	Unit Composition
Scout	4	4	4	4	1	4	1	8	4+	Infantry	4 Scouts
Scout Sergeant	4	4	4	4	1	4	1	8	4+	Infantry (Character)	1 Scout Sergeant
Veteran Scout Sergeant	4	4	4	4	1	4	2	9	4+	Infantry (Character)	

WARGEAR:
- **Boltgun**
- **Bolt pistol**
- **Frag grenades**
- **Krak grenades**

SPECIAL RULES:
- **And They Shall Know No Fear**
- **Combat Squads** (pg 148)
- **Grim Resolve** (pg 148)
- **Infiltrate**
- **Move Through Cover**
- **Scout**

OPTIONS:
- May include up to five additional Scouts .... *11 pts/model*
- The entire squad may take camo cloaks (pg 151) .... *2 pts/model*
- Any model may replace its boltgun with a Space Marine shotgun or close combat weapon .... *free*
- Any model may replace his boltgun with a sniper rifle .... *1 pt/model*
- One Scout may replace his boltgun with one of the following:
  - Heavy bolter .... *8 pts*
    - May also take hellfire shells (pg 152) .... *5 pts*
  - Missile launcher (with frag and krak missiles) .... *15 pts*
    - May also take flakk missiles .... *10 pts*
- May upgrade the Scout Sergeant to a Veteran Scout Sergeant .... *10 pts*
- The Scout Sergeant or Veteran Scout Sergeant may take items from the **Melee Weapons** and/or **Ranged Weapons** lists.
- The Scout Sergeant or Veteran Scout Sergeant may take melta bombs .... *5 pts*

COMPANY VETERANS SQUAD

90 POINTS

Moving with unhurried menace, their robes flowing in the ash-clogged winds of war, the Company Veterans advance toward their objective. Their eye-lenses blaze from beneath heavy cowls as the foe comes into sight; their weapons are raised – the full fury of the Rock's Armoury primed and ready. Taking careful aim, the Veterans let fly, their solemn silence broken by the sudden thunder of their guns. Plasma blasts howl through the air to explode amid the foe with ruinous force. Hails of bolts and gouts of flame reduce enemy warriors to scorched and blasted corpses. The Veterans raise their weapons in a warrior's salute, a moment's honour spared not for the detestable foe, but for the Lion who gave his sons the strength to slay them. Then, with oaths of vengeance upon their lips, the Company Veterans charge.

	WS	BS	S	T	W	I	A	Ld	Sv	Unit Type	Unit Composition
Veteran	4	4	4	4	1	4	2	9	3+	Infantry	4 Veterans
Veteran Sergeant	4	4	4	4	1	4	2	9	3+	Infantry (Character)	1 Veteran Sergeant

WARGEAR:
- **Boltgun**
- **Bolt pistol**
- **Frag grenades**
- **Krak grenades**

SPECIAL RULES:
- **And They Shall Know No Fear**
- **Combat Squads** (pg 148)
- **Grim Resolve** (pg 148)

OPTIONS:
- May include up to five additional Veterans .... *18 pts/model*
- Any model may take items from the **Melee Weapons** and/or **Ranged Weapons** lists.
- For every five models in the squad, one Veteran may take an item from the **Special Weapons** list.
- One Veteran may take an item from the **Heavy Weapons** list.
- Any model may take melta bombs .... *5 pts/model*
- Any model may take one of the following:
  - Combat shield (pg 152) .... *5 pts/model*
  - Storm shield (pg 153) .... *10 pts/model*
- The unit may select a Drop Pod (pg 122), Rhino (pg 120) or Razorback (pg 121) as a Dedicated Transport.

COMMAND SQUAD

90 POINTS

Beneath the ancient glory of one of their Chapter's honoured banners, the Command Squad fights with cold determination. Acting as bodyguards to a hero of the Chapter's Inner Circle, these hand-picked Veterans are pledged to follow their master's every command without a second's hesitation. Should brothers fall wounded, the Apothecary tends their hurts and gets them back into the fight. Should a mighty warrior of the foe bar their path, the Company Champion steps forth to do battle, the honour of his brothers mantled upon his broad shoulders. Meanwhile, the remaining Veterans maintain a constant hail of fire directed into the foe, picking out crucial targets at their lord's direction and sealing their victims' doom with a barrage of bolt shells and plasma blasts.

	WS	BS	S	T	W	I	A	Ld	Sv	Unit Type	Unit Composition
Veteran	4	4	4	4	1	4	2	9	3+	Infantry	5 Veterans
Company Champion	5	4	4	4	1	4	2	9	3+	Infantry (Character)	
Apothecary	4	4	4	4	1	4	2	9	3+	Infantry (Character)	

WARGEAR:
- **Bolt pistol**
- **Chainsword**
- **Frag grenades**
- **Krak grenades**

SPECIAL RULES:
- **And They Shall Know No Fear**
- **Grim Resolve** (pg 148)

Honour or Death (Company Champion only)**:** A model with this special rule must issue and accept a challenge whenever possible. If there is more than one friendly model in a combat with this rule, you may select which model issues or accepts the challenge.

OPTIONS:
- One Veteran may take an item from the **Dark Angels Standards** list.
- One Veteran may be upgraded to a Company Champion, replacing his chainsword with a Blade of Caliban and combat shield (pg 152) .... *15 pts*
- One Veteran may be upgraded to an Apothecary, taking a narthecium (pg 152) .... *15 pts*
- Any Veteran may take melta bombs .... *5 pts/model*
- Any Veteran may take a storm shield (pg 153) .... *10 pts/model*
- Any Veteran may take items from the **Melee Weapons**, **Ranged Weapons** and/or **Special Weapons** lists.
- The unit may select a Drop Pod (pg 122), Rhino (pg 120) or Razorback (pg 121) as a Dedicated Transport.

DREADNOUGHTS

100 POINTS

Enemies are scattered before the blazing heavy weapons of a Dreadnought like leaves in a gale. If still-living Dark Angels are severe and vengeful, the revenant pilots of these war machines are even more so. They advance unflinching into the heaviest enemy fire, war-hymnals booming from their vox-amps with all the righteous anger of the Lion. Some Dreadnoughts relive their warrior-duels of old, crushing the foe with their mighty power fists before grinding their broken bodies underfoot. Others act as implacable walking tanks, scything down enemy infantry with hails of heavy bolter or assault cannon fire, or blasting armoured war engines apart with searing swathes of burning promethium and swarms of super-krak missiles. Whichever role these armoured walkers choose, they are lethal in the extreme.

				Armour							
	WS	BS	S	F	S	R	I	A	HP	Unit Type	Unit Composition
Dreadnought	4	4	6	12	12	10	4	4	3	Vehicle (Walker)	1 Dreadnought

WARGEAR:
- **Multi-melta**
- **Power fist with built-in storm bolter**
- **Searchlight**
- **Smoke launchers**

SPECIAL RULES:
- **Grim Resolve** (pg 148)

OPTIONS:
- May include up to two additional Dreadnoughts.. *100 pts/model*
- Any model may take items from the **Dreadnought Weapons** list.
- Any model may replace its power fist with built-in storm bolter with one of the following:
  - Missile launcher.. *10 pts/model*
  - Twin-linked autocannon.. *15 pts/model*
- Any model may replace its built-in storm bolter with a built-in heavy flamer........ *10 pts/model*
- Any model may take extra armour.. *10 pts/model*
- If the unit contains no additional Dreadnoughts, it may select a Drop Pod (pg 122) as a Dedicated Transport.

VENERABLE DREADNOUGHTS

125 POINTS

Armour painted in the bone white of the Deathwing, Dark Angels Venerable Dreadnoughts are invaluable weapons in the war against the Fallen. These are the eldest and most determined members of the Inner Circle, warriors who have fought to absolve their Chapter's shame for – in many cases – thousands of years. Though it takes much to rouse these timeless heroes from their slumbers, once on the field of battle they are the embodiment of the Dark Angels' vengeful wrath. Their every shot is perfectly placed, punching through weak spots in enemy armour to blow tanks sky high or fell the greatest champions of the foe. Their every blow in close combat hits like a strike from the Primarch himself, hurling broken enemies through the air. None can stand before these ancients and live, not even the mightiest of the Fallen.

	WS	BS	S	Armour F	Armour S	Armour R	I	A	HP	Unit Type	Unit Composition
Venerable Dreadnought	5	5	6	12	12	10	4	4	3	Vehicle (Walker)	1 Venerable Dreadnought

WARGEAR:
- **Multi-melta**
- **Power fist with built-in storm bolter**
- **Searchlight**
- **Smoke launchers**

SPECIAL RULES:
- **Deathwing** (pg 148)
- **Grim Resolve** (pg 148)

Venerable: If a Venerable Dreadnought suffers a penetrating hit, you can make your opponent re-roll the result on the Vehicle Damage table. You must accept the second result, even if it is worst than the first.

OPTIONS:
- May include up to two additional Venerable Dreadnoughts.................................... *125 pts/model*
- Any model may take items from the **Dreadnought Weapons** list.
- Any model may replace its power fist with built-in storm bolter with one of the following:
  - Missile launcher .... *10 pts*
  - Twin-linked autocannon... *15 pts*
- Any model may replace its built-in storm bolter with a built-in heavy flamer... *10 pts*
- Any model may take extra armour .... *10 pts*
- If the unit contains no additional Venerable Dreadnoughts, it may select a Drop Pod (pg 122) as a Dedicated Transport.

DEATHWING TERMINATOR SQUAD

200 POINTS

Whether teleporting into battle amid a great corona of crackling energy discharge or striding down the assault ramp of a hulking Land Raider, the Terminators of the Deathwing obliterate all before them. Their firepower is a storm of death, shredding the enemy with such fury that many do not even realise they are under attack before they are turned into smoking offal. Striding over the ruin of their foes, the Deathwing press the attack with merciless efficiency, return fire rebounding from the super-dense plates of their bone white Terminator armour. Those who seek to meet these avenging angels at close quarters fare no better, for every mighty swing of the Terminators' power fists sees another victim splattered in pieces across their comrades. Soon, nothing remains of the foe but mangled, smouldering remnants.

	WS	BS	S	T	W	I	A	Ld	Sv	Unit Type	Unit Composition
Deathwing Terminator	4	4	4	4	1	4	2	9	2+	Infantry	4 Deathwing Terminators
Deathwing Sergeant	4	4	4	4	1	4	2	9	2+	Infantry (Character)	1 Deathwing Sergeant

WARGEAR:
- **Terminator armour** (pg 154)
- **Storm bolter**
- **Power fist** (Deathwing Terminator only)
- **Power sword** (Deathwing Sergeant only)

SPECIAL RULES:
- **Deathwing** (pg 148)
- **Grim Resolve** (pg 148)
- **Split Fire**

OPTIONS:
- May include up to five additional Deathwing Terminators .... *40 pts/model*
- Any model may replace all of its weapons with:
  - Two lightning claws.. *free*
  - Thunder hammer and storm shield (pg 153).. *10 pts/model*
- Any model may replace its power fist with a chainfist.. *5 pts/model*
- For every five models in the squad, one Deathwing Terminator may take an item from the **Terminator Heavy Weapons** list.
- The unit may take a perfidious relic of the Unforgiven (pg 153) .... *15 pts*
- The unit may select a Land Raider (pg 136), Land Raider Crusader (pg 137) or Land Raider Redeemer (pg 138) as a Dedicated Transport.

DEATHWING COMMAND SQUAD

200 POINTS

Armoured boots crushing bone and rubble to dust, the warriors of the Deathwing Command Squad advance at the side of their commanding officer and lend their might to his own. With their penchant for deploying by mass teleport straight into the heart of the enemy army, the Deathwing often finds itself beset from all sides. At such times, the Deathwing Command Squad provide a rock-solid rallying point, their standard flying proud above the maelstrom of screaming faces and clashing blades. Armed for close range annihilation of the foe, these elite battle-brothers support the hero to whom they have been assigned, tearing through every threat that stands in his path.

	WS	BS	S	T	W	I	A	Ld	Sv	Unit Type	Unit Composition
Deathwing Terminator	4	4	4	4	1	4	2	9	2+	Infantry	5 Deathwing Terminators
Deathwing Sergeant	4	4	4	4	1	4	2	9	2+	Infantry (Character)	
Deathwing Apothecary	4	4	4	4	1	4	2	9	2+	Infantry (Character)	
Deathwing Champion	5	4	4	4	1	4	2	9	2+	Infantry (Character)	

WARGEAR:
- **Terminator armour** (pg 154)
- **Storm bolter**
- **Power fist**

SPECIAL RULES:
- **Deathwing** (pg 148)
- **Grim Resolve** (pg 148)
- **Honour or Death** (pg 113) (Deathwing Champion only)
- **Split Fire**

OPTIONS:
- One Deathwing Terminator may be upgraded to a Deathwing Sergeant, replacing his power fist with a power sword .... *free*
- One Deathwing Terminator in the army may take:
  - Deathwing Company Banner (pg 152) .... *20 pts*
  - Sacred Standard (pg 153) .... *35 pts*
- One Deathwing Terminator in the army may be upgraded to the Deathwing Champion, replacing all of his weapons with the Halberd of Caliban (pg 151) .... *5 pts*
- One Deathwing Terminator in the army may be upgraded to the Deathwing Apothecary, replacing his power fist with a narthecium (pg 152) .... *5 pts*
- Any Deathwing Terminator may replace all of his weapons with:
  - Two lightning claws .... *free*
  - Thunder hammer and storm shield (pg 153) .... *10 pts/model*
- Any Deathwing Terminator may replace his power fist with a chainfist .... *5 pts/model*
- One Deathwing Terminator may take an item from the **Terminator Heavy Weapons** list.
- The unit may take a perfidious relic of the Unforgiven (pg 153) .... *15 pts*
- The unit may select a Land Raider (pg 136), Land Raider Crusader (pg 137) or Land Raider Redeemer (pg 138) as a Dedicated Transport.

DEATHWING KNIGHTS

235 POINTS

Shields locked and maces of absolution glowing, the Deathwing Knights advance upon their quarry with the inevitability of death. A cold fury burns within their hearts, for these warriors know of Luther, of his heresies and of the stain he and his followers have left upon their Chapter's honour. Their anger at this betrayal is channelled into every battle; the Deathwing Knights swing their maces with a strength born of hatred for all those who impede their quest for redemption. These warriors are their Chapter's ultimate weapon against the Fallen, capable of crushing any resistance and subduing even the mightiest foes. Neither Warp-infused Daemon nor rampaging Tyranid monstrosity can stand against their righteous wrath, for the Deathwing Knights fight for the very soul of their Chapter.

	WS	BS	S	T	W	I	A	Ld	Sv	Unit Type	Unit Composition
Deathwing Knight	5	4	4	4	1	4	2	9	2+	Infantry	4 Deathwing Knights
Knight Master	5	4	4	4	1	4	3	9	2+	Infantry (Character)	1 Knight Master

WARGEAR:
- **Terminator armour** (pg 154)
- **Mace of absolution** (pg 151) (Deathwing Knight only)
- **Flail of the Unforgiven** (pg 151) (Knight Master only)
- **Storm shield** (pg 153)

SPECIAL RULES:
- **Deathwing** (pg 148)
- **Grim Resolve** (pg 148)
- **Hammer of Wrath**
- **Precision Strikes**

Fortress of Shields: Any model in this unit that is equipped with a storm shield (including models with the Independent Character special rule that have joined it) and is in base contact with at least two other models from this unit has +1 Toughness.

OPTIONS:
- May include up to five additional Deathwing Knights .... *45 pts/model*
- The unit may take a perfidious relic of the Unforgiven (pg 153) .... *15 pts*
- The unit may select a Land Raider (pg 136), Land Raider Crusader (pg 137) or Land Raider Redeemer (pg 138) as a Dedicated Transport.

RAVENWING COMMAND SQUAD

120 POINTS

Roaring into battle at the side of one of their Chapter's greatest heroes, the Black Knights of the Ravenwing Command Squad ride down all who bar their path. Like the Knights of old Caliban, these pitch-clad warriors thunder out of the gloom in the wake of their heroic leader to smite their monstrous foes. Plasma talons rake the enemy ranks, blasting even heavily armoured warriors to drifting ash, while every swing of a corvus hammer sees another chest crushed, another head sent spinning through the air. Beneath the shadow of their fluttering standard, the warriors of the Ravenwing Command Squad form a rallying-point for one of the most fearsome fast-strike forces in the galaxy, their heroic example leading their brothers to greatness time and again.

	WS	BS	S	T	W	I	A	Ld	Sv	Unit Type	Unit Composition
Ravenwing Black Knight	4	4	4	5	1	4	2	9	3+	Bike	3 Ravenwing Black Knights
Ravenwing Apothecary	4	4	4	5	1	4	2	9	3+	Bike (Character)	
Ravenwing Champion	5	4	4	5	1	4	2	9	3+	Bike (Character)	

WARGEAR:
- **Bolt pistol**
- **Plasma talon** (pg 150)
- **Corvus hammer** (pg 150)
- **Frag grenades**
- **Krak grenades**
- **Teleport homer** (pg 153)

SPECIAL RULES:
- **And They Shall Know No Fear**
- **Grim Resolve** (pg 148)
- **Honour or Death** (pg 113) (Ravenwing Champion only)
- **Hit & Run**
- **Ravenwing** (pg 148)
- **Scout**
- **Skilled Rider**

OPTIONS:
- May include up to three additional Ravenwing Black Knights.................................... *40 pts/model*
- One Ravenwing Black Knight in the army may take:
  - Ravenwing Company Banner (pg 153) .... *20 pts*
  - Sacred Standard (pg 153) .... *35 pts*
- Up to two Ravenwing Black Knights may replace their plasma talon with a Ravenwing grenade launcher (pg 150) .... *free*
- One Ravenwing Black Knight in the army may be upgraded to the Ravenwing Apothecary, taking a narthecium (pg 152).. *30 pts*
- One Ravenwing Black Knight in the army may be upgraded to the Ravenwing Champion, replacing his corvus hammer with a Blade of Caliban (pg 150) .... *5 pts*

RHINO

35 POINTS

With a tireless determination to match that of the warriors they carry into battle, the Rhino APCs of the Dark Angels shrug off incoming fire and plough through obstacles that bar their way. The storm bolters of these dauntless transports play left and right, spitting streams of shells into the foe and scouring them from the Rhinos' path. Only once they have reached their destination do the Rhinos skid to a halt, engines rumbling and storm bolters continuing to roar. With a whine of hydraulics, the Rhinos' hatches swing open, squads of Dark Angels deploying to gun down their foes with ruthless efficiency. Swift, reliable and resilient, the Rhino APC is as stoic a steed as the Sons of the Lion could hope for, and it forms an indispensable part of their arsenal.

		Armour					
	BS	F	S	R	HP	Unit Type	Unit Composition
Rhino	4	11	11	10	3	Vehicle (Tank, Transport)	1 Rhino

WARGEAR:
- **Storm bolter**
- **Searchlight**
- **Smoke launchers**

SPECIAL RULES:
Repair: If a Rhino is Immobilised, then in subsequent turns, it may attempt to repair itself instead of shooting. To make the attempt, roll a D6 in the Shooting phase; on the roll of a 6+, the vehicle is no longer Immobilised. Note that a successful Repair does no restore a Hull Point.

TRANSPORT:
- **Transport Capacity:** Ten models. It cannot carry models with the Bulky, Very Bulky or Extremely Bulky special rules.
- **Fire Points:** Two models can fire from the Rhino's top hatch.
- **Access Points:** The Rhino has one Access Point on each side of the hull and one at the rear.

OPTIONS:
- May take items from the **Dark Angels Vehicle Equipment** list.

RAZORBACK

55 POINTS

Blasts of potent firepower precede the Razorback into battle, its turret swivelling rapidly as it hammers the foe with salvoes of fire. A hybrid of battle tank and transport, the Razorback serves as the preferred mount for Company Veterans and Command Squads alike. As it roars forward, the Razorback provides fast-moving fire support for those forces advancing alongside it. This role continues after its passengers have disembarked; thanks to its turret-mounted weaponry, the Razorback is able to eliminate armoured threats, cull large numbers of enemy infantry, or blast open gaps in the foe's defences through which its accompanying warriors can charge. Few vehicles can boast this level of tactical versatility, making the Razorback an ideal transport for the fast-moving, elite forces of the Dark Angels.

		Armour					
	BS	**F**	**S**	**R**	**HP**	**Unit Type**	**Unit Composition**
Razorback	4	11	11	10	3	Vehicle (Tank, Transport)	1 Razorback

WARGEAR:
- **Twin-linked heavy bolter**
- **Searchlight**
- **Smoke launchers**

TRANSPORT:
- **Transport Capacity:** Six models. It cannot carry models with the Bulky, Very Bulky or Extremely Bulky special rules.
- **Fire Points:** None.
- **Access Points:** The Razorback has one Access Point on each side of the hull and one at the rear.

OPTIONS:
- May take items from the **Dark Angels Vehicle Equipment** list.
- May replace its twin-linked heavy bolter with one of the following:
  - Twin-linked heavy flamer .... *free*
  - Twin-linked assault cannon .... *20 pts*
  - Twin-linked lascannon .... *20 pts*
  - Lascannon and twin-linked plasma gun .... *20 pts*

DROP POD

35
POINTS

Fired from the launch bays of orbiting Strike Cruisers, Dark Angels Drop Pods plummet toward the planet below. Within, squads of battle-brothers meditate upon the battle to come, ignoring the violent shaking of the pods' atmospheric re-entry as they recite mantras of readiness and renew oaths of detestation. Plunging towards the battlefield, the Drop Pods fire their retros at the last moment, the armoured capsules slamming down amidst the panicked enemy with sledgehammer force. Within, electro-candles flare from amber to green, warriors raise their heads from prayer, and bolters are hefted in readiness. A second later, the Drop Pods' locking bolts release with a bang, their hatches crash down, and the Sons of the Lion charge forth like a storm of vengeance to slaughter the unworthy.

		Armour					
	BS	F	S	R	HP	Unit Type	Unit Composition
Drop Pod	4	12	12	12	3	Vehicle (Open-topped, Transport)	1 Drop Pod

WARGEAR:
- **Storm bolter**

SPECIAL RULES:
Drop Pod Assault: Drop Pods and units embarked upon them must be held in Deep Strike Reserve. At the beginning of your first turn, half of your Drop Pods (rounding up) automatically arrive from Reserve. The arrival of remaining Drop Pods is rolled for normally. Once a Drop Pod lands, all passengers must disembark and no models can embark for the rest of the game.

Immobile: A Drop Pod cannot move once it has entered play, and counts in all respects as a vehicle that has suffered an Immobilised result that cannot be repaired in any way. This does not cause it to lose a Hull Point.

Inertial Guidance System: If a Drop Pod scatters on top of impassable terrain or another model (friend or foe), reduce the scatter distance by the minimum required in order to avoid the obstacle. If the Drop Pod scatters off the edge of the board, it suffers a Deep Strike Mishap.

TRANSPORT:
- **Transport Capacity:** Ten models or one Dreadnought of any type.

OPTIONS:
- May replace storm bolter with a deathwind launcher (pg 149) .... *15 pts*
- May take a locator beacon (pg 154) .... *10 pts*

ASSAULT SQUAD

70 POINTS

Chanting mantras of wrath and vengeance, the warriors of the Dark Angels Assault Squads strike their foes like a breaking storm. Beneath the Assault Marines' veneer of monastic solemnity lies a passion every bit as fierce as that of their counterparts in other Chapters, a fire that burns all the hotter for being strictly controlled. Where a less disciplined warrior might rain a flurry of wasteful, reckless blows upon his foe, a Dark Angel will target his enemy's weak-points with a focussed fury; each blade-swing will be perfectly placed, and driven with all the strength and hatred the battle-brother can muster. In this way, Dark Angels Assault Marines hew through armour and flesh, hacking down their foes with the unstoppable might of the righteous.

	WS	BS	S	T	W	I	A	Ld	Sv	Unit Type	Unit Composition
Space Marine	4	4	4	4	1	4	1	8	3+	Infantry	4 Space Marines
Space Marine Sergeant	4	4	4	4	1	4	1	8	3+	Infantry (Character)	1 Space Marine Sergeant
Veteran Sergeant	4	4	4	4	1	4	2	9	3+	Infantry (Character)	

WARGEAR:
- **Bolt pistol**
- **Chainsword**
- **Frag grenades**
- **Krak grenades**

SPECIAL RULES:
- **And They Shall Know No Fear**
- **Combat Squads** (pg 148)
- **Grim Resolve** (pg 148)

OPTIONS:
- May include up to five additional Space Marines .... *14 pts/model*
- The entire squad may take jump packs (pg 152) .... *3 pts/model*
- Up to two Space Marines may replace their bolt pistols with one of the following:
  - Flamer .... *5 pts/model*
  - Plasma pistol .... *15 pts/model*
- For every five models in the unit, one model may replace its bolt pistol and chainsword with an eviscerator .... *25 pts*
- May upgrade the Space Marine Sergeant to a Veteran Sergeant .... *10 pts*
- The Space Marine Sergeant or Veteran Sergeant may take items from the **Melee Weapons** and/or **Ranged Weapons** lists.
- The Space Marine Sergeant or Veteran Sergeant may take a combat shield (pg 152) and/or melta bombs .... *5 pts each*
- If the squad does not take jump packs, it may then take a Drop Pod (pg 122), Rhino (pg 120) or Razorback (pg 121) as a Dedicated Transport.

RAVENWING BIKE SQUAD

75 POINTS

Speeding through the smoke-wreathed hell of battle come the warriors of the Ravenwing. The throaty roar of Space Marine bikes is the only warning their foes have before the black-clad huntsmen of the 2nd Company descend upon them in force. Following strict doctrines of lightning warfare, the Ravenwing slice like blackened blades through the ranks of the foe before breaking off and speeding away once more. As their panicked victims struggle to process the destruction wrought in their midst, the Ravenwing strike again and again. Even the mightiest foes are cut apart and eventually massacred, left as tattered, bloody remnants in the bikers' wake. So do the Ravenwing ride their prey to ground and seal their doom.

	WS	BS	S	T	W	I	A	Ld	Sv	Unit Type	Unit Composition
Ravenwing Biker	4	4	4	5	1	4	1	8	3+	Bike	2 Ravenwing Bikers
Ravenwing Sergeant	4	4	4	5	1	4	1	8	3+	Bike (Character)	1 Ravenwing Sergeant
Ravenwing Veteran Sgt.	4	4	4	5	1	4	2	9	3+	Bike (Character)	
Ravenwing Attack Bike	4	4	4	5	2	4	2	8	3+	Bike	

WARGEAR:
- **Bolt pistol or chainsword**
- **Heavy bolter** (Attack Bike only)
- **Frag grenades**
- **Krak grenades**
- **Space Marine bike** (pg 153)
- **Teleport homer** (pg 153)

SPECIAL RULES:
- **And They Shall Know No Fear**
- **Combat Squads** (pg 148)
- **Grim Resolve** (pg 148)
- **Hit & Run**
- **Ravenwing** (pg 148)
- **Scout**

OPTIONS:
- May include up to three additional Ravenwing Bikers .... *25 pts/model*
- Up to two Ravenwing Bikers may each take one item from the **Special Weapons** list.
- May upgrade the Ravenwing Sergeant to a Ravenwing Veteran Sergeant .... *10 pts*
- The Ravenwing Sergeant or Ravenwing Veteran Sergeant may:
  - Take items from the **Melee Weapons** and/or **Ranged Weapons** lists.
  - Take melta bombs .... *5 pts*
- May include one Ravenwing Attack Bike (pg 125) .... *45 pts*
  - The Ravenwing Attack Bike may replace its heavy bolter with a multi-melta .... *10 pts*

RAVENWING ATTACK BIKE SQUAD

45 POINTS

Those designated as the Ravenwing's quarry are dangerous foes, possessed of potent weapons and armoured fighting vehicles that can wreak havoc amongst the ranks of the 2nd Company. To neutralise such threats, Ravenwing Attack Squadrons frequently include whole squads of heavily armed Attack Bikes. Speeding alongside their battle-brothers, the crews of these swift gun-platforms play the devastating fire of their weapons across the foe. Attack Bikes armed with heavy bolters punch volleys of shells into infantry, tearing ragged wounds in the enemy battle line through which their comrades race. Meanwhile, those Attack Bikes that mount multi-meltas direct their fire towards the enemy's armoured vehicles, vaporising massive battle tanks with each roaring shot.

	WS	BS	S	T	W	I	A	Ld	Sv	Unit Type	Unit Composition
Ravenwing Attack Bike	4	4	4	5	2	4	2	8	3+	Bike	1 Ravenwing Attack Bike

WARGEAR:
- **Bolt pistol**
- **Heavy bolter**
- **Frag grenades**
- **Krak grenades**
- **Space Marine bike** (pg 153)
- **Teleport homer** (pg 153)

SPECIAL RULES:
- **And They Shall Know No Fear**
- **Grim Resolve** (pg 148)
- **Hit & Run**
- **Ravenwing** (pg 148)
- **Scout**

OPTIONS:
- May include up to two additional Ravenwing Attack Bikes ....*45 pts/model*
- Any Ravenwing Attack Bike may replace its heavy bolter with a multi-melta.................... *10 pts*

RAVENWING LAND SPEEDERS

50 POINTS

Skimming fast and low over the battlefield, Ravenwing Land Speeders sweep above their prey like murderous shadows. Mixed marks of Land Speeders make up these squadrons, standard attack craft holding formation with Tornado and Typhoon support skimmers as they race toward the foe. The amount of firepower generated by these squadrons is tremendous, each pass engulfing the foe in a cauldron of explosions that leaves blazing wreckage and smoking corpses in their wake. Wherever the bikers of the Ravenwing face overwhelming odds, the Land Speeders swoop down to even them. Wherever the quarry looks set to escape, the skimmers race after them, arrow swift, crippling their transports with pinpoint fire. To the foe, the Land Speeders seem to strike everywhere at once, always with deadly speed and violence.

		Armour					
	BS	F	S	R	HP	Unit Type	Unit Composition
Ravenwing Land Speeder	4	10	10	10	2	Vehicle (Fast, Skimmer)	1 Ravenwing Land Speeder

WARGEAR:
- **Heavy bolter**

SPECIAL RULES:
- **Deep Strike**
- **Ravenwing** (pg 148)

Anti-grav Upwash: Whilst this unit includes at least three Ravenwing Land Speeders, it can move an additional 6" when moving Flat Out.

OPTIONS:
- May include up to four additional Ravenwing Land Speeders .... *50 pts/model*
- Any Ravenwing Land Speeder may replace its heavy bolter with one of the following:
  - Heavy flamer .... *free*
  - Multi-melta .... *10 pts*
- Any Ravenwing Land Speeder may take one of the following:
  - Heavy bolter .... *5 pts/model*
  - Heavy flamer .... *5 pts/model*
  - Multi-melta .... *15 pts/model*
  - Assault cannon .... *20 pts/model*
  - Typhoon missile launcher (pg 150) .... *25 pts/model*

RAVENWING DARKSHROUD

80 POINTS

The Ravenwing Darkshroud skims low across the battlefield, wreathed in a crackling nimbus of gloaming shadow. This strange energy rolls in waves from the sepulchral statue that looms at the vehicle's rear, enshrined upon its armoured dais. Advancing around it, the Dark Angels fade in and out of sight as fearsome, half-seen wraiths with fire in their eyes. Enemy fire directed at the Darkshroud – or at those engulfed by its pall-like energy field – simply flickers out of being, searing bolts of energy reduced to dying glimmers while missiles and rockets fall out of the air. Meanwhile, the Darkshroud draws ever closer, its ominous presence shielding and inspiring the Sons of the Lion even as it terrifies the foe.

		Armour					
	BS	**F**	**S**	**R**	**HP**	**Unit Type**	**Unit Composition**
Ravenwing Darkshroud	4	10	10	10	3	Vehicle (Fast, Skimmer)	1 Ravenwing Darkshroud

WARGEAR:
- **Heavy bolter**

SPECIAL RULES:
- **Deep Strike**
- **Ravenwing** (pg 148)
- **Scout**
- **Shrouded**

Icon of Old Caliban: Friendly units with the Dark Angels Faction within 6" of one or more Ravenwing Darkshrouds gain the Fear and Stealth special rules (though this does not affect the Darkshrouds themselves). Furthermore, enemy units cannot fire Overwatch at friendly units with the Dark Angels Faction that are within 6" of one or more Ravenwing Darkshrouds at the start of the Assault phase.

OPTIONS:
- May replace heavy bolter with an assault cannon .... *15 pts*

NEPHILIM JETFIGHTER

170 POINTS

Swift, agile and heavily armed, the Nephilim makes for an exceptional air superiority fighter. Whether dogfighting amid the tangled spires of an industrial world, or screaming through the storm-lashed canyons of a mountain range, the Nephilim is winged death to enemy flyers. Dark Angels make for tenacious pilots, and once a battle-brother of the Ravenwing has an aircraft in his sights the target's destruction is almost guaranteed. Foes hurl their craft into ever more desperate evasive manoeuvres, their panic reaching fever pitch just moments before a salvo of blacksword missiles punches them from the sky in a tumbling ball of flame. Ground vehicles are no safer, for the strafing runs of these agile fighter craft leave tanks and transports crippled and blazing – easy game for the ground-based huntsmen of the Ravenwing.

		Armour					
	BS	**F**	**S**	**R**	**HP**	**Unit Type**	**Unit Composition**
Nephilim Jetfighter	4	11	11	11	3	Vehicle (Flyer)	1 Nephilim Jetfighter

WARGEAR:
- **Twin-linked heavy bolter**
- **Avenger mega bolter** (pg 149)
- **Six blacksword missiles** (pg 149)

SPECIAL RULES:
- **Missile Lock**
- **Ravenwing** (pg 148)
- **Strafing Run**

Unrelenting Hunter: When shooting at enemy vehicles, a Nephilim Jetfighter can choose to treat any Weapon Destroyed result as an Immobilised result instead.

OPTIONS:
- May replace avenger mega bolter with a twin-linked lascannon .... *5 pts*

RAVENWING DARK TALON

160 POINTS

The Ravenwing Dark Talon glides through the skies like a great bird of ill omen. As its shadow passes overhead, the enemy cower in terror, for here is the most horrific weapon that the Ravenwing have at their disposal. The Dark Talon is their killing blow, the final grim and terrible sight that their prey will see, and it is equipped accordingly. Alongside racks of hurricane bolters for shredding the worshippers of the Fallen, the Dark Talon mounts weapons based upon ancient technology from the depths of the Rock. The first of these, the stasis bomb, is used to disrupt the flow of time itself in order to weaken and disorient its prey. Far more extreme is the rift cannon, a monstrous weapon that rips asunder the very fabric of reality in order to cast its victims into the void beyond.

		Armour					
	BS	F	S	R	HP	Unit Type	Unit Composition
Ravenwing Dark Talon	4	11	11	11	3	Vehicle (Flyer, Hover)	1 Ravenwing Dark Talon

WARGEAR:
- **Two hurricane bolters** (pg 149)
- **Rift cannon** (pg 150)
- **Stasis bomb**

SPECIAL RULES:
- **Ravenwing** (pg 148)
- **Strafing Run**

STASIS BOMB

The stasis bomb combines explosives with ancient and little understood technology that causes any not slain by the blast to become frozen in time. At battle's end, these unfortunate souls will be handed over to the Interrogator-Chaplains for judgement.

Range	S	AP	Type
-	4	5	Bomb 1, Large Blast, Vast Stasis Anomaly, One Use Only

Vast Stasis Anomaly: Any unit hit by one or more weapons with this special rule reduces its Weapon Skill and Initiative by 3 (to a minimum of 1) until the end of the turn. Furthermore, if a model suffers one or more unsaved Wounds from this weapon, it must pass a separate Initiative test for each Wound suffered or be removed from play as a casualty.

RAVENWING BLACK KNIGHTS

120 POINTS

Terrifying figures upon snarling, armoured steeds, the Black Knights of the Ravenwing ride down their foes without mercy. In their gauntlets they grip weighty corvus hammers, a single blow from which can smash the head from a traitor Space Marine. Those foes not struck from their feet at close quarters are instead gunned down at range, the searing blasts of the Knights' plasma talons making short work of even the largest beasts. Yet more terrifying still than all of their vaunted weaponry is the sheer, single-minded conviction of these grim hunters. Nothing can deter the Black Knights once their hunt has begun, and if they must hack their way through an ocean of foes to reach their prey then they will do so without the slightest hesitation.

	WS	BS	S	T	W	I	A	Ld	Sv	Unit Type	Unit Composition
Ravenwing Black Knight	4	4	4	5	1	4	2	9	3+	Bike	2 Ravenwing Black Knights
Ravenwing Huntmaster	4	4	4	5	1	4	2	9	3+	Bike (Character)	1 Ravenwing Huntmaster

WARGEAR:
- **Bolt pistol**
- **Plasma talon** (pg 150)
- **Corvus hammer** (pg 150)
- **Frag grenades**
- **Krak grenades**
- **Teleport homer** (pg 153)

SPECIAL RULES:
- **And They Shall Know No Fear**
- **Grim Resolve** (pg 148)
- **Hit & Run**
- **Ravenwing** (pg 148)
- **Scout**
- **Skilled Rider**

OPTIONS:
- May include up to seven additional Ravenwing Black Knights.............................. *40 pts/model*
- For every three models in the unit, one Ravenwing Black Knight may replace his plasma talon with a Ravenwing grenade launcher (pg 150) ....*free*
- The Ravenwing Huntmaster may replace his corvus hammer with a power weapon....... *12 pts*
- The Ravenwing Huntmaster may take melta bombs ....*5 pts*

RAVENWING LAND SPEEDER VENGEANCE

120 POINTS

A low, sinister hum fills the air as the Land Speeder Vengeance bears down upon the foe. Cold light flares, the speeder's menacing plasma storm battery glowing ever brighter as its power cores cycle rapidly up to full force. The hum becomes a crackling moan, and then a nerve-shredding howl as the Vengeance opens fire. Fierce white light strobes across the battlefield, momentarily transforming the warriors of both sides into monochrome shadows. Then the Vengeance's plasma salvo slams home into its target, completely obliterating it and leaving nothing behind but glowing vapour and a glassy crater. Such firepower would be frightening enough from a ponderous battle tank. Mounted on a lightning fast attack skimmer it is more terrifying still, clear proof that the vengeance of the Dark Angels is inescapable.

		Armour					
	BS	F	S	R	HP	Unit Type	Unit Composition
Land Speeder Vengeance	4	10	10	10	3	Vehicle (Fast, Skimmer)	1 Land Speeder Vengeance

WARGEAR:
- **Heavy bolter**
- **Plasma storm battery** (pg 149)

SPECIAL RULES:
- **Deep Strike**
- **Ravenwing** (pg 148)

OPTIONS:
- May replace heavy bolter with an assault cannon .... *15 pts*

DEVASTATOR SQUAD

70 POINTS

The firepower of a Dark Angels Devastator Squad can tear apart even the mightiest enemy war engine, or scour whole squads of infantry from the battlefield amid thunderous explosions. The Sons of the Lion take well to the use of heavy weaponry, for the power to annihilate targets with a single, well-aimed volley tallies with the methodical and considered teachings of Lion El'Jonson. The Devastators of the Dark Angels stand unflinching in the midst of incoming enemy fire, steadily waiting to take the perfect shot that will lay their enemies low. Only when such an opportunity presents itself do their mighty weapons speak as one, unleashing death and destruction upon the Emperor's foes. Such a way of war takes all the training and discipline a battle-brother can muster, but these are qualities which no Dark Angel lacks.

	WS	BS	S	T	W	I	A	Ld	Sv	Unit Type	Unit Composition
Space Marine	4	4	4	4	1	4	1	8	3+	Infantry	4 Space Marines
Space Marine Sergeant	4	4	4	4	1	4	1	8	3+	Infantry (Character)	1 Space Marine Sergeant
Veteran Sergeant	4	4	4	4	1	4	2	9	3+	Infantry (Character)	

WARGEAR:

- **Boltgun**
- **Bolt pistol**
- **Frag grenades**
- **Krak grenades**
- **Signum** (pg 153) (Space Marine Sergeant and Veteran Sergeant only)

SPECIAL RULES:

- **And They Shall Know No Fear**
- **Combat Squads** (pg 148)
- **Grim Resolve** (pg 148)

OPTIONS:

- May include up to five additional Space Marines .... *14 pts/model*
- Up to four Space Marines may take items from the **Heavy Weapons** list.
- The unit may take an armorium cherub (pg 151) .... *5 pts*
- May upgrade the Space Marine Sergeant to a Veteran Sergeant .... *10 pts*
- The Space Marine Sergeant or Veteran Sergeant may take items from the **Melee Weapons** and/or **Ranged Weapons** lists.
- The Space Marine Sergeant or Veteran Sergeant may take melta bombs .... *5 pts*
- The unit may select a Drop Pod (pg 122), Rhino (pg 120) or Razorback (pg 121) as a Dedicated Transport.

PREDATORS

75 POINTS

Barging forward through the wreckage of the battlefield, the Predator battle tanks of the Dark Angels crush the unrighteous beneath their grinding treads. Some Chapters' warriors, most notably the individualistic and impulsive Space Wolves, scorn Dark Angels tank crews as stolid and unimaginative. Yet what some mistake for a lack of initiative is in fact a well-drilled and methodical approach to battle that sees their Predator squadrons act with impressive synchronicity. The tanks roll into battle, their fire-patterns carefully calculated to provide cover for one another's advance. When a choice target comes into sight the Predators triangulate their targeting augurs before laying down barrage of fire that no foe can survive.

	BS	Armour F	Armour S	Armour R	HP	Unit Type	Unit Composition
Predator	4	13	11	10	3	Vehicle (Tank)	1 Predator

WARGEAR:
- **Autocannon**
- **Searchlight**
- **Smoke launchers**

SPECIAL RULES:
Killshot: Whilst this unit includes three Predators, all Predators in the unit have the Monster Hunter and Tank Hunters special rules.

OPTIONS:
- May include up to two additional Predators .... *75 pts/model*
- Any Predator may replace its autocannon with a twin-linked lascannon .... *25 pts/model*
- Any Predator may take two side sponsons which are both armed with one of the following:
  - Heavy bolters .... *20 pts/model*
  - Lascannons .... *40 pts/model*
- Any Predator may take items from the **Dark Angels Vehicle Equipment** list.

WHIRLWINDS

65 POINTS

Behind the relentless advance of the Dark Angels, Whirlwind tanks rumble into position. Their multiple missile launchers swivel to the skies before spitting forth a roaring volley of lethal warheads. Screaming in over the Dark Angels lines, the Whirlwinds' missiles pummel enemy positions, throwing fire and bodies high into the air amid great gouts of flame and ruptured earth. Finally, the bombardment stops, leaving a pall of thick black smoke drifting over a fire-blasted hellscape of bloody meat and burning wrecks. The Dark Angels stalk forward into this riven wasteland, bolters barking as they put down the shell-shocked survivors. Meanwhile, the Whirlwinds are already on the move, cogitators calculating a new firing solution as they prepare to unleash the Lion's fury once again.

		Armour					
	BS	**F**	**S**	**R**	**HP**	**Unit Type**	**Unit Composition**
Whirlwind	4	11	11	10	3	Vehicle (Tank)	1 Whirlwind

WARGEAR:
- **Whirlwind multiple missile launcher** (pg 150)
- **Searchlight**
- **Smoke launchers**

SPECIAL RULES:
Suppressive Bombardment: Whilst this unit includes three Whirlwinds, each model's Whirlwind multiple missile launcher has the Pinning and Shred special rules.

OPTIONS:
- May include up to two additional Whirlwinds .... *65 pts/model*
- Any Whirlwind may take items from the **Dark Angels Vehicle Equipment** list.

VINDICATORS

120 POINTS

Peering over their barricades, the enemy's eyes widen in horror as they see the bulky silhouettes of Vindicators grinding toward them. Gunners rake the Dark Angels siege-tanks with panicked fire, yet they can do little more than scratch their dark green paintwork. Horrified troopers throw down their weapons and turn to flee, but they are too late. As one, the muzzles of the tanks' demolisher cannons belch fire, lobbing their massive shells at the enemy lines. The earth-shaking force of the blast that follows seems apocalyptic to those nearby. White fire roars outward. Plasteel, rockcrete, and screaming defenders are all vapourised in an instant. As the smoke clears, all that remains is a blazing rent in the enemy's defences, through which the Dark Angels continue their implacable advance.

		Armour					
	BS	**F**	**S**	**R**	**HP**	**Unit Type**	**Unit Composition**
Vindicator	4	13	11	10	3	Vehicle (Tank)	1 Vindicator

WARGEAR:
- **Demolisher cannon** (pg 149)
- **Searchlight**
- **Smoke launchers**

SPECIAL RULES:
Linebreaker Bombardment: Whilst this unit includes three Vindicators that can all fire their demolisher cannons, the unit can fire a single Linebreaker Bombardment instead of firing normally. To do so, nominate one model in the unit as the firer; the firer's demolisher cannon changes its type from Large Blast to Apocalyptic Blast and gains the Ignores Cover special rule.

OPTIONS:
- The squadron may include up to two additional Vindicators....................................... *120 pts/model*
- Any Vindicator may take a siege shield (pg 154) .... *10 pts/model*
- Any Vindicator may take items from the **Dark Angels Vehicle Equipment** list.

LAND RAIDER

250 POINTS

Like a tracked fortress, the Land Raider rolls into battle with enemy fire bouncing harmlessly from its mighty hull. Within, its Dark Angel crewmen maintain a constant mantra, reciting the Thousand and One Canticles of Enforced Absolution as they guide their relic war engine towards the foe. An ancient and belligerent presence, the Land Raider's machine spirit echoes their chant in the snarl of its engine and the pulsing thunder of its guns. Foes disintegrate before its fury, while within the tank's transport bay its passengers offer solemn praise to their armoured protector. Whether painted the green of the old Calibanite forests, or clad in the bone white of the elite Deathwing, the Land Raider is a force of both destruction and deliverance upon the field of battle.

		Armour					
	BS	**F**	**S**	**R**	**HP**	**Unit Type**	**Unit Composition**
Land Raider	4	14	14	14	4	Vehicle (Tank, Transport)	1 Land Raider

WARGEAR:
- **Twin-linked heavy bolter**
- **Two twin-linked lascannons**
- **Searchlight**
- **Smoke launchers**

SPECIAL RULES:
- **Assault Vehicle**
- **Power of the Machine Spirit**

TRANSPORT:
- **Transport Capacity:** Ten models.
- **Fire Points:** None.
- **Access Points:** The Land Raider has one Access Point on each side of the hull and one at the front.

OPTIONS:
- May take a multi-melta .... *10 pts*
- May take items from the **Dark Angels Vehicle Equipment** list.

LAND RAIDER CRUSADER

250 POINTS

Roaring through no-man's land, the Land Raider Crusader smashes over ruins and wreckage without slowing. As it nears the enemy lines, the armoured behemoth swings its guns to bear, raking the foe's defences with a howling storm of fire. Enemy infantry are blown off their feet or flash-blasted to ash, moments before the massive tank crashes straight through their sundered ranks like a battering ram. With a whine, the Crusader's assault ramp hinges open, clouds of incense billowing forth from its shadowed interior. Striding through this coiling smoke come the Dark Angels, weapons already raised and spitting death into the reeling foe. No battle cries accompany this grim spectacle, just the roar of gunfire and the screams of the dying as the enemy's defences collapse.

		Armour					
	BS	**F**	**S**	**R**	**HP**	**Unit Type**	**Unit Composition**
Land Raider Crusader	4	14	14	14	4	Vehicle (Tank, Transport)	1 Land Raider Crusader

WARGEAR:
- **Twin-linked assault cannon**
- **Two hurricane bolters** (pg 149)
- **Frag assault launchers** (pg 154)
- **Searchlight**
- **Smoke launchers**

SPECIAL RULES:
- **Assault Vehicle**
- **Power of the Machine Spirit**

TRANSPORT:
- **Transport Capacity:** Sixteen models.
- **Fire Points:** None.
- **Access Points:** The Land Raider Crusader has one Access Point on each side of the hull and one at the front.

OPTIONS:
- May take a multi-melta .... *10 pts*
- May take items from the **Dark Angels Vehicle Equipment** list.

LAND RAIDER REDEEMER

240 POINTS

A terror weapon without equal, the Land Raider Redeemer grinds through the anarchic tangle of urban warfare with its flamestorm cannons blazing. Wherever the foe dig in to resist the Dark Angels' attack, white-hot sheets of flame boil through their ranks. Warriors reel from their strongpoints, enveloped in crackling shrouds of flame. Ash billows upon the wind, the enemy choking upon the blasted remnants of their own comrades as they fall back before the Redeemer's terrifying wrath. The Dark Angels gunners remain unmoved by the horrors they inflict, solemnly intoning rites of purgation as they watch the enemy shrivel and blacken before their eyes. Redemption is the ultimate goal of the Lion's sons, and under their direction this mighty tank lives up to its name.

		Armour					
	BS	**F**	**S**	**R**	**HP**	**Unit Type**	**Unit Composition**
Land Raider Redeemer	4	14	14	14	4	Vehicle (Tank, Transport)	1 Land Raider Redeemer

WARGEAR:
- **Twin-linked assault cannon**
- **Two flamestorm cannons**
- **Frag assault launchers** (pg 154)
- **Searchlight**
- **Smoke launchers**

SPECIAL RULES:
- **Assault Vehicle**
- **Power of the Machine Spirit**

TRANSPORT:
- **Transport Capacity:** Twelve models.
- **Fire Points:** None.
- **Access Points:** A Land Raider Redeemer has one Access Point on each side of the hull and one at the front.

OPTIONS:
- May take a multi-melta .... *10 pts*
- May take items from the **Dark Angels Vehicle Equipment** list.

AZRAEL

215 POINTS

SUPREME GRAND MASTER OF THE DARK ANGELS

Amid the whirling storm of battle, with screaming foes on all sides, Supreme Grand Master Azrael remains icily calm. Face set in a scowl of righteous disgust, he sweeps the Sword of Secrets in killing arcs. His foes fall dismembered, their dying blows glancing from Azrael's ornate armour to no avail. All the while, the Supreme Grand Master issues a steady stream of concise commands, conducting his brothers to form a single, mighty weapon to smite the foe. Azrael's strategic skills are second to none, his operations faultlessly planned down to the most minute detail. His abilities in battlefield command are no less stellar, the Supreme Grand Master responding with decisive genius to every ebb and flow of battle. Azrael is never surprised, never caught off guard, and rarely faced with any situation for which he has not already planned several cunning contingencies. This heroic leader fights with the strength, skill and presence of the Primarch himself, knowing that every foe slain is another step taken along the never-ending path to absolution.

	WS	BS	S	T	W	I	A	Ld	Sv	Unit Type	Unit Composition
Azrael	6	5	4	4	4	5	4	10	2+	Infantry (Character)	1 (Unique)

WARGEAR:
- **Master-crafted combi-plasma**
- **Bolt pistol**
- **Frag grenades**
- **Krak grenades**

SPECIAL RULES:
- **Deathwing** (pg 148)
- **Feel No Pain**
- **Grim Resolve** (pg 148)
- **Independent Character**

Master Tactician: An army that includes Azrael adds +1 to any Seize the Initiative rolls it makes.

Rites of Battle: All friendly models with the Dark Angels Faction can use Azrael's Leadership value in place of their own.

Supreme Strategist: When determining Warlord Traits for Azrael, choose any trait from the Dark Angels Warlord Traits table (pg 148).

RELICS OF CALIBAN

Sword of Secrets: *First of the mighty Heavenfall blades, the Sword of Secrets is an incredibly powerful weapon.*

Range	S	AP	Type
-	+2	3	Melee, Master-crafted

Lion Helm: *An ancient artefact said to have been worn by El'Jonson himself, this helm generates a powerful force field.*

The Lion Helm is carried by a Relic Bearer (see perfidious relic of the Unforgiven on page 153). The Lion Helm confers a 4+ invulnerable save to Azrael, all models in his unit, and any vehicle he is embarked in.

BATTLE DEMI-COMPANY

Composed of grim, resolute and utterly determined warriors, the Battle Demi-companies of the Dark Angels are the obsidian-hard foundations around which the Chapter's strike forces are built. Even a single Dark Angels battle-brother is a force to be reckoned with, his discipline, fortitude and ability a match for dozens of lesser men. A squad of these monastic master-combatants is more terrifying still. When gathered into whole Battle Demi-companies, the Dark Angels are the equal of any foe in the galaxy. Rigorously drilled, bound together by unbreakable ties of rhetoric and brotherhood, these warriors operate upon the battlefield like a single, lethally efficient machine. Objectives are held with stoic determination, the enemy breaking like waves against the indomitable cliffs of the Dark Angels' ranks.

FORMATION:

- 1 Company Master (pg 106) or Chaplain (pg 107)
- 0-1 Command Squad (pg 113)
- 0-1 Company Veterans Squad (pg 112)
- 3 Tactical Squads (pg 110)
- 1 Assault Squad (pg 123)
- 1 Devastator Squad (pg 132)
- 0-1 unit of Dreadnoughts (pg 114)

RESTRICTIONS:

None.

SPECIAL RULES:

Fire Discipline: Unless Jinking, all models in this Formation that have the Grim Resolve special rule count their Ballistic Skill as 3 instead of 2 when firing Overwatch.

Objective Secured: A unit with this special rule controls Objective Markers even if an enemy scoring unit is within range of the Objective Marker, unless the enemy unit also has this special rule.

DEATHWING REDEMPTION FORCE

Though they fight to defend Humanity, the brethren of the Dark Angels' Inner Circle know that their hunt for the Fallen must always be foremost in their thoughts. The Deathwing Redemption Force stands ready to strike en masse at their command – a weapon meant to crush the strength of the Fallen and their followers with a single thunderous blow. It is a measure of how seriously the capture of the Fallen is taken by the Dark Angels that the Deathwing Redemption Force has might enough to swing the course of an entire war; when not actively on the hunt, it is the Chapter's ultimate weapon against the most terrible of enemy threats. When the fate of whole worlds hangs in the balance, these warriors deploy with sudden, devastating force to destroy their foes utterly.

FORMATION:

- 1 model chosen from the following list:
  - Belial (pg 99)
  - Company Master (pg 106)
  - Interrogator-Chaplain (pg 102)
  - Librarian (pg 104)
- 2-5 Deathwing Terminator Squads (pg 116)
- 0-1 Deathwing Command Squad (pg 117)
- 0-1 units of Deathwing Knights (pg 118)
- 0-1 units of Venerable Dreadnoughts (pg 115)

RESTRICTIONS:

If it is taken, the unit of Venerable Dreadnoughts in this Formation may only include one model, which must be given a Drop Pod (pg 122) as a Dedicated Transport. All Independent Characters in this Formation must have Terminator armour (pg 154).

SPECIAL RULES:

- **Preferred Enemy (Chaos Space Marines)**

Deathwing Assault: All units in this Formation must be placed in Deep Strike Reserve. Immediately after determining Warlord Traits, make a secret note of which of your turns you would like each Deathwing Redemption Force in your army to arrive: your turn 2, 3 or 4. All units in this Formation automatically arrive by Deep Strike at the start of the chosen turn.

If this Formation includes a Venerable Dreadnought embarked in a Drop Pod, the Drop Pod automatically arrives at the start of the chosen turn, and ignores the normal rules that determine when a Drop Pod arrives.

Take the Fight to the Enemy: Units from this Formation can either shoot and then Run, or Run and then shoot, in the Shooting phase of the turn they arrive by Deep Strike.

RAVENWING ATTACK SQUADRON

Dust clouds billow behind the Ravenwing Attack Squadron as it hurtles into battle. Striking swiftly, the 2nd Company huntsmen drive hard into the midst of the enemy, many foes falling before they even realise their danger. With massed firepower, the Attack Squadron mow their victims down in huge numbers. They plough a bloody furrow through the heart of battle, bursting from the foe's rear ranks before wheeling about and diving back into the fray once more. It is these high-speed attacks for which the Ravenwing are rightly feared, yet this is not the only trick they have to play. Should some vital quarry be sighted, or a mighty enemy strongpoint need to be purged, the hunters activate their teleport homers and – amid a crackling storm of light – summon the merciless warriors of the Deathwing to join the fight.

FORMATION:

- 1 Ravenwing Bike Squad (pg 124) or 1 Ravenwing Attack Bike Squad (pg 125)
- 1 unit of Ravenwing Land Speeders (pg 126) or 1 Ravenwing Land Speeder Vengeance (pg 131)

RESTRICTIONS:

The unit of Ravenwing Land Speeders may only include one model.

SPECIAL RULES:

- **Scout**

Attack Squadron: If the Ravenwing Land Speeder or Ravenwing Land Speeder Vengeance from this Formation scores one or more hits upon an enemy unit in the Shooting phase, then all models in this Formation's Ravenwing Bike Squad or Ravenwing Attack Bike Squad add 1 to their Ballistic Skill characteristic when shooting at the same target for the rest of the phase.

Summon the Deathwing: Friendly units composed entirely of models with the Deathwing special rule do not scatter when they Deep Strike, so long as the first model is placed within 12" of a model from this Formation. For this to work, the model from this Formation must have been on the battlefield at the start of the turn.

RAVENWING SUPPORT SQUADRON

If the Attack Squadrons are the sword of the Ravenwing, then the Support Squadrons are their shield. Skimming fast and low over the field of battle, the Land Speeders of the Support Squadrons scan constantly for anything that might threaten the mission. Where heavily armoured war engines or entrenched artillery attempt to devastate the Ravenwing formations, the Support Squadrons swoop low overhead, missiles and plasma blasts reducing the weapons of the foe to blazing scrap. Where infantry mass in sufficient quantities to swamp the huntsmen of the 2nd Company, the Support Squadron's Land Speeders pass back and forth, raking the enemy with bullets, bolts and fiery blasts. In this way, the Support Squadrons combine their strength with their land-bound brothers to crush the foe completely.

FORMATION:

- 1 unit of Ravenwing Land Speeders (pg 126)
- 1 Ravenwing Land Speeder Vengeance (pg 131) or 1 Ravenwing Darkshroud (pg 127)

RESTRICTIONS:

The unit of Ravenwing Land Speeders must include at least 3 models.

SPECIAL RULES:

- **Grim Resolve** (pg 148)
- **Interceptor**
- **Strafing Run**

Ravenshield: When an enemy unit declares a charge against a friendly unit with the Ravenwing special rule, models from this Formation within 24" of that friendly unit can choose to fire Overwatch against the charging unit (even though vehicles cannot normally fire Overwatch). Template weapons can only use the Wall of Death special rule if they are within 6" of the friendly unit. Remember that a unit can still only fire Overwatch once per turn.

Support Squadron: All vehicles in this Formation must form a single Vehicle Squadron as described in *Warhammer 40,000: The Rules.* However, this Vehicle Squadron counts as two units for the purposes of calculating Victory Points if it is completely destroyed.

RAVENWING SILENCE SQUADRON

At the culmination of the hunt, the Ravenwing's prey must be snatched from the field of battle. No enemy reinforcements can be allowed to rescue them, and none must slip the net to tell of what they have witnessed. It is the task of the Ravenwing Silence Squadron to ensure these rules are adhered to. A single ominous Dark Talon screams down from the skies with a dedicated wing of Nephilim escorts in tow. While the Dark Talon captures its vital target – ideally a Fallen Dark Angel – the Nephilim Jetfighters peel off to cover the extraction. Arrowing through the skies, they cripple escaping transports, mow down fleeing foes and eliminate airborne threats. Utterly merciless in their purge, the Nephilim ensure that no enemy gets close to the Dark Talon while it executes its capture-run, and that no-one lives to tell the tale.

FORMATION:

- 2 Nephilim Jetfighters (pg 128)
- 1 Ravenwing Dark Talon (pg 129)

RESTRICTIONS:

None.

SPECIAL RULES:

Capture Run: When making a Bombing Run (see *Warhammer 40,000: The Rules*) with the stasis bomb of this Formation's Ravenwing Dark Talon, do not roll for scatter; the stasis bomb hits automatically. Furthermore, enemy models that suffer an unsaved Wound from the stasis bomb must roll two dice and pick the highest result when taking their Initiative tests to see if they are removed as casualties.

In missions that use Victory Points to determine the winner, the Slay the Warlord Secondary Objective is worth D3 additional Victory Points to the controlling player at the end of the game if the enemy Warlord was removed as a casualty as a result of a Capture Run.

Fighter Escort: When making Reserve Rolls, make a single roll for this entire Formation, which you can choose to re-roll. On a successful Reserve Roll, all of the units in this Formation arrive from Reserve.

THE HAMMER OF CALIBAN

Only the mightiest foes are worthy of the death dealt by the Hammer of Caliban. Named for the beast-slaying weapons once wielded by the Knights of the Order, this formation concentrates the fury of the Rock's Armoury into a single, mighty hammerblow. Comprising multiple squadrons of heavily armoured battle tanks under the auspices of the Chapter's finest Techmarines, the Hammer of Caliban is most often deployed when the enemy have multiple monstrous beasts or war engines in the field. Like the knights of their ancient home world, the tank-crews of the Hammer of Caliban ride their armoured steeds to war, charging down their massive prey and blasting them apart with the fire of their heavy weapons.

FORMATION:

- 1 Techmarine (pg 108)
- 1 unit chosen from the following list:
  - Land Raider (pg 136)
  - Land Raider Crusader (pg 137)
  - Land Raider Redeemer (pg 138)
- 1 unit chosen from the following list:
  - Predators (pg 133)
  - Whirlwinds (pg 134)
  - Vindicators (pg 135)

RESTRICTIONS:

This Formation's unit of Predators, Whirlwinds or Vindicators must include three models.

SPECIAL RULES:

- **Monster Hunter**
- **Tank Hunters**

Hammer of Heretics: This Formation's Techmarine must begin the game embarked upon this Formation's Land Raider, Land Raider Crusader or Land Raider Redeemer. Whilst the Techmarine from this Formation is embarked upon the Transport vehicle from this Formation, that vehicle's Ballistic Skill is increased to 5.

Might of the Lion: All vehicles in this Formation must form a single Vehicle Squadron as described in *Warhammer 40,000: The Rules.* However, this Vehicle Squadron counts as 2 units for the purposes of calculating Victory Points if it is completely destroyed.

APPENDIX

This section of the book details many of the rules for using an army of Dark Angels in your games of Warhammer 40,000, including their unique Warlord Traits, wargear, psychic powers, Tactical Objectives and additional Detachments. The profiles page at the end provides a list of unit and weapon profiles for reference during your games.

DARK ANGELS SPECIAL RULES

There are a number of special rules that are common to several Dark Angels units, which are collected here for your convenience. Special rules that are unique to particular units are presented in the relevant unit entry instead. Other rules are simply listed by name – these are all described in the Special Rules section of *Warhammer 40,000: The Rules.*

Combat Squads

It is sound doctrine for Space Marine units to remain flexible, splitting into two entities as the tactical situation dictates.
A full strength, ten-man unit with this special rule can break down into two five-man units, called combat squads, considered to be two five-man squads of the same type. For example, a ten-man Tactical Squad can split into two five-man Tactical Squads using the Combat Squads special rule.

You must decide which units are splitting into combat squads, and which models go into each combat squad, immediately before determining your Warlord Traits. A unit split into combat squads therefore is now two separate units for all game purposes, including calculating the total number of units in the army and determining the number of units you can place in Reserve. Then proceed with deployment as normal. In an exception to the normal rules, two combat squads split from the same unit can embark in the same transport vehicle, providing its Transport Capacity allows. Once you have decided whether or not to split a unit into combat squads, it must remain that way for the entire battle. It cannot split up or join back together later on in the battle, nor can you use a redeployment to split up a unit or join it back together.

Note that Ravenwing Bike Squads count as being at full strength when they include seven models. If split into combat squads, this unit will divide into three units: two units of three models and a single Ravenwing Attack Bike.

Deathwing

No traitor can stay the wrath of the Dark Angels 1st Company.
A model with this special rule has the Fearless and Hatred (Chaos Space Marines) special rules.

Grim Resolve

The Sons of the Lion are renowned for their ruthless tenacity, composure and fire discipline in battle.
Models with this special rule have the Stubborn special rule and, unless Jinking, count their Ballistic Skill as 2 when firing Overwatch.

Ravenwing

The Dark Angels 2nd Company are the hunstmen of the Chapter, and undisputed masters of mounted combat.
A model with this special rule can re-roll failed cover saves when it Jinks.

WARLORD TRAITS

When generating Warlord traits for a Warlord with the Dark Angels Faction, you can either roll on one of the Warlord Traits tables in *Warhammer 40,000: The Rules* or roll on the table below.

Warlord Traits Table

D6	WARLORD TRAIT
1	**The Hunt:** *This Warlord is renowned for rooting out members of the Fallen from their hiding places – no heretic is safe from his fierce scrutiny.* Your Warlord has the Precision Shots special rule. In addition, your Warlord's shooting attacks have the Ignores Cover special rule.
2	**Courage of the First Legion:** *The Dark Angels have ever been famous for standing fast beside their leaders, for their loyalty never falters.* Your Warlord, and all friendly units with the Dark Angels Faction within 12" of him, have the Fearless special rule.
3	**For the Lion!:** *It is deeds, not words, that truly stoke a Dark Angel to cold fury. This leader inspires his battle-brothers through the courage of his actions.* Your Warlord and his unit have the Furious Charge special rule.
4	**Brilliant Planning:** *The commanders of the Dark Angels share a measure of their Primarch's vaunted ability to coordinate attacks.* While your Warlord is alive and on the battlefield, you can add 1 to or subtract 1 from any of your Reserve Rolls (choose after you roll the dice).
5	**Rapid Manoeuvre:** *This Warlord is known for his ability to swiftly redeploy into ideal attack positions, outmanoeuvring the foe before crushing them utterly.* Your Warlord and his unit add 3" to their maximum move distance when they move Flat Out, Turbo-boost, Run and make charge moves.
6	**Hold At All Costs:** *A Dark Angels commander can call upon the famed tenacity of his Chapter's warriors to defend crucial objectives.* Your Warlord and his unit have the Feel No Pain special rule whilst they are within 3" of an Objective Marker.

ARMOURY OF THE ROCK

This section of *Codex: Dark Angels* lists the weapons and equipment used by the Dark Angels, along with the rules for using them in your games of Warhammer 40,000. Equipment that is carried by named characters is detailed in the appropriate entry in the datasheets (pages 99 to 139), while equipment used by all other types of units are detailed here.

RANGED WEAPONS

Profiles for the following ranged weapons are listed on the profiles page (pg 160). Their full rules can be found in *Warhammer 40,000: The Rules*.

Assault cannon	Grav-gun	Multi-melta
Autocannon	Grav-pistol	Plasma cannon
Boltgun	Grav-cannon	Plasma gun
Bolt pistol	Heavy bolter	Plasma pistol
Combi-weapon	Heavy flamer	Sniper rifle
Flamer	Lascannon	Space Marine
Flamestorm	Meltagun	shotgun
cannon	Missile launcher	Storm bolter

Avenger Mega Bolter

The avenger mega bolter opens up with a thunderous roar, filling the air with a deadly hail of heavy bolt shells. Jutting from the nose of the Nephilim Jetfighter, this weapon is the ideal tool for tearing apart light aircraft, or shredding infantry with high-speed strafing runs.

Range	S	AP	Type
48"	6	4	Heavy 5

Blacksword Missiles

Streaking through the air like blades of vengeance, blacksword missiles leave ominous dark contrails in their wake. Each missile impacts with a deafening crack, swatting enemy aircraft from the sky as spinning fireballs.

Range	S	AP	Type
36"	7	3	Heavy 1, One Use Only

Cyclone Missile Launcher

Borne on the broad shoulders of a Terminator battle-brother, the cyclone missile launcher spits salvoes of high impact warheads. Triggered with a thought, the weapon can fire either frag missiles for slaughtering tightly-packed enemy infantry, or krak missiles capable of punching through the thickest armour.

A Terminator can fire his cyclone missile launcher in addition to his storm bolter.

	Range	S	AP	Type
Frag missile	48"	4	6	Heavy 2, Blast
Krak missile	48"	8	3	Heavy 2

Deathwind Launcher

Explosions ripple outward in a furious storm as the deathwind launcher opens up. Designed to purge Drop Pod landing zones, these missile launchers are short-ranged but punishingly effective.

Range	S	AP	Type
12"	5	-	Heavy 1, Large Blast

Demolisher Cannon

Few weapons command the terror evoked by the blunt maw of the demolisher cannon. Firing ferociously destructive high explosive shells, the demolisher can level an enemy bunker or reduce a battle tank to a crater with a single shot.

Range	S	AP	Type
24"	10	2	Ordnance 1, Large Blast

Hurricane Bolter

The aptly named hurricane bolter spews forth a torrential barrage of shots, reducing whole squads to red mist in seconds.

A hurricane bolter consists of three twin-linked boltguns fired as a single weapon.

Plasma Storm Battery

Like a supernova born amid the fires of battle, the blast of the plasma storm battery annihilates anything it touches. Whether spitting multiple bolts of energy or loosing a single, monstrous blast, this weapon spells death to all before it.

	Range	S	AP	Type
Burst mode	36"	7	2	Heavy 3, Gets Hot
Charged mode	36"	7	2	Heavy 1, Gets Hot, Large Blast

Plasma Talon

Armour melts away and flesh turns to seething vapour as the plasma talons of the Black Knights let fly. Lesser victims are simply erased from existence by the fire of these terrifying weapons, while even the most resilient foes are left wounded and reeling, wide open for the Black Knights' devastating charge.

Range	S	AP	Type
18"	7	2	Rapid Fire, Gets Hot, Twin-linked

Ravenwing Grenade Launcher

Calibrated to maintain lethally accurate fire at extreme speeds, this weapon pummels the enemy with spreads of explosive munitions.

	Range	S	AP	Type
Frag shell	24"	3	6	Rapid Fire, Blast
Krak shell	24"	6	4	Rapid Fire
Rad shell	12"	3	-	Assault 1, Blast, Rad Poisoning
Stasis shell	12"	3	-	Assault 1, Blast, Stasis Anomaly

Rad Poisoning: When attacking with a weapon that has this special rule, a To Wound roll of 6 causes 2 Wounds on the target unit, regardless of the target's Toughness. Each Wound is allocated and saved against separately.

Stasis Anomaly: All models in a unit hit by one or more weapons with this special rule suffer a -1 penalty to their Weapon Skill and Initiative (to a minimum of 1) until the end of the turn.

Rift Cannon

The scintillating beam of the rift cannon cracks a hole in reality itself, creating a deadly implosion. Those not dragged screaming into the breach are left temporarily blinded, their vision a surreal, static image of the moment before the rift howled into existence.

Range	S	AP	Type
18"	10	2	Heavy 1, Blast, Blind, Rift Vortex

Rift Vortex: If any double is rolled when rolling for scatter for an attack made by this weapon, resolve the rest of the attack as if the weapon had the Vortex special rule.

Typhoon Missile Launcher

This versatile weapon is specially adapted for high-speed assaults.

	Range	S	AP	Type
Frag missiles	48"	4	6	Heavy 2, Blast
Krak missiles	48"	8	3	Heavy 2

Whirlwind Multiple Missile Launcher

Whirlwind multiple missile launchers suppress the foe with punishing salvoes of long range warheads.

Whirlwind multiple missile launchers have two different profiles. All Whirlwind multiple missile launchers in the squadron must use the same profile each time the squadron fires.

	Range	S	AP	Type
Vengeance	12"-48"	5	4	Ordnance 1, Barrage, Large Blast
Incendiary castellan	12"-48"	4	5	Ordnance 1, Barrage, Ignores Cover, Large Blast

MELEE WEAPONS

Profiles for the following Melee weapons are listed on the profiles page (pg 160). Their full rules can be found in *Warhammer 40,000: The Rules*.

Chainfist
Chainsword
Close combat weapon
Eviscerator
Force weapon
Lightning claw
Power fist
Power weapon
Thunder hammer

Blade of Caliban

Ancient and lethal relics of war, the Blades of Caliban are carried only by those heroic Company Champions who have earned the right in battle. Heavy, ornate weapons graven with the names of their previous wielders, these energised swords cut through all but the thickest armour with ease.

Range	S	AP	Type
-	+1	3	Melee

Corvus Hammer

Swung with vengeful might by its Black Knight wielder, the corvus hammer smashes its victim from their feet in a shocking spray of blood. Adapted from the traditional monster-slaying weapons of the old Calibanite knights, these sharp-beaked hammers punch through armour and crush bone to powder.

Range	S	AP	Type
-	+1	-	Melee, Rending

Crozius Arcanum

The crozius serves as both a sacred staff of office and a weapon for Dark Angels Chaplains. An energy field boosts the crozius arcanum's mauling power.

Range	S	AP	Type
-	+2	4	Melee, Concussive

Flail of the Unforgiven

Lashing through the air with cruel force, the flail of the Unforgiven tears great strips from armour, flesh and bone alike. Wielded by the leaders of the Deathwing Knights, these archaic weapons are used with furious force to castigate all unworthy scum that stand in the Dark Angels' path, and foreshadow the horrific fate that awaits those Fallen who are taken to the dungeons of the Rock.

Range	S	AP	Type
-	+2	3	Melee, Concussive, Fleshbane

Halberd of Caliban

The Company Champion of the Deathwing traditionally carries this massive weapon, reforged from a Blade of Caliban shattered in battle long ago and incorporating the same grim technologies that power the weapons of the Deathwing Knights. The name of every brother to wield this weapon is microscopically etched into its blade, while the ground finger bones of the Fallen burn amid everlasting flames within censers fitted in the weapon's haft.

Range	S	AP	Type
-	+2	2	Melee, Two-handed

Mace of Absolution

Wreathed in glowing smoke, these massive weapons are as sinister in aspect as they are lethal in application, and are capable of obliterating even the mightiest heretics in a blaze of killing light.

Range	S	AP	Type
-	+2	3	Melee, Concussive, Smite

Smite: When a model equipped with this weapon makes its close combat attacks, it can choose instead to make a single Smite attack. If it does so, roll To Hit as normal but resolve the Attack at Strength x2, AP2.

Relic Blade

The relic blades of the Dark Angels are solemnly bestowed upon their greatest warriors. Few foes can stay the wrath of these coldly glowing blades, or endure their scything blows.

Range	S	AP	Type
-	+2	3	Melee, Two-handed

Servo-arm

These massive articulated utility-claws are primarily used to facilitate battlefield repairs, but are strong enough to crush the life from a foe and wreck armoured vehicles, should the need arise.

Range	S	AP	Type
-	x2	1	Melee, Specialist Weapon, Unwieldy

SPECIAL ISSUE WARGEAR

Rules for the following items can be found in *Warhammer 40,000: The Rules.*

Frag grenades*	Melta bombs
Krak grenades	Psychic hood

* *See assault grenades*

Armorium Cherub

Cherubim are cyborg constructs created to assist the Emperor's servants. Among the Adeptus Astartes they are rarely seen outside of the Librarius, save for those few that relay targeting data and carry spare ammunition for Devastator Squads.

One use only. One model in a unit equipped with an armorium cherub can re-roll all failed To Hit rolls in one Shooting phase. An armorium cherub is represented by a separate miniature that will always remain as close as possible to the unit that selected it. The model itself is purely decorative and is always ignored for game purposes – just move it to one side if it gets in the way. Remove the armorium cherub once it has been used or once the unit that selected it has been completely destroyed.

Auspex

A short-ranged scanning device, the auspex detects hidden heretics no matter where they hide.

A model with an auspex can use it in place of making a shooting attack. If he does so, target an enemy unit within 12" (this does not count as choosing a target for his unit to shoot at). A unit that is targeted by one or more auspexes has its cover save reduced by 1 until the end of the phase.

Camo Cloak

Dark Angels Scouts clad in camo cloaks slip unseen across the battlefield. The material of these garments absorbs light and shifts its hue and texture to match its surroundings, allowing the novitiate warriors to remain unseen until the moment they strike.

A model wearing a camo cloak has +1 cover save. If it does not already have a cover save, it gains a 6+ cover save.

Chapter Banner

The Dark Angels' Chapter Banner is a relic that dates back to the days of the Great Crusade – they will fight like heroes to defend it, determined not to dishonour themselves in its presence.

Friendly units with the Dark Angels Faction within 12" of a model equipped with the Chapter banner re-roll failed Morale checks, Pinning tests and Fear tests. In addition, all friendly models with the Dark Angels Faction in the same unit as this banner have +1 Attack whilst the bearer is alive.

Combat Shield
Often styled after those carried by the Knights of the Order, these lightweight shields are wreathed in potent force fields capable of turning aside even the most devastating blow.

A combat shield confers a 6+ invulnerable save.

Company Standard
The company standards of the Dark Angels are precious heirlooms, hand-crafted over the millennia by skilled artisans and heavy with the honour of the Chapter.

Friendly units with the Dark Angels Faction within 12" of a model equipped with the company standard re-roll failed Morale checks, Pinning tests and Fear tests.

Conversion Field
Crackling and sparking like a miniature version of the force field around the Rock itself, this strange shield enfolds its wearer in its protective energies. Shots and blows that strike the field are converted instantly into a flash of energy that leaves assailants blinded and reeling.

A conversion field confers a 4+ invulnerable save. At the end of a phase in which the bearer passes one or more invulnerable saves granted by the conversion field, all units within D6" of the bearer must test as if they had been hit by a weapon with the Blind special rule. Friendly units can re-roll this test.

Deathwing Company Banner
Depicting a shattered tower and a fallen angel, the Deathwing Company Banner is redolent with veiled meanings. It is one of the most precious relics of the Dark Angels 1st Company, whose battle-brothers will protect it with their lives.

Friendly units with the Dark Angels Faction within 12" of a model equipped with the Deathwing Company Banner re-roll failed Morale checks, Pinning tests and Fear tests. In addition, all friendly models with the Deathwing special rule in the same unit as this banner have +1 Attack whilst the bearer is alive.

Storm shield

Corvus hammer

Digital Weapons
Stabbing light and sudden agony are the enemy's only warning as these miniature weapons trigger. Fitted into gauntlets, rings and the like, digital weapons are extremely short-ranged lasers that give their wielder a lethal edge in close combat.

A model armed with digital weapons can re-roll a single failed roll To Wound in each Assault phase.

Grav-amp
The grav-amp is a wonder of archeotech that focusses and strengthens the field of the bearer's grav-weapons.

When rolling to Wound with a grav-weapon, or to determine its effects on a vehicle, the bearer can re-roll the result.

Hellfire Shells
Each hellfire shell contains a reservoir of concentrated bio-acid. Upon detonation, this incredibly caustic substance sprays across its targets, burning away flesh and sinew with hideous speed.

Each time a weapon equipped with hellfire shells fires, the controlling player can choose whether to fire a hellfire shell or to use the ordinary profile for that weapon.

Range	S	AP	Type
24"	1	-	Heavy 1, Blast, Poisoned (2+)

Iron Halo
The iron halo is a symbol of exceptional bravery and wisdom. It contains a powerful energy field that acts as a ward against the weapons of the enemy. An iron halo is capable of rendering useless even the most potent of attacks.

An iron halo confers a 4+ invulnerable save.

Jump Pack
A jump pack enables the wearer to take great bounding leaps across the battlefield and make a boosted flight over short distances. Space Marines often enter battle via airdrop deployment, wearing jump packs and leaping from low-flying Thunderhawk Gunships, issuing controlled bursts to slow their descent to the ground.

Models equipped with jump packs gain the Jump unit type as described in *Warhammer 40,000: The Rules.*

Narthecium
This device, along with the reductor, is employed to heal wounded Dark Angels or, if this is impossible, to remove the progenoid gland containing the battle-brother's precious gene-seed.

As long as the bearer of the narthecium is alive, all models in his unit have the Feel No Pain special rule.

Perfidious Relic of the Unforgiven

Ancient relics from the old Legion that have been recaptured by the Deathwing are sometimes carried into battle by the wraith-like figures known as Watchers in the Dark. The exact nature or function of most of these revered relics is unknown – they are as mysterious as the cowled figures that bear them. What is known is their effect on the battlefield – their presence alone dampens the power of enemy psykers and fills the Dark Angels' opponents with feelings of dread.

A perfidious relic of the Unforgiven is borne to battle by a Relic Bearer. A Relic Bearer is represented by a separate miniature that will always remain as close as possible to the unit that selected it. The model itself is purely decorative and is always ignored for game purposes – just move it to one side if it gets in the way. Remove the Relic Bearer once the unit that selected it has been completely destroyed.

Models in a unit that includes a Relic Bearer carrying a perfidious relic of the Unforgiven have the Adamantium Will and Fear special rules.

Ravenwing Company Banner

Flying proud from its adamantine banner-pole, the standard of the Ravenwing shows a cowled figure slaying a horned, skull-headed serpent that, unbeknownst to most, represents the Fallen.

Friendly units with the Dark Angels Faction within 12" of a model equipped with the Ravenwing Company Banner re-roll failed Morale checks, Pinning tests and Fear tests. In addition, all friendly models with the Ravenwing special rule in the same unit as this banner automatically pass Initiative tests when attempting to Hit & Run and roll one additional dice when determining the distance of a Hit & Run move whilst the bearer is alive.

Rosarius

A rosarius is a gorget or amulet worn by Dark Angels Chaplains, both for protection and as a symbol of office. A rosarius emits a protective energy field around the wearer, and is capable of deflecting blows and shots that would smash a ferrocrete bunker. It is believed that the stronger its bearer's belief in the might of the Emperor, the stronger a rosarius' force field will be.

A rosarius confers a 4+ invulnerable save.

Sacred Standard

Hanging in the Great Hall of the Rock, there are those standards of the Dark Angels that are precious works of art. Since before the Horus Heresy the Dark Angels have guarded icons such as the Standard of Fortitude, the Standard of Devastation and the Standard of Retribution, all of which command fanatical levels of devotion from the warriors of the Chapter. These relics are borne into only the most desperate of battles, for though their effect upon the Dark Angels is truly inspiring, each one is irreplaceable. More than once, whole strike forces of Unforgiven have been deployed simply to recover such a banner lost upon the field of battle.

Friendly units with the Dark Angels Faction within 12" of a model equipped with a sacred standard re-roll failed Morale checks, Pinning tests and Fear tests. In addition, all friendly models with the Dark Angels Faction in the same unit as this banner have the Counter-attack and Relentless special rules whilst the bearer is alive.

Servo-harness

Pistons hissing and actuators whining, the servo-harness enfolds its wearer in the manifest blessings of the Omnissiah. Bearing a multitude of crushing claws and hissing plasma torches, this multi-limbed harness aides its wearer by repairing Dark Angels vehicles, not to mention tearing apart the foe.

A servo-harness gives the bearer two servo-arms, a plasma cutter and a flamer. In the Shooting phase, the bearer can fire both harness-mounted weapons, or one harness-mounted weapon and another weapon.

	Range	S	AP	Type
Plasma cutter	12"	7	2	Assault 1, Gets Hot, Twin-linked

Signum

A targeting auto-cogitator of prodigious power, the signum swiftly calculates optimal trajectories and imparts the data directly to the machine spirits of weapons within its bearer's squad.

At the start of the Shooting phase, a model with a signum can choose to use it instead of shooting. If he does so, one model in his unit is Ballistic Skill 5 for the remainder of the Shooting phase. Declare that the signum is being used before any rolls To Hit are made.

Space Marine Bike

Engines snarling like the beasts of old Caliban, the bikes of the Ravenwing bear their riders into battle with speed and surety. Well armoured and able to traverse even the densest terrain, the Space Marine bike is a versatile, durable and faithful steed.

Models equipped with Space Marine bikes change their unit type to Bike, as described in *Warhammer 40,000: The Rules*. Space Marine bikes are fitted with a twin-linked boltgun.

Storm Shield

A storm shield is a solid shield that has an energy field generator built into it. Though the bulk of the shield offers some physical protection, much more impressive is the energy field. It is capable of deflecting almost any attack – blows that would normally cut through even Terminator armour fail to make a scratch.

A storm shield confers a 3+ invulnerable save. In addition, a model equipped with a storm shield can never claim the +1 Attack for being armed with two Melee weapons in an assault.

Teleport Homer

Teleport homers emit a powerful signal enabling orbiting Strike Cruisers to lock on to them with their teleportation equipment.

Friendly units composed entirely of models in Terminator armour do not scatter when they Deep Strike, so long as the first model is placed within 6" of the teleport homer's bearer. For this to work, the bearer of the teleport homer must have been on the battlefield at the start of the turn.

ARMOUR

Artificer Armour

Embellished by the finest artificers in the Dark Angels Armoury, these lavish suits afford the wearer protection to rival even Terminator armour.

Artificer armour confers a 2+ Armour Save.

Terminator Armour

Terminator armour is the best protection a Space Marine can be equipped with. It is even said that Terminator armour can withstand the titanic energies at a plasma generator's core, and that this was, in fact, the armour's original purpose.

Terminator armour confers a 2+ Armour Save and a 5+ invulnerable save. Furthermore, models in Terminator armour have the Bulky, Deep Strike and Relentless special rules, and may not make Sweeping Advances.

Vengeful Strike: A model with the Deathwing special rule that arrives by Deep Strike treats all of its ranged weapons as having the Twin-linked special rule until the end of the turn.

DARK ANGELS VEHICLE EQUIPMENT

Rules for the following vehicle upgrades can be found in *Warhammer 40,000: The Rules.*

Dozer blade	Searchlight
Extra armour	Smoke launchers
Hunter-killer missile	Storm bolter

Frag Assault Launchers

The hulls of Land Raider Crusaders and Land Raider Redeemers are studded with explosive charges designed to hurl shrapnel at the enemy as the troops inside charge out.

Any unit charging into close combat on the same turn as it disembarks from a transport vehicle equipped with frag assault launchers counts as having frag grenades.

Locator beacon

The locator beacon is a signalling package that contains a teleport homing device, broad-spectrum communicators and geo-positional tracking. When activated, the locator beacon streams detailed positional uploads in Adeptus Astartes coded signals, allowing for precision reinforcement by reserve forces.

Friendly units do not scatter when they Deep Strike, so long as the first model is placed with 6" of a model equipped with a locator beacon. The locator beacon must have been on the battlefield at the start of the turn in order for it to be used.

Siege Shield

Due to their effectiveness in rubble-strewn city fights and urban assaults, Vindicators are often fitted with enormous siege shields which enable them to bulldoze through obstacles with impunity.

A vehicle with a siege shield automatically passes Dangerous Terrain tests.

RELICS OF CALIBAN

These artefacts are ancient heirlooms that are maintained in places of honour on the Rock. Only the mightiest of Dark Angels are worthy of using such storied items, and having their heroics and deeds added to the continuing legends of the items themselves. Only one of each of the following relics may be chosen per army.

Foe-smiter

This ornate storm bolter was wrought by Fedorovich the Great, one of the greatest Martian weaponsmiths of the era of the Great Crusade. Fedorovich forged many of the master-crafted weapons still prized by the Imperium today. Even by comparison to these, Foe-smiter has always been considered special. It was presented with honour to the first Grand Master of the Deathwing, and continues to lay low the enemies of the Chapter to this day.

Range	S	AP	Type
24"	4	4	Assault 4, Master-crafted, Shred

Lion's Roar

One of the most unusual pieces in the arsenal of the Rock is the combi-weapon known as the Lion's Roar. The single-shot plasma blast it fires is accompanied by a devastating roar, from whence the weapon gets its name. The Lion's Roar is issued to heroes of the Chapter and over the years it has proven to be an ideal weapon for those leading boarding missions, bunker assaults or a forlorn hope. Whether its heroic bearer survives the battle or not, the Lion's Roar has always been recovered and returned to its place of honour in the Rock's armouries.

The Lion's Roar is a Master-crafted combi-weapon. The secondary weapon has the following profile:

Range	S	AP	Type
24"	7	2	Assault 1, Blast, Gets Hot, Master-crafted, One Use Only

Mace of Redemption

The Mace of Redemption is perhaps the greatest of the weapons forged by the Dark Angels to hunt their traitorous comrades. Blessed with incantations of vengeance, the hollow centre of this sacred power maul flares white-hot when it smites a foe. It is said that, with the mace in hand, Supreme Grand Master Raphael struck down the Daemon Prince ruler of the blasphemous world of New Caliban, allowing the arch-heretic to be captured. Of all the Dark Angels who have ever hunted the Fallen, none has bested this heroic deed.

Range	S	AP	Type
-	+3	3	Melee, Bane of the Traitor, Blind, Concussive

Bane of the Traitor: When the Mace of Redemption is used to attack a unit with the Chaos Space Marines Faction, its AP is increased to 1.

Monster Slayer of Caliban

This ancient weapon was traditionally bestowed upon the most honourable Knight of the Order before the onset of a long quest into the wilds of Caliban. Its well-honed blade is empowered by a force generator of magnificent strength; however, over the ages, it has grown somewhat temperamental, and the know-how to fix such ancient technology is now beyond the Techmarines of the Dark Angels. It is believed that as long as its owner stays pure of mind, the Monster Slayer of Caliban will strike down even the greatest of foes.

At the start of each Fight sub-phase in which the wielder is locked in combat, roll a D6 to determine which profile the Monster Slayer of Caliban uses that turn.

D6	Range	S	AP	Type
1	-	User	3	Melee
2-4	-	+1	3	Melee
5-6	-	+2	3	Melee, Instant Death

Shroud of Heroes

The rites of the Dark Angels dictate that when one of their mightiest is slain in glorious battle, his recovered remains are wrapped in a death shroud until he can be interred within the crypts of the Lion's Sanctum deep within the Rock. Pieces of this fabric, stained in the blood of heroes, are then continually stitched into a single set of robes known as the Shroud of Heroes. It is customary for the Shroud of Heroes to be presented to a noble warrior of the Chapter, who will wear it for the duration of a battle or ongoing campaign before passing the revered robes on to another worthy aspirant of the Chapter. Those who wear the Shroud of Heroes claim they can feel the protective powers of their predecessors swirling around them, still eager to aid the Chapter.

The bearer of the Shroud of Heroes has the Feel No Pain special rule. In addition, while he is not in a unit, the bearer has the Shrouded special rule.

The Eye of the Unseen

This ancient augmetic was first bequeathed to Interrogator-Chaplain Enoch by the Watchers in the Dark, and has since been extracted and re-implanted in a string of Dark Angels heroes. It is said that no secret can escape the gaze of the Eye, nor guilt, lies or any obfuscation. Those fixed by the glowing lens of the Eye of the Unseen have their deepest wants and fears laid bare, and their every weakness exposed. The sensation is said to be akin to Catachan harpoon-bugs crawling across the inside of the skull, and it is all the victim can do not to drop to their knees and confess all.

The bearer of the Eye of the Unseen has the Fear and Preferred Enemy special rules.

INTERROMANCY DISCIPLINE

In order to aid the Interrogator-Chaplains in their cruel labours, the Librarians of the Dark Angels have mastered a sinister and invasive form of telepathy. Few sensations are more horrific for a victim than the insidious slither of the Librarian's thoughts as they writhe through the gaps in his mental defences, flaying and twisting his psyche at will.

PRIMARIS POWER

MIND WORM .... WARP CHARGE 1

The Librarian burrows his consciousness into the screaming victim's brain, ripping free their secrets in a spray of gore.

Mind Worm is a **focussed witchfire** power with the following profile:

Range	S	AP	Type
12"	6	2	Assault 1, Ignores Cover, Sap Will

Sap Will: If a model suffers any unsaved Wounds from *Mind Worm*, its Weapon Skill, Ballistic Skill, Initiative and Leadership characteristics are reduced by 3 (to a minimum of 1) for the rest of the battle.

1. SEED OF FEAR .... WARP CHARGE 1

The Librarian inveigles his way into the minds of his foes. Subtly, he twists and heightens their fears, inciting first unease, then paranoia, then outright, overwhelming terror.

Seed of Fear is a **malediction** that targets all enemy units within 9". Whilst the power is in effect, all target units must take Morale checks as well as Pinning and Fear tests on 3D6.

2. RIGHTEOUS REPUGNANCE .... WARP CHARGE 1

Reaching into the minds of his brothers, the Librarian stokes the fires of their hate. Conditioned and receptive to such manipulation by their leaders, the Dark Angels respond with a surge of cold, furious violence.

Righteous Repugnance is a **blessing** that targets a single friendly unit within 24". Whilst the power is in effect, the target unit has the Rage special rule.

3. AVERSION .... WARP CHARGE 1

The Librarian sends waves of cold fear washing outwards. The foe find themselves unable to focus upon the psyker, their subconscious screaming at them to look away for fear of what they will see.

Aversion is a **malediction** that targets a single enemy unit within 24". Whilst the power is in effect, the target unit can only fire Snap Shots.

4. MAELSTROM OF MISERY .... WARP CHARGE 2

The Librarian focusses his disgust for the foe into a potent assault. All enemies in the vicinity experience agonising pain as their brains implode, then fall to the ground without a mark on them.

Maelstrom of Misery is a **witchfire** power with the following profile:

Range	S	AP	Type
24"	1	2	Assault 1, Blast, Neural Shock

Neural Shock: Hits caused by this psychic power always wound on a 4+. This special rule has no effects on vehicles or buildings.

5. TREPHINATION .... WARP CHARGE 2

The Librarian gathers his thoughts into a white hot spike to plunge straight into his victim's mind. There is no subtlety here, just a vicious psychic thrust that leaves the foe's sanity in tatters and their brain matter dribbling from ears, nose and eyes.

Trephination is a **focussed witchfire** power with a range of 18". The affected model must roll 2D6+2 and subtract their Leadership. That model suffers a number of Wounds equal to the result. Armour and cover saves cannot be taken against Wounds caused by *Trephination*.

6. MIND WIPE .... WARP CHARGE 3

Like a barbed lash, the Librarian's mind scourges that of his foe, dragging out every memory, secret and thought that makes them who they are. For some foes, this theft of identity is momentary, a fearful but temporary blank. Others are permanently reduced to glassy-eyed walking corpses – hollow shells of what they once were.

Mind Wipe is a **malediction** that targets a single enemy unit within 24". All models in the target unit have their Weapon Skill and Ballistic Skill reduced to 1 until the end of their next turn, at which point the unit must take a Leadership test. If the Leadership test is failed, the effects of *Mind Wipe* last for the rest of the game.

TACTICAL OBJECTIVES

Codex: Dark Angels **describes six Tactical Objectives to use in your games that are exclusive to Dark Angels players and reflect their secretive, but incredibly single-minded and resolute method of war.**

If your Warlord has the Dark Angels Faction, these Tactical Objectives replace the Capture & Control Tactical Objectives (numbers 11-16) described in *Warhammer 40,000: The Rules.*

If a Warhammer 40,000 mission has the Tactical Objectives special rule, players use the normal rules for using Tactical Objectives with the following exception: when a Dark Angels player generates a Capture & Control objective (numbers 11, 12, 13, 14, 15 or 16), the Dark Angels player instead generates the corresponding Dark Angels Tactical Objective, as shown in the table (right). Other Tactical Objectives (numbers 21-66) are generated normally.

D66	RESULT
11	Not One Step Backwards
12	No Forgiveness
13	Let None Escape Your Gaze
14	Apprehend and Interrogate
15	Flawless Strategy
16	The Path of Redemption

11 NOT ONE STEP BACKWARDS

TYPE: DARK ANGELS

Intractable and immovable, you must stand firm in the face of the foe no matter what horrors they unleash.

When this Tactical Objective is generated secretly choose either your next turn, your next two turns or your next three turns; score 1, D3 or D3+3 Victory points respectively if this Tactical Objective is still Active at the end of the number of turns you chose. This Tactical Objective is immediately discarded if any friendly unit fails a Morale Check. If the game ends before this Tactical Objective is achieved, no Victory Points are scored.

12 NO FORGIVENESS

TYPE: DARK ANGELS

Be implacable in your hatred of the foe. Root them out and scour them from existence, wherever they may hide.

Score 1 Victory Point at the end of your turn if you completely destroyed 1 or more enemy units that were controlling an Objective Marker at the start of your turn.

13 LET NONE ESCAPE YOUR GAZE

TYPE: DARK ANGELS

Tear aside the flimsy veil that hides the thoughts of the foe. Rip free their secrets from the darkest hollows of their minds, and prove to them that there is no escape from vengeance.

Score 1 Victory Point at the end of your turn if you successfully manifested one or more psychic powers from the Interromancy discipline during your turn.

14 APPREHEND AND INTERROGATE

TYPE: DARK ANGELS

The path of one of the Fallen has crossed this battlefield – more information must be extracted from enemy leaders.

Score 1 Victory Point at the end of your turn if at least one enemy character was slain in a challenge during your turn. If your opponent's Warlord was slain in a challenge during your turn, score D3 Victory Points instead.

15 FLAWLESS STRATEGY

TYPE: DARK ANGELS

Honour the Lion in the perfect application of battlefield tactics.

Score 1 Victory Point at the end of your turn if one or more friendly units with the Deathwing or Ravenwing special rule arrived from Reserve during your turn. If one or more friendly units with the Deathwing special rule used a teleport homer to arrive by Deep Strike within 6" of a friendly unit with the Ravenwing special rule during your turn, score D3 Victory Points instead.

16 THE PATH OF REDEMPTION

TYPE: DARK ANGELS

Prove your faith and loyalty in the Emperor by fulfilling your duty, no matter the cost.

Score 1 Victory Point at the end of your turn if, during your turn, a friendly unit with the Dark Angels Faction charged an enemy unit that, at the start of the Charge sub-phase, included more models than their own unit.

Secret Agenda: If your Warlord has the Dark Angels Faction, hide your dice roll when generating Tactical Objectives. If the Tactical Objective generated does not have the Dark Angels Type, reveal both the dice roll and the Tactical Objective to your opponent as normal (unless the mission you are playing instructs you otherwise). If the Tactical Objective generated has the Dark Angels Type, keep the dice roll and Tactical Objective hidden; reveal these Tactical Objectives only when achieving them.

DESIGNER'S NOTE – TACTICAL OBJECTIVES CARD DECK

If you own a deck of Dark Angels Tactical Objective Cards, you can generate your Tactical Objectives by shuffling the deck and drawing the top card instead of rolling a D66. These should be kept face up, so your opponent can see which Tactical Objectives you have generated, unless the mission you are playing instructs you otherwise, or they have Dark Angels Type (see Secret Agenda, above).

DEATHWING STRIKE FORCE

Codex: Dark Angels* details two further Detachments, the first of which is based upon the mighty 1st Company of the Dark Angels – the Deathwing – which specialises in devastating teleportation strikes into the heart of the enemy army. This Detachment follows all of the rules for Detachments as presented in *Warhammer 40,000: The Rules.

Compulsory	Optional
1 HQ	2 HQ
2 Elites	10 Elites

RESTRICTIONS:

All units in this Detachment must have the Deathwing special rule (pg 148) or be Dedicated Transports. Units of Venerable Dreadnoughts in this Formation may only include one model, which must be given a Drop Pod (pg 122) as a Dedicated Transport.

COMMAND BENEFITS:

Summoned to War: All units in this Detachment must begin the game in Deep Strike Reserve. If your army includes a Ravenwing Attack Squadron (pg 142) or a Ravenwing Strike Force (see opposite), you can choose to automatically pass or fail any Reserve Rolls you make for units in this Detachment; there is no need to roll.

First Knight of Caliban: If this Detachment is your Primary Detachment, you can re-roll the result when rolling on the Dark Angels Warlord Traits table (pg 148).

Take the Fight to the Enemy: Units from this Detachment can either shoot and then Run, or Run and then shoot, in the Shooting phase of the turn they arrive by Deep Strike.

RAVENWING STRIKE FORCE

The final Detachment in *Codex: Dark Angels* focusses on the 2nd Company – the Ravenwing – and their highly mobile style of warfare. As the eyes and ears of the Chapter, it is the Ravenwing who are tasked with running the Fallen to ground. This Detachment follows all of the rules for Detachments as presented in *Warhammer 40,000: The Rules*.

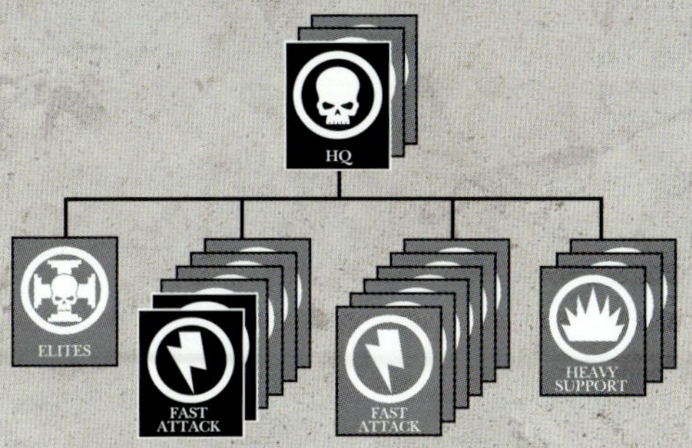

COMPULSORY
1 HQ
2 Fast Attack

OPTIONAL
2 HQ
1 Elites
10 Fast Attack
3 Heavy Support

RESTRICTIONS:

All units in this Detachment must have the Ravenwing special rule (pg 148).

COMMAND BENEFITS:

First Huntsman: If this Detachment is your Primary Detachment, you can re-roll the result when rolling on the Dark Angels Warlord Traits table (pg 148).

Speed of the Raven: During your first turn (or your second turn if the units in this Detachment were placed in Reserve – see below), any units from this Detachment that Turbo-boost or move Flat Out count as Jinking until your next turn. However, units from this Detachment that do so can still fire their guns normally in your next turn; they do not have to fire Snap Shots.

Strike as One: All of the units in this Detachment must either be placed in Reserve or deployed as normal. If placed in Reserve, all units in this Detachment automatically arrive at the start of your second turn.

PROFILES

HQ

	WS	BS	S	T	W	I	A	Ld	Sv	Unit Type	Pg
Asmodai	6	5	4	4	3	5	3	10	3+	In (ch)	103
Belial	6	5	4	4	3	5	4	10	2+	In (ch)	99
Chaplain	5	4	4	4	2	4	2	10	3+	In (ch)	107
Company Master	6	5	4	4	3	5	3	10	3+	In (ch)	106
Ezekiel	5	5	4	4	3	5	3	10	2+	In (ch)	105
Interrogator-Chaplain	5	5	4	4	3	5	3	10	3+	In (ch)	102
Librarian	5	4	4	4	2	4	2	10	3+	In (ch)	104
Sammael	6	5	4	5	3	5	3	10	3+	Jb (ch)	100
Servitor	3	3	3	3	1	3	1	8	4+	In	108
Techmarine	4	5	4	4	2	4	2	9	2+	In (ch)	108

TROOPS

	WS	BS	S	T	W	I	A	Ld	Sv	Unit Type	Pg
Space Marine	4	4	4	4	1	4	1	8	3+	In	110
Space Marine Sergeant	4	4	4	4	1	4	1	8	3+	In (ch)	110
Veteran Sergeant	4	4	4	4	1	4	2	9	3+	In (ch)	110
Scout	4	4	4	4	1	4	1	8	4+	In	111
Scout Sergeant	4	4	4	4	1	4	1	8	4+	In (ch)	111
Veteran Scout Sergeant	4	4	4	4	1	4	2	9	4+	In (ch)	111

ELITES

	WS	BS	S	T	W	I	A	Ld	Sv	Unit Type	Pg
Apothecary	4	4	4	4	1	4	2	9	3+	In (ch)	113
Company Champion	5	4	4	4	1	4	2	9	3+	In (ch)	113
Deathwing Apothecary	4	4	4	4	1	4	2	9	2+	In (ch)	117
Deathwing Champion	5	4	4	4	1	4	2	9	2+	In (ch)	117
Deathwing Terminator	4	4	4	4	1	4	2	9	2+	In	116
Deathwing Sergeant	4	4	4	4	1	4	2	9	2+	In (ch)	116
Deathwing Knight	5	4	4	4	1	4	2	9	2+	In	118
Knight Master	5	4	4	4	1	4	3	9	2+	In (ch)	118
Ravenwing Apothecary	4	4	4	5	1	4	2	9	3+	Bk (ch)	119
Ravenwing Black Knight	4	4	4	5	1	4	2	9	3+	Bk	119
Ravenwing Champion	5	4	4	5	1	4	2	9	3+	Bk (ch)	119
Veteran	4	4	4	4	1	4	2	9	3+	In	112
Veteran Sergeant	4	4	4	4	1	4	2	9	3+	In (ch)	112

FAST ATTACK

	WS	BS	S	T	W	I	A	Ld	Sv	Unit Type	Pg
Ravenwing Attack Bike	4	4	4	5	2	4	2	8	3+	Bk	125
Ravenwing Biker	4	4	4	5	1	4	1	8	3+	Bk	124
Ravenwing Black Knight	4	4	4	5	1	4	2	9	3+	Bk	130
Ravenwing Huntmaster	4	4	4	5	1	4	2	9	3+	Bk (ch)	130
Ravenwing Sergeant	4	4	4	5	1	4	1	8	3+	Bk (ch)	124
Ravenwing Veteran Sgt.	4	4	4	5	1	4	2	9	3+	Bk(ch)	124
Space Marine	4	4	4	4	1	4	1	8	3+	In	123
Space Marine Sergeant	4	4	4	4	1	4	1	8	3+	In (ch)	123
Veteran Sergeant	4	4	4	4	1	4	2	9	3+	In (ch)	123

VEHICLES

				Armour							
	WS	BS	S	F	S	R	I	A	HP	Unit Type	Pg
Dreadnought	4	4	6	12	12	10	4	4	3	W	114
Drop Pod	-	4	-	12	12	12	-	-	3	O, T	122
Land Raider	-	4	-	14	14	14	-	-	4	Tk, T	136
Land Raider Crusader	-	4	-	14	14	14	-	-	4	Tk, T	137
Land Raider Redeemer	-	4	-	14	14	14	-	-	4	Tk, T	138
Land Speeder Vengeance	-	4	-	10	10	10	-	-	3	F, S	131
Nephilim Jetfighter	-	4	-	11	11	11	-	-	3	Fl	128
Predator	-	4	-	13	11	10	-	-	3	Tk	133
Ravenwing Dark Talon	-	4	-	11	11	11	-	-	3	Fl, H	129
Rhino	-	4	-	11	11	10	-	-	3	Tk, T	120
Ravenwing Darkshroud	-	4	-	10	10	10	-	-	3	F, S	127
Ravenwing Land Speeder	-	4	-	10	10	10	-	-	2	F, S	126
Razorback	-	4	-	11	11	10	-	-	3	Tk, T	121
Sableclaw	-	5	-	14	14	10	-	-	2	F, S (ch)	101
Venerable Dreadnought	5	5	6	12	12	10	4	4	3	W	115
Vindicator	-	4	-	13	11	10	-	-	3	Tk	135
Whirlwind	-	4	-	11	11	10	-	-	3	Tk	134

HEAVY SUPPORT

	WS	BS	S	T	W	I	A	Ld	Sv	Unit Type	Pg
Space Marine	4	4	4	4	1	4	1	8	3+	In	132
Space Marine Sergeant	4	4	4	4	1	4	1	8	3+	In (ch)	132
Veteran Sergeant	4	4	4	4	1	4	2	9	3+	In (ch)	132

UNIT TYPES

Bike = Bk, *Character* = (ch), *Fast* = F, *Flyer* = Fl, *Hover* = H, *Infantry* = In, *Jetbike* = Jb, *Open-topped* = O, *Skimmer* = S, *Tank* = Tk, *Transport* = T, *Walker* = W

LORDS OF WAR

	WS	BS	S	T	W	I	A	Ld	Sv	Unit Type	Pg
Azrael	6	5	4	4	4	5	4	10	2+	In (ch)	139

RANGED WEAPONS

Weapon	Range	S	AP	Type
Assault cannon	24"	6	4	Heavy 4, Rending
Autocannon	48"	7	4	Heavy 2
Avenger mega bolter	48"	6	4	Heavy 5
Blacksword missiles	36"	7	3	Heavy 1, One Use Only
Boltgun	24"	4	5	Rapid Fire
Bolt pistol	12"	4	5	Pistol
Cyclone missile launcher				
- Frag missile	48"	4	6	Heavy 2, Blast
- Krak missile	48"	8	3	Heavy 2
Deathwind launcher	12"	5	-	Heavy 1, Large Blast
Demolisher cannon	24"	10	2	Ordnance 1, Large Blast
Frag grenade	8"	3	-	Assault 1, Blast
Flamer	Template	4	5	Assault 1
Flamestorm cannon	Template	6	3	Assault 1
Grav-cannon	24"	*	2	Salvo 3/5, Concussive, Graviton
Grav-gun	18"	*	2	Salvo 2/3, Concussive, Graviton
Grav-pistol	12"	*	2	Pistol, Concussive, Graviton
Heavy bolter	36"	5	4	Heavy 3
- Hellfire shells	24"	1	-	Heavy 1, Blast, Poisoned (2+)
Heavy flamer	Template	5	4	Assault 1
Hunter-killer missile	Infinite	8	3	Heavy 1, One Use Only
Krak grenade	8"	6	4	Assault 1
Lascannon	48"	9	2	Heavy 1
Meltagun	12"	8	1	Assault 1, Melta
Missile launcher				
- Frag missile	48"	4	6	Heavy 1, Blast
- Flakk missile	48"	7	4	Heavy 1, Skyfire
- Krak missile	48"	8	3	Heavy 1
Multi-melta	24"	8	1	Heavy 1, Melta
Plasma cannon	36"	7	2	Heavy 1, Blast, Gets Hot
Plasma cutter	12"	7	2	Assault 1, Gets Hot, Twin-linked
Plasma gun	24"	7	2	Rapid Fire, Gets Hot
Plasma pistol	12"	7	2	Pistol, Gets Hot
Plasma storm battery				
- Burst mode	36"	7	2	Heavy 3, Gets Hot
- Charged mode	36"	7	2	Heavy 1, Gets Hot, Large Blast
Plasma talon	18"	7	2	Rapid Fire, Gets Hot, Twin-linked
Ravenwing grenade launcher				
- Frag shell	24"	3	6	Rapid Fire, Blast
- Krak shell	24"	6	4	Rapid Fire
- Rad shell	12"	3	-	Assault 1, Blast, Rad Poisoning
- Stasis shell	12"	3	-	Assault 1, Blast, Stasis Anomaly
Rift cannon	18"	10	2	Heavy 1, Blast, Blind, Rift Vortex
Sniper rifle	36"	X	6	Heavy 1, Sniper
Space Marine shotgun	12"	4	-	Assault 2
Storm bolter	24"	4	5	Assault 2
Typhoon missile launcher				
- Frag missiles	48"	4	6	Heavy 2, Blast
- Krak missiles	48"	8	3	Heavy 2
Whirlwind multiple missile launcher				
- Vengeance	12"-48"	5	4	Ordnance 1, Barrage, Large Blast
- Incendiary castellan	12"-48"	4	5	Ordnance 1, Barrage, Ignores Cover, Large Blast

MELEE WEAPONS

Weapon	Range	S	AP	Type
Blade of Caliban	-	+1	3	Melee
Chainfist	-	x2	2	Melee, Armourbane, Specialist Weapon, Unwieldy
Chainsword	-	User	-	Melee
Close combat weapon	-	User	-	Melee
Corvus hammer	-	+1	-	Melee, Rending
Crozius arcanum	-	+2	4	Melee, Concussive
Eviscerator	-	x2	2	Melee, Armourbane, Two-handed, Unwieldy
Flail of the Unforgiven	-	+2	3	Melee, Concussive, Fleshbane
Force axe	-	+1	2	Melee, Force, Unwieldy
Force stave	-	+2	4	Melee, Concussive, Force
Force sword	-	User	3	Melee, Force
Halberd of Caliban	-	+2	2	Melee, Two-handed
Krak grenade	-	6	4	-
Lightning claw	-	User	3	Melee, Shred, Specialist Weapon
Mace of absolution	-	+2	3	Melee, Concussive, Smite
Melta bomb	-	8	1	Armourbane, Unwieldy
Power axe	-	+1	2	Melee, Unwieldy
Power fist	-	x2	2	Melee, Specialist Weapon, Unwieldy
Power lance	-	+1/User	3/4	Melee
Power maul	-	+2	4	Melee, Concussive
Power sword	-	User	3	Melee
Relic blade	-	+2	3	Melee, Two-handed
Servo-arm	-	x2	1	Melee, Specialist Weapon, Unwieldy
Thunder hammer	-	x2	2	Melee, Concussive, Specialist Weapon, Unwieldy